Relocating Shakespeare and Austen on Screen

Also by Lisa Hopkins:

ELIZABETH I AND HER COURT (1990)

WOMEN WHO WOULD BE KINGS: FEMALE RULERS OF
THE SIXTEENTH CENTURY (1991)

JOHN FORD'S POLITICAL THEATRE (1994)

THE SHAKESPEAREAN MARRIAGE: MERRY WIVES AND
HEAVY HUSBANDS (1998)

CHRISTOPHER MARLOWE: A LITERARY LIFE (2000)

THE FEMALE HERO IN ENGLISH RENAISSANCE TRAGEDY (2002)

WRITING RENAISSANCE QUEENS: TEXTS BY AND
ABOUT ELIZABETH I AND MARY, QUEEN OF SCOTS (2002)

GIANTS OF THE PAST: POPULAR FICTIONS AND
THE IDEA OF EVOLUTION (2004)

SCREENING THE GOTHIC (2005)

SHAKESPEARE ON THE EDGE: BORDER-CROSSING IN
THE TRAGEDIES AND THE HENRIAD (2005)

CHRISTOPHER MARLOWE: AN AUTHOR CHRONOLOGY (2005)

BEGINNING SHAKESPEARE (2005)

THE RENAISSANCE (co-authored with Matthew Steggle, 2006)

BRAM STOKER: A LITERARY LIFE (2007)

SHAKESPEARE'S THE TEMPEST:
THE RELATIONSHIP BETWEEN TEXT AND FILM (2008)

CHRISTOPHER MARLOWE, DRAMATIST (2008)

THE CULTURAL USES OF THE CAESARS ON
THE ENGLISH RENAISSANCE STAGE (2008)

Relocating Shakespeare and Austen on Screen

Lisa Hopkins

Professor of English
Sheffield Hallam University, UK

First published 2009 by
PALGRAVE MACMILLAN

Palgrave Macmillan in the UK is an imprint of Macmillan Publishers Limited, registered in England, company number 785998, of Houndmills, Basingstoke, Hampshire RG21 6XS.

Palgrave Macmillan in the US is a division of St Martin's Press LLC, 175 Fifth Avenue, New York, NY 10010.

Palgrave Macmillan is the global academic imprint of the above companies and has companies and representatives throughout the world.

Palgrave® and Macmillan® are registered trademarks in the United States, the United Kingdom, Europe and other countries.

ISBN-13: 978–0–230–57955–2 hardback
ISBN-10: 0–230–57955–8 hardback

This book is printed on paper suitable for recycling and made from fully managed and sustained forest sources. Logging, pulping and manufacturing processes are expected to conform to the environmental regulations of the country of origin.

A catalogue record for this book is available from the British Library.

A catalog record for this book is available from the Library of Congress.

10 9 8 7 6 5 4 3 2 1
18 17 16 15 14 13 12 11 10 09

Printed and bound in Great Britain by
CPI Antony Rowe, Chippenham and Eastbourne

Contents

Acknowledgements

Whatever I know about India, I know because of the kindness and hospitality of Indian friends. I want to thank particularly Dr Shalini Sikka and her husband Dr Pawan Sikka, Manjit Singh and the late Dr Singh, Professor Bhim S. Dahiya of Kurukshetra University, and above all Professor R.W. Desai, for his friendship and generosity. I am also grateful to Suzanne Speidel for alerting me to *Kandukondain Kandukondain*, to Roger Lloyd-Jones, Merv Lewis and Peter Cain for help with Japanese history, to Tony Taylor for knowing more about old films than any human should, and to my mother, Monica Sant, and Teresa Friggieri for help with obtaining information about the Mountbattens in Malta. I would also like to thank the anonymous reader for Palgrave.

Introduction: Moving Pictures

What is a screen adaptation? At the most basic level, it involves taking a work of art originally conceived for one medium and 'translating' it to fit another. If Marshall McLuhan was right in his famous dictum that the medium is the message (McLuhan 1964: 1), this ought to be an impossible task, especially since there is, as Kamilla Elliot observes, a fundamental disjunction between the aesthetic of film and the aesthetic of literary texts, in that one centres on images and the other on the written word: 'Filmmakers regard verbal imagery as unnecessary beside film's perceptual images and scorn it as a type of braille for visually impaired readers' (Elliot 2003: 218). Nor does the suspicion come from one side alone: Deborah Cartmell observes that 'literature on screen has a history of being rejected by both the proponents of literature who felt it contributed to a decline in reading and thinking but, more subtly and persuasively, these movies were spurned by filmmakers and film enthusiasts, indeed writers themselves, who wanted film to have an identity all of its own' (Cartmell 2006: 1154). Moreover, in the cases of the two authors on whom I am going to focus in this book, Shakespeare and Jane Austen, there are several specific problems that seriously complicate the process of adapting the work of either of them for the screen. Indeed it would be fair to say that both of these authors think in almost every respect in ways which are entirely antithetical to the priorities and protocols of screenwriters, producers and directors.

Firstly, except on very rare occasions, neither Shakespeare nor Austen says much about how characters are dressed (and when they do, it is usually only in order to make fun of them, as with Malvolio's yellow stockings in *Twelfth Night* or the conversation between Catherine and Mrs Allen at the Pump Room in *Northanger Abbey*). Shakespeare in particular tends to say even less about the surroundings in which his

1

characters find themselves (as Sarah Hatchuel notes, 'Shakespeare plays provide very few stage directions' [Hatchuel 2004: 128]), and in Jane Austen, too, although we may sometimes be given the dimensions of, for example, a room that is to be used as a ballroom, descriptions of furniture and decoration are few and far between. For both Shakespeare and Austen, things like clothes and furnishings can be taken for granted, and need only to be touched on; for Austen in particular, who set all her novels in the present, these were things that her readers had in common with her characters, rather than things that made them different. This meant not only that the readers of her books were invited to engage with and judge the characters as peers, but also that they could be relied on to understand how those characters were likely to look and live with minimal explanation, since they could be trusted to fill in such details from their own imagination.

For us, though, costumes and settings are precisely what are most exotic in film adaptations of Austen, in particular, and are a fundamental element of their communal identity as 'heritage films' (see for instance Harris 2003: 44–45); thus Ariane Hudelet notes 'the attention to sensuous period details' (Hudelet 2005: 175) in recent adaptations and comments on Colin Firth's Mr Darcy, for instance, almost never failed to mention the fact that he wore breeches. Similarly, much attention was focused on Jennifer Ehle's Wonderbra and on Billie Piper's corset when she played Fanny Price, and both recent film versions of *Pride and Prejudice* have been accompanied by publicity splurges on the great houses in which they were partly filmed, Lyme Park in Cheshire and Chatsworth House in Derbyshire respectively (Chatsworth House now has the bust of Matthew MacFadyen as Mr Darcy on permanent display in its sculpture gallery, as an enduring reminder of the link). Equally notable are the many catalogues that use 'Jane Austen' as a brand to sell clothes, jewellery and trinkets, and much of the tie-in merchandise for the hugely successful 1995 BBC/A&E *Pride and Prejudice* also took the form of clothes and decorative objects, precisely the things that are least important for Austen herself. With the famous exceptions of the cross which William gives Fanny in *Mansfield Park* and the two rival chains she receives for it from Mary and Edmund, and of the pianoforte which Frank Churchill sends to Jane Fairfax, Austen has relatively little to say about material possessions: what is important for her is, above all, capital and income, in the shape of hard, realised or realisable cash sums rather than valuable objects. It is, for instance, notable how few things her heroines buy during the course of the novels: even Emma, the richest, is seen shopping only once. Things that were wholly peripheral for Austen herself, then, are likely to be the first and most urgent concern for film-makers, and also one of the things reviewers are most likely to fasten on, so much so indeed that the producer Tim Bevan has termed this genre of film the frock flick (Higson 2003: 14).

Secondly, film-makers must inevitably make decisions of the kind that both Shakespeare and Austen, although perhaps for slightly different reasons, deliberately avoid. One of Austen's most characteristic techniques is the use of free indirect speech, in which what may on the surface appear to be the narrator's own voice is in fact coloured by the views and perceptions of one or more of the characters, as in the famous strawberry-picking scene in *Emma*:

> strawberries, and only strawberries, could now be thought or spoken of. – 'The best fruit in England – every body's favourite – always wholesome. – These the finest beds and finest sorts. – Delightful to gather for one's self – the only way of really enjoying them. – Morning decidedly the best time – never tired – every sort good – hautboy infinitely superior – no comparison – the others hardly eatable – hautboys very scarce – Chili preferred – white wood finest flavour of all – price of strawberries in London – abundance about Bristol – Maple Grove – cultivation – beds when to be renewed – gardeners thinking exactly different – no general rule – gardeners never to be put out of their way – delicious fruit – only too rich to be eaten much of – inferior to cherries – currants more refreshing – only objection to gathering strawberries the stooping – glaring sun – tired to death – could bear it no longer – must go and sit in the shade.' (353–354)

Who is speaking here? Apart from the reference to 'Maple Grove', which must definitely have come from Mrs Elton, it would be impossible to attribute any one of these remarks to any individual speaker confidently. Perhaps the point, in fact, is that social discourse of this sort operates almost independently of individual speakers: just as Euripides' *Bacchae* explores the operation of group psychology, so Austen at moments like this can be seen as effectively exploring group language. Film as a medium inevitably has difficulty replicating or even approximating to this technique, because although it can of course offer point-of-view shots, it is likely to be obvious that we are seeing events from a particular character's point of view, so the ambiguity, play of irony and sense of the quasi-independent and free-floating power of social discourse which are so crucial a part of the Austen effect are inevitably closed down. Shakespeare presents a different but analogous problem in that he habitually underwrites characters: he does not make clear what motivates Iago or why Hamlet delays and if he did we would not be so interested in the plays as we are. Many film actors, trained in the tenets of method acting, simply cannot tolerate these ambiguities: they regard it as being of the essence of their art to 'fill out' the gaps in the script in a way simply unnecessary to the acting conventions of Shakespeare's own time.

Finally, a third problem is that neither Shakespeare's nor Austen's personages behave in the ways that most modern film directors want their characters to. They do not, for instance, have sex, because Shakespeare was writing for a theatre in which all the female parts were played by boys, and because for Austen it would have been simply unthinkable for such a thing to happen. Indeed Austen's characters do not even kiss, something that has posed problems for film directors, who either ignore this fact and then get pilloried by critics for doing so (as in the case of Roger Michell's 1995 TV film of *Persuasion*) or obey it and pay the price of a curiously flat feeling in crucial scenes, as in the proposal scene of the BBC / A&E *Pride and Prejudice*. The 2005 Joe Wright version of *Pride and Prejudice* shows itself acutely aware of this tension in that it actually supplies two endings: one without a kiss, which was screened in UK cinemas and forms the main feature on the UK version of the DVD, and an alternative that closes with a kiss in the grounds of Chatsworth, which was screened in the US and is available as an extra feature on the UK version of the DVD. More directly, Dan Zeff's *Lost in Austen* (2008), true to its status as an unashamed wish-fulfilment fantasy, does not hesitate to give its audience what it knows they want by concluding with a kiss. In the case of Shakespeare, meanwhile, the response of many directors to the absence of sex scenes is simply to invent them, by inserting scenes that are not there in the original and indeed never could have been, such as the sequences of Hamlet and Ophelia in bed in Kenneth Branagh's 1996 *Hamlet*, which, for all that it vaunts its status as a so-called 'full text' version of the play, has no qualms about leaving the actual text of the play a long, long way behind in this respect. In the case of both authors, these additions and interventions make the narratives of the films significantly different in both content and texture from those of the original texts. Linda Troost and Sayre Greenfield argue in their introduction to the groundbreaking collection *Jane Austen in Hollywood* that 'Much of the indeterminacy that powers our delight in arguments about Austen gets too settled by the films' (Troost and Greenfield 1998: 10), and the same is, even if perhaps to a slightly lesser extent, true too of Shakespeare. In all these respects, then, the two media seem hopelessly at odds with one another, with each of its very nature forced to privilege an aspect of any given work that the other would deliberately choose to downplay.

Nevertheless, screen adaptations of classic texts have been popular since the earliest days of film as a medium, and presently appear to be increasing both in number and in cultural impact rather than diminishing. There are clearly a number of reasons for this, including the obvious facts that the plots are already tried and tested and the titles will spark recognition in audiences. Certainly, as Heidi Kaye and Imelda Whelehan observe,

> Since the beginnings of cinema, adaptations of classic fiction have been prominent. [At] the Oscars ... approximately three-quarters of the awards for Best Picture go to adaptations. Adaptations of 'classic' works have traditionally been seen as high-prestige enterprises for film-makers. (Kaye and Whelehan 2000: 2)

Although some of these adaptations have been commercially or critically unsuccessful or have simply sunk without trace, others (perhaps most notably the BBC/A&E *Pride and Prejudice* and Baz Luhrmann's *William Shakespeare's Romeo + Juliet* [1996]) have proved hugely popular, and a burgeoning industry in critical studies of adaptations has found many of them worthy of attention in their own right rather than just as versions of their original texts (see Giddings, Selby and Wensley 1990: 12–13) – something that is hardly surprising given that, as Martin Orkin discussing the ways in which 'local knowledges may additionally aid the reading of the Shakespeare text' suggests, 'cinema is arguably the major art form of the twentieth century and beyond' (Orkin 2005: 112). In 2001 it was calculated that the previous decade or so had seen some 250 articles and more than two dozen books devoted to adaptations of Shakespeare alone (Rothwell 2001: 91), a number that has since climbed steadily, and as I write an Association of Literature on Screen Studies has just been founded and has launched a new scholarly journal devoted entirely to the study of adaptations. This is timely, because it is a discipline that is growing steadily more complex and sophisticated: Sarah Hatchuel, discussing ways of defining and classifying screen adaptations, proposes 'four main types of adaptation, though their boundaries will often overlap' (Hatchuel 2004: 16) – those using a version of the original English text, those using a translation, those using a Shakespearean plot as a framework and those in which the characters are involved in teaching or producing Shakespeare – so that even the term 'adaptation' is no longer a stable one. Equally Deborah Cartmell writes of 'the extraordinary variety of adaptations, moving from "high" to "low" culture, or from what some would perceive as from the sublime to the ridiculous' (Cartmell 2000: xi), and elsewhere comments that 'Shakespeare on film seems to have established itself as an area in its own right, with little or no heed of the wider context of studies in literature on screen' (Cartmell 2006: 1150). Moreover, Kamilla Elliot also argues that despite the apparent differences between literature and film there is in fact an absolutely central relationship between the two genres, saying of the argument of her important book on the subject that 'The idea expressed here is not simply that the nineteenth-century novel influenced western film, but that it in some sense *became* film, while the modern novel evolved in a different direction' (Elliot 2003: 3).

What then makes for a successful adaptation, and how might it negotiate what Ariane Hudelet calls 'the complex and intricate relationships that inhabit the imaginary space linking the four cardinal points of adaptation: text, film, reader, authenticity' (Hudelet 2005: 176)? Early criticism of adaptations concentrated principally on the vexed question of fidelity: how close was the film to the book? Indeed as late as 2000, Erica Sheen wrote in her introduction to *The Classic Novel from Page to Screen*, which she co-edited with Robert Giddings, that 'All the essays in this volume take the question of fidelity as their primary critical point of reference' (Sheen 2000: 2). Over time, though, the reductiveness and unhelpfulness of this paradigm has become increasingly apparent; as Neil Sinyard remarks (ironically in the very volume in which Erica Sheen declared the commitment of all contributors to fidelity criticism), 'The very act of adaptation is an appropriation of a text from one medium to another and, in the best cases, from author to *auteur*' (Sinyard 2000: 160) – that is, the new work has a real claim to be considered as an entirely separate work of art in its own right, and as the conception of a creative mind, in the shape of the director, quite distinct from that of the author of the original work – while Brian McFarlane, noting that 'Fidelity criticism depends on a notion of the text as having and rendering up to the (intelligent) reader a single, correct "meaning" which the film-maker has either adhered to or in some sense violated or tampered with' (McFarlane 1996: 8), roundly declares that

The insistence on fidelity has led to a suppression of potentially more rewarding approaches to the phenomenon of adaptation. It tends to ignore the idea of adaptation as an example of convergence among the arts, perhaps a desirable – even inevitable – process in a rich culture; it fails to take into serious account what may be transferred from novel to film as distinct from what will require more complex processes of adaptation; and it marginalizes those production determinants which have nothing to do with the novel but may be powerfully. influential upon the film. Awareness of such issues would be more useful than those many accounts of how films 'reduce' great novels. (McFarlane 1996: 10)

As Kenneth Rothwell puts it, for many critics 'The question is no longer "Is it Shakespeare?" but "Is it film?"' (Rothwell 2001: 89), while Emma French notes that her book on the subject

tracks the commercial failure of several adaptations marketed as "faithful", particularly Kenneth Branagh's epic four-hour *Hamlet* and Michael Hoffman's *William Shakespeare's A Midsummer Night's Dream*, and the success of those adaptations that emphasised the hybrid nature of their product, such as *Shakespeare in Love* and *William Shakespeare's Romeo + Juliet*. (French 2006: 2)

French's concept of hybridity is an important one; many of the films I shall be discussing in this book do indeed highlight their affinities with genres, cultures or national traditions which would have been entirely foreign to their originals.

It has also become obvious that many of the film adaptations which work best in their own right are those which are not afraid to take bold decisions about elements of the original book which should be sacrificed or altered (for instance, scriptwriter Philippa Boyens explains in the ancillary material to *The Two Towers* (2002), the second in Peter Jackson's highly acclaimed *The Lord of the Rings* films, that they made Faramir initially more sinister than he is in the original book because you could not have the big build-up to his meeting with the hobbits culminate in nothing more climactic than a tea party; it was dramatically necessary to have a threat at this point). It is because even quite radical change can express something about a central concern of the original while liberating it from unhelpful details that many critics have found Amy Heckerling's *Clueless* (1995) to be the most 'faithful' version of *Emma* in spirit, even if it is the least so in letter (see for instance Dole 1998: 72; Nachumi 1998: 130; and Harris 2003: 53). John Wiltshire coins a term for this kind of creative alteration when he defines what is happening in another extremely free 'adaptation', *Bridget Jones's Diary* (dir. Sharon Maguire, 2001), as

> 'transcoding'. It is a kind of borrowing that plays fast and loose with the original but is, it might be argued, redeemed by its lightness of touch. Aware of the differences between our times and Austen's, it switches and changes and finds different ways to meet similar ends – which might be defined, roughly speaking, as exploring the pressures on young women to conform to the expectations of their culture. (Wiltshire 2001: 2)

Growing understanding of the ways in which alteration of the original can be benign and intelligent rather than simply an irreverence has meant that recent criticism is generally much more ready to engage with adaptations on their own terms and to treat them as independent artefacts with cultural work of their own to do rather than mangled versions of the original.

Of the two authors I am going to be discussing here, Shakespeare has the longer pedigree in film, unsurpringly since, as Denise Albanese has it, 'Shakespeare has a legible place in the tense priorities of commodity culture, where his name stands as a free-floating signifier for quality' (Albanese 2001: 207). Although the earliest feature-length talkie version of a Shakespeare play was *The Taming of the Shrew* (dir. Sam Taylor, 1929), the history of Shakespeare on screen began more than a hundred years ago, with William Pfeffer Dando and William K.L. Dickson's brief film advertising Sir Herbert Beerbohm Tree's theatrical production of *King John* (1899). Film was then in its infancy, and this early adaptation and the numerous others that followed close on its heels were short, flickering and highly selective in their choice of which bits of text to dramatise: in Percy Stow's 1908 film of *The Tempest*, for instance, the first four scenes all cover events that occurred before the play starts, neither Stephano nor Trinculo appears and there are no comic scenes. In the century that has followed, the art of adapting Shakespeare for screen has inevitably grown far more sophisticated (for a brief but perceptive overview of the history of Shakespeare on screen, see Davies 1994). Some films – Julie Taymor's *Titus* (1999) is perhaps the most notable example – have virtually eclipsed the fame of their source texts to become objects of cultural and critical enquiry in their own right (Baz Luhrmann's *William Shakespeare's Romeo + Juliet* might also be thought to fall into this category). Moreover the number and inventiveness of Shakespearean adaptations seems to gather ever more pace. Mark Thornton Burnett and Ramona Wray note that 'Since the mid-1990s, there has been an explosion of filmic interpretations offering major reassessments of Shakespearean drama' (Burnett and Wray 2000: 2), and as Courtney Lehmann and Lisa S. Starks observe,

> What shocked millions of people in 1999 – Whoopi Goldberg's quip at the Oscars that 'Little Willy is very large' – now seems anything but surprising, for in the years following the spectacular success of *Shakespeare in Love* (dir. John Madden, 1998), 'Little Willy' has become Hollywood's biggest screenwriting sensation. (Lehmann and Starks 2002: 9)

Shakespeare adaptations, it seems, are here to stay, and increasingly form a genre in their own right.

Obviously not all of Shakespeare's corpus has attracted equal attention from either film-makers or critics. Mark Thornton Burnett and Ramona Wray remark that 'the Shakespearean play that exercised the greatest imaginative engagement over the course of the 1990s was *Romeo and Juliet*, thanks, in part, to its reinvention in *Shakespeare in Love*' (Burnett and Wray 2000: 6), while Kenneth Rothwell analyses the focus of the first 100 or so essays to appear on Shakespeare films in *Literature/Film Quarterly* as follows: '*Hamlet* was the most frequently written about, with at least twenty-two, most of which were on Branagh's version ... *King Lear* ran a good second with fifteen articles, many of them on the Brook version. *Macbeth* and *Romeo and Juliet* came in third and fourth, with *Othello* running a poor fifth' (Rothwell 2001: 87). Broadly speaking, this critical emphasis reflects the very different degrees of attention which film-makers have paid to individual plays. *The Tempest*, for instance, has given rise to at least five innovative and noteworthy versions – Paul Mazursky's *Tempest* (1982), Fred Wilcox's *Forbidden Planet* (1956), Peter Greenaway's *Prospero's Books* (1991), Derek Jarman's *The Tempest* (1979), and Jack Bender's strange but not wholly uninteresting 1998 version – while *Coriolanus* and *Richard II* have remained virtually untouched apart from the stolid and uninspired treatments in the BBC's *Complete Shakespeare* series.

The Shakespeare plays which have proved most congenial to recent film-makers are by and large those which have proved most readily susceptible of updating or of being made to speak clearly to contemporary concerns. This can be seen even in the apparently anomalous case of a play set firmly in the past, *Richard III*, in Richard Loncraine's 1995 adaptation, in which the affairs of the fifteenth-century Plantagenets start to look eerily like those of the twentieth-century House of Windsor, with the initial disclaimer that '[t]he events and characters in this motion picture are fictitious. Any similarity to persons, living or dead, or to actual firms is purely coincidental' clearly inviting us to detect the obvious parallels between the film's characters and members of the modern royal family, which the Queen famously refers to as 'the firm'. The quest for contemporaneity, rather than fidelity, could indeed be described as the Holy Grail of the recent Shakespeare film and of its critics alike. Burnett and Wray observe of their collection that 'The essays gathered together in this volume argue that recent Shakespearean films are key instruments with which western culture confronts the anxieties attendant upon the transition from one century to another' (Burnett and Wray 2000: 4), and adaptations of Shakespeare have certainly proved a versatile and sharply focused mirror to hold up to the nature of our own times: Andrew Davies' adaptation of *Othello*, for instance (2001, dir. Geoffrey Sax), was able to map the events of Shakespeare's play almost seamlessly onto the fictional story of the first black commissioner of the London Metropolitan Police force. Indeed at times Shakespeare can come *too* close to our own historical moment: the release of Tim Blake Nelson's *O* (2001), an updated version of *Othello*, was postponed because the events it depicted came eerily close to those of the real-life Columbine High School massacre. A strongly distinguishing feature of the Shakespeare canon, much more than of the Austen canon, is how often films have been updated or recast in this way, with notable examples including *10 Things I Hate About You* (*The Taming of the Shrew*) (dir. Gil Junger, 1999) and *She's the Man* (*Twelfth Night*) (dir. Andy Fickman, 2006), as well as less extreme instances such as Julie Taymor's postmodern *Titus*; this partly reflects the fact that a strong element of Shakespeare's appeal has always been the perception that he was, as his friend Ben Jonson put it in the poem to Shakespeare's memory which he wrote for the First Folio, 'Not of an age but for all time', but it also testifies to the recurring phenomenon that when a significant cultural shift is felt to be taking place, particularly if it is a threatening or potentially destabilising one, many directors (and not only Western ones, as the films of Kurosawa and Kozintsev clearly show) have felt it important or at least appropriate to contextualise it within a Shakespearean frame.

This partly explains why adaptors of Shakespeare have in general been more willing to take risks than those of Jane Austen – take for instance the care taken to stay largely faithful to the book and to create a period atmosphere in the two versions of *Emma* (dir. Diarmuid Lawrence, 1996 and dir. Douglas McGrath, 1996) and *Sense and Sensibility* (dir. Ang Lee, 1995) as opposed to Julie Taymor's *Titus* (1999), Loncraine's *Richard III* (1995), *Forbidden Planet* (dir. Fred M. Wilcox, 1956), *My Kingdom* (dir. Don Boyd, 2001) and *Prospero's Books* (dir. Peter Greenaway, 1991). Even the more adventurous Austen adaptations, *Mansfield Park* (dir. Patricia Rozema, 1999) and *Northanger Abbey* (dir. Giles Foster, 1986), offer tweaks to Austen's narrative rather than wholesale shifts and leave the texts set firmly in their original historical period. At the same time, though, there is also a conservative pull at work in even the most apparently revolutionary Shakespearean adaptations: to situate something in the context of Shakespeare is, it seems, a way of coming to terms with it and constituting it as safe, contained and comprehensible. In the case of Austen, the appeal of conservatism – one might even say conservationism – has been even stronger, for 'Jane Austen' is a brand that speaks strongly of nostalgia, heritage and the supposed safety of a 'gentler age'. (Notoriously, she barely mentions the Napoleonic wars in her novels, despite having brothers serving in them, and it is notable that Roger Michell's 1995 adaptation of the one novel which does stress them, *Persuasion*, has pointedly not been updated; instead its ships and officers are filmed with the same emphasis on their pastness as is to be found in, say, *Master and Commander*.) Deborah Cartmell sees a fundamental difference in this respect between the predominant ethos of Shakespeare films and that of Austen films: 'Films of Shakespeare's plays are not escapist representations of an idyllic past in the same way that films of Jane Austen's novels can be' (Cartmell 2000: 3). Indeed the first words of *Lost in Austen* are 'It is a truth generally acknowledged that we are all longing to escape', and even *The Jane Austen Book Club* (dir. Robin Swicord, 2007), which fails to offer some of the normal pleasures of Jane Austen films – there are no period costumes, and the score gravitates to the modern rather than the classical – opens with a number of shots of people unable to cope with the technology and pace of modern life, and offers, even if ironically, the assurance that 'Jane Austen is the perfect antidote to ... life'.

Although film-makers came to Austen later than to Shakespeare (a 1938 TV adaptation of *Pride and Prejudice* being the earliest), they have embraced her just as wholeheartedly, not least because, as Pascoe observes in Reginald Hill's Dalziel and Pascoe novel *A Cure for All Diseases*, a cross between a continuation of *Sanditon* and a detective novel, 'she films surprisingly well' (Hill 2008: 362). Nora Nachumi quips that 'It is a truth universally acknowledged, that each of Austen's novels ought to make a good movie. Four of them already have' (Nachumi 1998: 130), and as Linda Troost and Sayre Greenfield observe,

> Between 1970 and 1986, seven feature-length films or television miniseries, all British, were produced based on Austen novels; in the years 1995 and 1996, however, six additional adaptations appeared, half of them originating in Hollywood and the rest influenced by it. (Troost and Greenfield 1998: 4)

As I write, new adaptations by ITV of *Persuasion* (dir. Adrian Shergold, 2007), *Mansfield Park* (dir. Iain B. MacDonald, 2007), *Northanger Abbey* (dir. Jon Jones, 2007) and *Sense and Sensibility* (dir. John Alexander, 2008) have all recently aired for the first time, in a period that also saw the release of the biopic *Becoming Jane* (dir. Julian Jarrold, 2007), starring Anne Hathaway, along with *The Jane Austen Book Club* and *Miss Austen Regrets* (Jeremy Lovering, 2008), while *Lost in Austen*, a time-travel fantasy in which a twenty-first century girl swaps places with Elizabeth Bennet, has just been screened and a Latino *Sense and Sensibilidad* is reported to be in production. The spate of Shakespeare and Austen adaptations, then, shows no signs of slowing down. There is, moreover, a discernible pattern of Austen-based films following close behind and taking their cue from Shakespeare-based ones: ITV's 2007 season of three 90-minute Austen adaptations mentioned above was like a deliberate echo in shape and to a certain extent in style of the BBC *Shakespeare Retold* series, first aired in 2005, which consisted of 90-minute versions of *Much Ado About Nothing* (dir. Brian Percival), *The Taming of the Shrew* (dir. David Richards), *Macbeth* (dir. Mark Brozel) and *A Midsummer Night's Dream* (dir. Ed Fraiman); *Shakespeare in Love* (1998) was a biopic about the young Shakespeare which saw the production of his works as rooted in the circumstances of his own life, *Becoming Jane* (2007) was a biopic about the young Jane Austen that saw the production of her works as rooted in the circumstances of her own life; in *Lost in Austen* Mr Bennet calls Mr Collins 'a preening Caliban', Wickham echoes Hamlet when he says that Amanda is the daughter of a fishmonger and Bingley echoes *Othello* when he observes that Mr Bennet thinks that he and Lydia have been 'making the beast with two backs'. Where Shakespeare films go, it seems, Austen films follow.

This is not surprising, because Shakespeare and Austen are not only two classics of the British literary canon, but there are strong intertextual connections between them. These are neatly emblematised by the fact that in her introduction to her father Geoffrey Kendal's book

The Shakespeare Wallah, the actress Felicity Kendal phrases her praise of this Shakespearean book in Austenian language, giving her 'considered opinion of my father's autobiography, offered with daughterly pride and prejudice' (Kendal and Colvin 1987: xi); it is perhaps suggestive that in the Merchant Ivory team's 1965 adaptation of the book the figure of the daughter, played by Felicity Kendal and based on her sister Jennifer Kendal, is renamed Lizzie. Similarly in the overtly Austenian *A Cure for All Diseases*, it is Shakespeare who provides a crucial clue: Franny Roote's 'Poor lady, she were better love a dream' (Hill 2008: 423), one of many Shakespearean quotations and allusions in the book, provides the first clue that two of the male characters are having an affair. Jane Austen herself was notably interested in Shakespeare. In *Mansfield Park*, for instance, Henry Crawford is able to read aloud from *Henry VIII* despite having not consciously looked at Shakespeare at all since his teens; he explains this by declaring that 'Shakespeare one gets acquainted with without knowing how. It is a part of an Englishman's constitution. His thoughts and beauties are so spread abroad that one touches them every where, one is intimate with him by instinct' (335); indeed Mrs Norris has already apparently unconsciously quoted Shakespeare earlier in the book when she says 'What a piece of work here is about nothing' (169). Also in *Mansfield Park*, it is a mark of the would-be actors' shallowness that 'All the best plays were run over in vain. Neither Hamlet, nor Macbeth, nor Othello, nor Douglas, nor the Gamester, presented any thing that could satisfy even the tragedians' (155), and Edmund even uses Henry Crawford's interest in Shakespeare as an argument that Fanny should marry him: 'Fanny, who that heard him read, and saw you listen to Shakespeare the other night, will think you unfitted as companions?' (345). Indeed John Wiltshire declares that 'An analogy to the contemporary remaking of Jane Austen, I suggest, is to be found in her own hardly reverent relation to Shakespeare' (Wiltshire 2001: 7).

Austen was of course aware that, even though not writing in the same form as Shakespeare, her novels did have something in common with the tone and structure of his comedies, and she surely also knew that her own writing was likely to achieve a place in the emerging literary canon, even if she would not have suspected that she would in fact eclipse her own favourite, Richardson. James Thompson comments on how in the nineteenth century Austen 'becomes, via Thomas Babington Macaulay, George Henry Lewes, and Richard Simpson, "the prose Shakespeare"' (Thompson 2003: 19), and certainly they are now often paired as twin icons of 'the classics'. John Wiltshire comments on the coupling of Shakespeare and Austen on a poster for Penguin Classics (58), cites critics and scholars who have linked the two (59–61) or pointed to instances of Shakespearean allusion or borrowing in Austen (68) and observes that 'In Patricia Rozema's film of *Mansfield Park* [1999] Fanny Price's horse – her escape from conformity – is even called Shakespeare' (62). This means that when it comes to Austen adaptations, there is an additional layer of referentiality to be considered, especially because many of those who have acted in notable adaptations of Austen already had a strong Shakespearean pedigree (for instance Laurence Olivier in the 1940 *Pride and Prejudice* (dir. Robert Z. Leonard), or Elliot Cowan in *Lost in Austen* playing Mr Darcy fresh from his stint as Henry V at the Royal Exchange in Manchester). However, there is almost always more than one layer of referentiality present anyway, because virtually every recent adaptation of Shakespeare or Austen is well aware that there is a previous history of existing adaptations of the same text, at or from which each successive version is likely at least to glance knowingly and perhaps to quote extensively: indeed Christine Geraghty argues that

> The term classic indicates the nature of the source in the canon of English literature ... and alerts us to the fact that these are adaptations that are generally strongly linked to a previous source not only by title but also by drawing on the author's name, the use of the original's illustrations, and often by an image of the book or pages from it appearing in the opening sequence ... It is in this explicit referencing of the original that the classic adaptation distances itself most clearly from the other genres with which it has strong overlaps – the costume drama, for instance, or the historical romance. (Geraghty 2008: 15)

Thus much of the point of the screen adaptation of *Bridget Jones's Diary* lies in the casting of Colin Firth, famous as Mr Darcy from the landmark BBC/A&E *Pride and Prejudice*. *Lost in Austen*, in which Elizabeth shows Darcy a picture of Colin Firth on her laptop, is even more aware of such intertextualities: its theme music is that of the 1995 version; Amanda echoes Mr Knightley in *Emma* when she says 'It was badly done, Bingley, badly done'; Hugh Bonneville, who featured as Jane Austen's rejected suitor in *Miss Austen Regrets*, reappears as Mr Bennet; and both the fight and some of Amanda's mannerisms recall *Bridget Jones's Diary*, although here America is not a threat but the place which offers Bingley and a divorced Jane an opportunity for a fresh start. The second Bridget Jones film, *Bridget Jones: The Edge of Reason* (dir. Beeban

Kidron, 2004), is also echoed in the fact that Miss Bingley proves to be a lesbian, just as Bridget's apparent rival for Mark's affections does. Even in the Merchant Ivory film *Shakespeare Wallah*, a first (and very free) adaptation of its source text, the issue of traditional and emerging performance styles is absolutely central, and is made so explicitly in relation to Shakespeare. This means that representation in these texts is also always metarepresentation, and this makes their signifying processes particularly rich and complex.

In this book, I shall focus on something that adds yet a further layer to these already multi-layered texts: what happens to texts by Austen or Shakespeare when they are transplanted to a new location. In a discussion of Jane Austen on screen, Elsa Solender boldly declares that 'Tolstoy's art may require Russia. Dumas's may require France. But Jane Austen's world, like Shakespeare's, need not be constrained by time or place' (Solender 2002: 103), and in his introduction to the screenplay of one of the films I shall be discussing here, *In the Bleak Midwinter* (1995), its director, Kenneth Branagh, implies that he himself feels that his films are transcultural and universal, since he remarks of backstage movies in general that 'The aspirations of the characters seem to remain the same regardless of the locale' (Branagh 1995: vi). Nevertheless, in *Brief Encounter* (dir. David Lean, 1945), the film which Vernon in *In the Bleak Midwinter* proposes to give to Joe for Christmas, Laura opines that 'I believe we should all behave quite differently if we lived in a warm, sunny climate all the time'. My argument is essentially that Laura is right, and that the cultural meanings of the original texts are indeed shifted and dislocated when they are transplanted to new geographical settings, although in the last chapter, the transpositions I am focusing on are rather different in that what has been changed here are cultural rather than geographical specifics. Already in all these films we are dealing with a past viewed through the lens of the present, but even more importantly, I shall be arguing here, these films are conditioned not only by temporality but also by location and cultural ambience and moving them to new locations allows them to speak in new ways.

Both Shakespeare and Austen function, albeit in slightly different ways, as culturally accessible icons of Englishness. At this point, a clarification of terms is perhaps in order. It is true that, as the work of Willy Maley and others has shown (Maley 2007), Shakespeare did not confine his attention to things specifically English but had a strongly developed British dimension, and it is certainly true that this distinction is one to which it behoves us all to be attentive. However, it is one which is not always well understood outside these islands – Elsa Solender, for instance, declares that 'I prefer not to struggle with the authentic but dismaying array of British accents that regional and class differences would require in a film with pretensions to linguistic authenticity' (Solender 2002: 104), although it is hard to to think of any character in Jane Austen whose accent would or could need to be Irish, Scots or Welsh – nor scrupulously observed even within them. I shall, therefore, be using 'English' in this book as a catch-all phrase for the national 'brand' which I see Shakespeare and Austen as being perceived to represent in the films I shall be discussing, as when, as Neil Sinyard notes, David Lean in *A Passage to India* (1984) changed the dialogue at one point – ' "We're being awfully English about this, aren't we?" says Adela (Forster says "British" in the novel)' (Sinyard 2000: 155) – or as when Christine Geraghty contends that 'Classic adaptations are ... often associated with a particular version of the English past' (Geraghty 2008: 17). In the case of Austen at least, the emphasis specifically on Englishness is in any case wholly appropriate, since she not only set all of her novels within England but wrote to her friend Alethea Bigg 'I hope your Letters from abroad are satisfactory. They would not be satisfactory to *me*, I confess, unless they breathed a strong spirit of regret for not being in England' (Austen 2004: 201).

Nevertheless, in the cases of the eight films discussed in my first four chapters (four focusing on Austen, four on Shakespeare), all are radically dislocated from their traditional contexts in ways that allow for a powerful interrogation not only of what these texts mean in the modern world but also, in many cases, of what 'Englishness' itself means, particularly in relation to two countries whose identities Britain helped to shape but which have now broken definitively away from it, the United States and India. Both Shakespeare and Austen wrote at crucial moments in what was to become the history of colonialism, Shakespeare at the time of the first fledgling colonies at Roanoke and Jamestown and Austen during the debates about slavery and about the legitimacy of taking profits from an estate such as Sir Thomas Bertram's in Antigua. Indeed John Wiltshire argues that in the eyes of some modern audiences, Austen effectively connotes imperialism, albeit of a slightly different sort:

For others, 'Jane Austen' signifies English imperialism, the dissemination of her work via the BBC and Miramax films, colonisation in a new form. This Jane Austen is perceived as an enemy of the indigenous, the literary queen (as Shakespeare is the king) of a dominant culture, her texts one arm of an oppressive educative project that inculcates the values of the 'mother country', her careful investigation of behavioural constrains and the inner life, confined to a small section of nineteenth-century society, absurdly anachronistic, inappropriate and fundamentally detrimental to nations, peoples and classes seeking their own identities. (Wiltshire 2001: 8–9)

So steeped in this context is Jane Austen, Wiltshire argues, that he says of Rozema's *Mansfield Park* that 'An attack on colonialism, it is itself a neo-colonialist enterprise, the promotion of "Jane Austen"' (Wiltshire 2001: 136). Both Shakespeare and Austen, then, can be seen as representing not only Englishness, but above all Englishness in relation to other national identities. Each of the first four chapters of this book therefore pairs an Austen-based film with a Shakespeare-based film to explore what happens when these classic texts are moved from their original contexts in ways that resonate with the rise and fall of the British colonial project.

It is of course worth noting that there is a further layer of referentiality generated in the cases of the Shakespeare adaptations I shall be discussing by the fact that all of their original plays are set abroad – *Hamlet* in Denmark, *Romeo and Juliet* in Verona, *A Midsummer Night's Dream* in Athens, *Macbeth* in Scotland and *Much Ado About Nothing* in Messina. Some film adaptations of these plays have been notably interested in that aspect: Olivier famously (and ill-advisedly) dyed his hair blond to look more Danish, Branagh took his entire cast and crew to Tuscany so that *Much Ado About Nothing* (1993) would feel suitably Italian. (Branagh's own *In the Bleak Midwinter* pokes fun at this kind of approach when the actor playing Fortinbras thinks about rollmop herrings in order to sound more Norwegian; his director caustically reminds him that Norwegians come from Planet Earth.) And yet, in all these cases, Shakespeare's foreign settings all have at least one eye firmly fixed on England. England is openly referred to in *Hamlet* and *Macbeth*, and it is clearly the source of such character names as Dogberry and Robin Goodfellow in *Much Ado About Nothing* and *A Midsummer Night's Dream* respectively. Even in *Romeo and Juliet* an event is apparently dated by an earthquake which had happened not in Italy but in England (see Everett 2001: 153–154). In fact, for the adaptations I discuss, the foreign settings are if anything a distraction (there is, for instance, a notable process of anglicisation at work in the BBC *Shakespeare Retold* series); for them, it is Shakespeare-as-English – indeed in chapter 4 specifically what Mark Thornton Burnett calls 'The Shakespeare-as-passport motif' (Burnett 2007: 12) – that matters.

Chapter 1, 'The West Coast', looks at Amy Heckerling's *Clueless* and Baz Luhrmann's *William Shakespeare's Romeo + Juliet*. Both of these films update and transpose their chosen text from its original country and setting to the late twentieth century west coast of America. (In the case of *William Shakespeare's Romeo + Juliet* this process is less clear cut, since its fictional locale is sometimes identified with Florida rather than California, but I shall be arguing for a 'West Coast sensibility', as well as a specifically Hollywood ethos, at work here.) In both cases, the move results in a smartly self-conscious and sophisticated meditation on the ways in which, even in this temple of self-fashioning, cultural heritage configures identities. Moreover, both of these films draw on source texts that had already been adapted. Although both of the two feature films of *Emma* postdate *Clueless*, a 1972 miniseries directed by John Glenister and starring Doran Godwin as Emma had already brought the story to the screen. In the case of *Romeo and Juliet*, since its first adaptation in 1908 there have been at least thirty screen versions, of which the most famous was Franco Zeffirelli's in 1968. Both films are therefore acutely aware of what they are not as well as what they are, and perhaps most importantly of *where* they are not.

Chapter 2, 'The East Coast', couples Merchant Ivory's *Jane Austen in Manhattan* (1980) with Michael Almereyda's *Hamlet* (2000). Ironically, considering that the East Coast was settled by people from the land of Shakespeare and Austen so long before the West Coast, the anxiety of influence weighs less heavily on these two films than on many adaptations of classic texts, and in different ways. Though Almereyda's *Hamlet* plays self-referentially with allusions to a wide range of previous films, most notably in the scene which is actually set in a Blockbuster video store, it does not, as Branagh's *Hamlet* does, stand in awe of any previous versions of itself; rather, it is confidently aware that however many previous films of *Hamlet* there have been (and there have been many: Deborah Cartmell notes that 'there are 104 versions listed on the Internet Movie Database' (Cartmell 2008: 175), not to mention others that are less obviously adaptations such as *101 Reykjavik*, *The Impostors*, *To Be or Not to Be* and *In the Bleak Midwinter*), there has never been one like this. *Jane Austen in Manhattan*, too, is well aware of alternative aesthetics – indeed that is its central point – but again it is comfortably committed to its own. However, despite their ostensible assuredness in their own stylish modernity, both films consciously pit a hurried, streetwise, culturally dislocated aesthetic against the image of a traditionalism that both reassures and threatens. In the competition for meaning thus staged, no one ultimately wins, but some exceptionally probing questions are asked about how the past relates to the present and how location relates to behaviour.

Chapter 3, 'Across the Pond', may seem out of step with the others because neither of the two texts on which it focuses, *In the Bleak Midwinter* and *Bridget Jones's Diary*, has been uprooted from England. In both cases, though, what these films show is not the England which either Shakespeare or Austen knew, which was one determined to claim both political and cultural dominance over territories both near and far, but a shrunken, embattled land whose cultural values are under threat and which can now be understood only in relation to America. In *Bridget Jones's Diary*, England is so far from being master of the world that its inhabitants find their property invaded by Bosnian immigrants and can only wring their hands over the plight of Chechnya; the days of gunboat diplomacy are long since gone. Most of all, though, America in both films looms across an unseen horizon as a place whose wealth dwarfs Britain's and to which the romantic hero is in serious danger of being lured, abandoning the sweet English heroine. Even though danger is ultimately averted for the hero, in each case one other character (Tom Newman in *In the Bleak Midwinter* and Natasha Glenville in *Bridget Jones's Diary*) does succumb to the lure of the States, confirming the reality of the temptation. Both of these films, then, are set not simply in the England in which they were originally conceived but in an England-which-is-not-America. Moreover, these films, too, are always aware of previous adaptations lying behind them. *In the Bleak Midwinter*, although not a direct adaptation, centres on a performance of *Hamlet* and constitutes, as I discuss, a conscious *hommage* to a number of other films, but of all the films I consider in this book, *Bridget Jones's Diary* is the one which plays the most complicated games with the previous history of adaptation of its source text. This is ironic because *Bridget Jones's Diary* is in fact the first (and to date the only) film of Helen Fielding's book of that name, but behind both the book and the film Jane Austen's *Pride and Prejudice* looms as a central, structuring presence. Thus in both *In the Bleak Midwinter* and *Bridget Jones's Diary* the vision of this compromised contemporary Englishness is thrown into stark relief by a backdrop of an older, more confident form of national identity (something stressed still further in *In the Bleak Midwinter* when we are reminded by Vernon of the clipped tones and stiff-upper-lip ethos epitomised in *Brief Encounter*).

America continues to loom large in Chapter 4, 'Across the Ocean', but here the really salient presence is India, a country which in its own right has a long history of engagement with Shakespeare on screen: Poonam Trivedi points out that 'The earliest Indian cinematic engagement with

Shakespeare goes back to the silent era and is generally recognized to be *Dil Farosh* (1927)' (Trivedi 2007: 148). In Merchant Ivory's *Shakespeare Wallah*, the story of a British Shakespearean acting troupe touring in India becomes an emblem of the decline of both the power and the cultural influence of the Raj, not least because the name of the real-life Kendal family has been changed to the resonant Buckingham (and the daughter, in a further sly gesture in the direction of Buckingham Palace and its inhabitants, becomes Lizzie), setting the scene for an examination of how that most enduring icon of Englishness, Shakespeare, intersects with the discourses of Empire and of Orientalism. In Gurinder Chadha's *Bride and Prejudice* (2004), in which the story of *Pride and Prejudice* is turned into a Bollywood musical, both the image of the Queen and the idea of the waning cultural influence of Britain recur, as the less wealthy Bingley character, a British Asian who lives near Windsor Castle, is eclipsed by the American Mr Darcy figure. For all the loudness of its music, this film is heavy with silences: Amritsar becomes just the place where the Golden Temple is situated rather than a place where a massacre occurred, and no one must mention the fact that Darcy is white. By its very refusal to discuss these things, *Bride and Prejudice* powerfully reveals what is at stake when a text by Austen or Shakespeare is uprooted and transplanted to a new location.

What is important in both of these films is less the previous history of adaptation of their source texts than the long history of British filmic engagement with India. The jewel in the crown of Britain's Empire has consistently offered film-makers the most telling of all trick mirrors for reflecting England back to itself (a trick that is neatly reversed in Shekhar Kapur's 1998 *Elizabeth* and its 2007 sequel *Elizabeth: the Golden Age*): as Mrs Moore says in *A Passage to India*, 'India forces one to come face to face with oneself. It can be rather disturbing'. Even in Peter Duffell's *The Far Pavilions* (1984), which is as close to pure tosh as a high-budget Anglo-Indian film or TV narrative ever comes, there is some rudimentary sense that the two cultures reflect on each other; in a subtler, better scripted work like *The Jewel in the Crown* (dir. Christopher Morahan and Jim O'Brien, 1984), the ironies are devastating. Perhaps most notably, in *A Passage to India*, David Lean found a highly amenable vehicle for his ongoing examination of the defining cultural characteristics of Englishness, which he finds best revealed under pressure. As Neil Sinyard notes,

> Both Forster and Lean share a fascinated horror with Englishness ... [they] are fascinated by what happens when you take [the English] from their usual habitat and put them somewhere hot where they

can lose their inhibitions, shed a skin as it were, but where they come face to face with themselves. As Mrs Moore will say in the film: 'India forces one to come to terms with oneself. It can be very disturbing'. (Sinyard 2000: 154)

In fact, as Sinyard notes, Lean 'felt Forster had too much of an anti-English bias in the novel, and he would try to balance it a little more, be more even-handed, which disquieted some critics who felt the novel's politics would be gutted and its anti-imperialist message lost' (Sinyard 2000: 151). In paying attention to this issue, Lean was very consciously following in a long tradition of fictional and filmic examinations of the relationship between India and Englishness, and this is a tradition into which, I shall argue, the Merchant Ivory team and Chadha are also very consciously tapping. In all of these films, then, the question of Englishness is at the fore, and Shakespeare and Austen, twin icons of Englishness, provide powerful tools of interrogating what it means to be English in a changing world and how English identities of the past relate to those of the present.

I have not, however, chosen Shakespeare and Austen simply because they are both so strongly identifiable as icons of Englishness and as particularly richly charged repositories of its accumulated cultural capital, nor even because the one was influenced by the other. Rather I focus on these two authors because, partly as a result of Shakespeare's influence on Austen and partly because they are independently interested in exploring many of the same genres and issues, they can be, and in the instances which I discuss have been, made to speak to the same concerns. In Chapter 1, I show how two entirely different directors, of different nationalities and genders and with different histories, have found in Shakespeare and Austen respectively a story of the importance of choice in love and of the strength of genuine emotional commitment which each uses to great effect as a counterweight to the stereotypical glamour and self-absorption of Californian culture: in these two films, Shakespeare and Austen can stand in the same way as symbols of the 'classic' in the sense of the long-lived versus the ephemeral. In Chapter 2, the Shakespeare and Austen canons are ransacked for narratives that are very different in genre and also in weight and degree of cultural capital – *Hamlet* is widely recognised as the consummate work of art of the world's greatest playwright and has exerted a huge influence on world literature, while Austen's adaptation of Richardson's *Sir Charles Grandison* is an unregarded dramatic skit by someone known only as a novelist, and was not published or even really known about until shortly before the Merchant Ivory film was made. Nevertheless, Merchant Ivory's and Almereyda's adaptations reveal a profound and unexpected kinship between their two source texts, in that both have a fundamentally metatheatrical sensibility that can work very interestingly as a stimulus and point of departure for metacinematic ideas. These films, then, use Shakespeare and Austen in a rather different way from the films in Chapter 1, but again they find that Shakespeare and Austen can be put to the same cultural work as each other: each can be used as a representative of the old and European in the face of the new and American, although I shall be suggesting that for Merchant Ivory, the old and European is cast as bad, while for Almereyda, what is old and non-American (represented both by Shakespeare himself and also by Almereyda's intertextual engagement with the Japanese director Akira Kurosawa's earlier take on *Hamlet* in *The Bad Sleep Well*, 1960) is a valuable and stabilising cultural counterweight to the bewildering maze that is Manhattan.

In Chapter 3, 'Across the Pond', the same source text, *Hamlet*, recurs, but this time this famously most polyvalent and interpretable of plays, to which an entire journal was once devoted, is made to speak to another of its many concerns as Branagh's film examines not only the metatheatrical element of *Hamlet* but also the degree of personal involvement which it elicits (perhaps most famously emblematised when Daniel Day-Lewis played the part in the theatre and fled the stage after seeing his own father's ghost). Here, too, an Austen text proves to speak the same language as a Shakespeare one, for *Bridget Jones's Diary*, my second text in this chapter, hinges on the way in which *Pride and Prejudice* too, both in its original and its adapted forms, proves able to elicit a sense of personal engagement from readers and audiences alike. For all their very obvious differences, then, both *Hamlet* and *Pride and Prejudice* allow for an acutely probing examination of the emotional appeal of classic narratives and the ways in which they can still underpin readers' and audiences' sense of both emotional and national identities, as has most recently been seen in *Lost in Austen*, which is all about the emotional engagement of a reader with a classic text.

In Chapter 4, 'Across the Ocean', it is the Austen rather than the Shakespeare text which recurs, as *Pride and Prejudice* is adapted to very different effect and in the context of a different country, and this time it is paired with a heady mixture of Shakespearean texts rather than any single one, as *Romeo and Juliet*, *Antony and Cleopatra* and *Othello* are all called into play. This is clearly because although the respective authors' actual texts are of course important here, even more so is the simple fact of their iconic status as emblems of Englishness, and above all of the rôle that cultural capital played in the long history of British presence in the subcontinent. Equally important, though, is the fact that all of the texts drawn on here are classic love stories, all of them centring on a relationship that is for one reason or another exogamous to a degree that the society of the play presents as excessive, and, as I show in this chapter, the idea of cross-cultural romance has proved a crucial *topos* of films about the British in India.

Finally, after four chapters of mapping the extent to which the cultural footprints of Shakespeare and Austen share many of the same contours, I turn my attention in Chapter 5, 'Modernity', to perhaps the principal difference between them, which is that Austen texts find themselves much less at home in the modern world than Shakespeare's have often done. (Even *Lost in Austen*, for all its cheerfully modern and indeed postmodern self-consciousness, depends on this idea.) This is, I think, not merely an accident, but revelatory of a constitutive fact about modern readers' and viewers' perception of Austen, and one which is indeed grounded in her own writing: Austen stands for the past, and a past, moreover, which is seen as in many ways safer, more decorous and more morally serious than the present – as Audrey says in Whit Stillman's *Metropolitan* (1990), 'Today, looked at from Jane Austen's perspective, would look even worse'. Shakespeare's texts, by contrast, have often found themselves very interestingly adapted as mirrors of the future, as is perhaps most memorably seen in the uses made of *The Tempest* in *Brave New World* and *Forbidden Planet* respectively. It is perhaps this contrast between the two authors which more than anything else illustrates most clearly why apparently quite disparate texts of Shakespeare and Austen have so often been brought to bear on the same issues: when one speaks so powerfully of the past and the other is so intriguingly associated with the future, it is not surprising that they can so often be seen functioning as in effect twinned halves of a two-pronged attack on such central cultural concerns as the causes and consequences of choice of partners, the ways in which theatrical and cinematic performance styles feed off each other, the rôle of classic narratives in modern society, and present and former colonial and quasi-colonial relationships.

1
The West Coast:
William Shakespeare's
Romeo + Juliet and *Clueless*

In this chapter, I want to look at two films that certainly or arguably take Shakespeare and Austen to the west coast of America. I say arguably because in the case of one of the films, Baz Luhrmann's *William Shakespeare's Romeo + Juliet* (1996), there is in fact considerable ambiguity about the setting. The film was shot in Mexico City and Veracruz, so the source of its actual landscape is clear enough, but there have been various schools of thought about the landscape it is supposed to be seen as representing. Denise Albanese remarks that 'part of the reason Luhrmann chose Mexico City for the setting of this film is that, given the country's recent economic crises, "Everything was for sale there"' (Albanese 2001: 217), although it is unclear whether she means this to apply intradiegetically or extradiegetically. Alfredo Michel Modenessi certainly reads the Mexican setting as intradiegetic as well as extradiegetic: 'Verona Beach is built upon signs easily recognizable as originating on *either* side of the U.S.-Mexico border, but *most* of them are rooted in the Mexican landscape and religious iconography' (Modenessi 2002: 69), and certainly 'Abra, a Capulet' is dressed as a skeleton, clearly an image derived from Mexican iconography.

However, Modenessi also sees the film as deliberately departing from the reality of Mexico City itself, declaring that '*William Shakespeare's Romeo + Juliet* reduces its Mexican landscape to a trope for the postmodern city' (Modenessi 2002: 70), as when it shows 'the statue of Christ, nicely digitalized on top of the monument to the Independence of Mexico' (Modenessi 2002: 71): the point here is not that both of these structures are actually to be found standing in Mexico City, but that the conjunction of the two brings together such incongruously different symbols in the classic postmodern manner. Modenessi also remarks on

> The variety of definitions of 'Verona Beach' to which Luhrmann's film gives rise ... The CD-ROM version of *William Shakespeare's Romeo+Juliet* defines Verona Beach as a 'mythical city similar to Los Angeles or other contemporary cities in the world.' David Gates somewhat debatably suggests that 'while it evokes Rio, Mexico City, L.A. and Miami, it's absolutely Elizabethan.' An abstract from Samuel Crowl's 1997 Shakespeare Association of America seminar on 'Kenneth Branagh and his Contemporaries' dubs Verona Beach an 'imaginary South American Verona, a place of magical realism,' overplaying a widespread but fragile card pertaining to Latin American literature. The editors of the recent collection *Shakespeare, the Movie* call the setting of *William Shakespeare's Romeo+Juliet* 'a Cuban American community.' And finally, the anonymous review in *The Economist* talks of 'an imaginary American resort,' betraying a frankly European confusion. (Modenessi 2002: 70)

Modenessi himself introduces a further complication when he declares that 'the film is ... influenced by the style of the TV series *Miami Vice*; and ... the fashion sense of the Montague Boys is partly "Floridian"' (Modenessi 2002: 81).

There is certainly a similarity of tone between *William Shakespeare's Romeo + Juliet* and another film of the same year – and in some ways the same plot – which draws a sustained contrast between hot Florida and the frozen North: Mike Nichols' *The Birdcage* (1996), itself a 'translation' of the classic French comedy *La Cage aux Folles* (dir. Edouard Molinaro, 1978), offers scenes very similar to Mercutio's drag act, also references the Kennedys and foregrounds the rôle of the media and plays off what Agador splendidly calls 'my Guatamalanness' against white conservatism. Despite such parallels, though, a significant number of critics see the setting and ambience of Luhrmann's film as distinctively Californian: Courtney Lehmann remarks that '"Verona Beach" [is] itself a curious hybrid of Shakespeare's Veronese setting, LA's Venice Beach, and the film's on-location shots of Mexico City' (Lehmann 2002: 134), and Maurice Hindle suggests that 'Verona Beach and Sycamore Grove bear a similar relationship to each other as do Los Angeles and Venice Beach' (Hindle 2007: 178). Most of all, though, *William Shakespeare's Romeo + Juliet* insistently recalls California-based or California-produced TV shows: Elsie Walker observes that 'the materialism and fierce glamour of Luhrmann's Verona reminds us of *Dallas, Beverly Hills 90210* and countless other productions by Aaron Spelling' (Walker 2000: 134). In one respect, then, *William Shakespeare's Romeo + Juliet* does indeed unmistakably show us California, for it shows us a society entirely conditioned by the films and TV produced there.

There are in any case no such doubts about the setting of the second film I want to discuss here, Amy Heckerling's *Clueless* (1995). As it loudly proclaims, *Clueless* is set in Los Angeles, and is, moreover, very aware of the specificities of place: Cher dismisses the possibility that the wedding shown in the closing scene might be her own with the mocking 'This is California, not Kentucky', and Heckerling visited Beverly Hills High School as research for the film. As Lesley Stern points out, it is therefore borne in upon us that '*Clueless* has a fine lineage; it belongs not only to a group of films that feature girls coming of age, but more specifically to a group of such films set in LA: *Valley Girl, Earth Girls Are Easy,* and *Buffy the Vampire Slayer*' (Stern 2000: 230). Although Laura Carroll classes *Clueless* with Whit Stillman's *Metropolitan* (1990) because 'Both are set in North American cities, within enclaves of money, fashion, and privilege, and focus on the doings of a small set of adolescent men and women' (Carroll 2003: 169), the differences are far more significant than the similarities, and not least is the difference between the East Coast, where *Metropolitan* is set, and the California of *Clueless*. Both of these films, then, take a classic English text and transplant it to a new location which is either overtly or arguably identifiable as the prosperous, sunny West Coast. In this chapter, I want to explore the effects of that transposition, beginning with *William Shakespeare's Romeo + Juliet*.

William Shakespeare's Romeo + Juliet

As we have seen, *William Shakespeare's Romeo + Juliet* transforms the structuring logic of its source text, which hinges on a feud between two families in a small town, and instead plays on extradiegetic tensions between various locations and intradiegetic tensions between very different communities. Most obviously, it sets Hispanic America, in the shape of Fulgencio and Gloria Capulet, against white establishment America, in the shape of Ted and Caroline Montague, who both have names associated with the politically influential Kennedy clan (appropriately enough since although Arnold Schwarzenegger, who is married to JFK's niece Maria Shriver, was not elected Governor of California until 2003, his political career had been well under way since 1990). More subtly, the film's inevitable allusions to *West Side Story* (dir. Jerome Robbins and Robert Wise, 1961), an earlier adaptation of *Romeo and Juliet*, are neatly counterpointed when Lady Capulet at the ball dresses as Cleopatra, icon of the *east*, while Katherine Rowe detects an analogous game with polarities when she declares that 'Romeo's stale Petrarchisms travel West as we look East through the center of a proscenium arch, into the rising sun'; she also refers to Mercutio's death in 'a Western shootout' (Rowe), reminding us of a further set of associations activated by the ways in which the film evokes the West Coast. In addition, the film also glances repeatedly at England, home of Shakespeare: Romeo, like Tom in Patricia Rozema's *Mansfield Park* (1999), casts himself as a knight, and is thus an icon of English chivalry in contrast with Dave Paris's (Paul Rudd, who also plays Josh in *Clueless*) astronaut, emblem of American achievement. Equally Pete Postlethwaite as the Friar and Miriam Margolyes as the Nurse, both English actors, are the nurturing figures, with Margolyes' Spanish accent here reprising the one she made immortal as the Spanish Infanta in the first series of the classic British comedy *Blackadder*.

All of these characters thus represent very different histories and heritages, and yet they jostle together in close proximity, because *William Shakespeare's Romeo + Juliet* is, like *Clueless*, above all a film of the city, and of the postmodern city at that, bringing together images and sounds in a heady mixture: as Elsie Walker points out,

> The many musical quotations of this film establish important tonal shifts, alluding to films of diverse genres – everything from music associated with Spaghetti Westerns, John Woo action movies to classical Hollywood Max Steiner-pastiche – in order to tell one story in a highly self-conscious, intertextual way. (Walker 2003: 3)

The trappings of modern, cosmopolitan, stressed city life are in evidence as never before in a Shakespeare film, and yet in a way which does, I think, resonate with the original play. Zeffirelli's sumptuous recreation of Renaissance Verona had made us acutely aware of the urban setting of *Romeo and Juliet* (Pilkington 1994: 165 and 173–4), but had presented us with an environment rich in all the beauties and civic amenities of the Italian Renaissance. Although this is of course chronologically accurate, it nevertheless presents an image of such beauty and such obvious exoticism that we are hardly likely to associate living there with difficulty or deprivation of any kind. Nevertheless, in

Shakespearean drama the city does indeed tend to be associated precisely with distress and worry. In the Athens of *A Midsummer Night's Dream*, Hermia could be condemned to death if she does not bow to her father's will and accept Demetrius as her husband, whereas when she runs away to the woods she manages to escape both these alternatives; in the Vienna of *Measure for Measure*, lust and disease run riot; in the Milan of *The Two Gentlemen of Verona*, Proteus betrays his friend Valentine. In all of these cases, the comic resolution can be brought about only by a remove to the 'green world' – the wood, the grange, the forest – where the laws and constraints of civic life can be shaken off or outmanoeuvred. The world of *Romeo and Juliet* affords no such respite: even Romeo's exile is to another city, Mantua, and thus the play can indeed be justly termed a 'city tragedy', to borrow the useful term coined by Verna Ann Foster (Foster 1988).

Lurhmann's film powerfully reinforces our sense of the pervasiveness of this all-important urban environment and of the manic nature of urban living. Helicopters whirr, guns blaze, prostitutes ply their trade and the characters use phones and cars and find their every move recorded on TV; indeed the film both opens and closes on the resonant image of a blank TV screen, which, neatly framed within our own screen, insistently reminds us of our own complicity and implication in this sophisticated, wired world and of the hi-tech equipment on which we ourselves are probably watching the film. This sense of the powerful, shaping force of culture, as opposed to the nature symbolised by the green world, is further underpinned by the fact that the film foregrounds not only visual images, plentiful and striking though these may be, but also words, in ways which both underline its own status as filmic adaptation of a literary text and also echo the play's own intense concern with the rôle of language in culture. In a fundamental sense, *Romeo and Juliet* is a play about the condition of being implicated in language, and that emphasis is directly picked up in Luhrmann's film. It is also further underlined there by the fact that the language spoken by the characters in the film is not only delivered in obviously American (and hence not typically Shakespearean) accents but is also supplemented by such extensive use of written language: Barbara Hodgdon points out that 'nearly half the speech turns into print headlines or graphic poster art, further fragmented through flash edits and slammed at viewers' (Hodgdon 2001: 130). Most particularly, we are made insistently aware that much of the written text we see consists of adverts, that is, words that are written to be repeated and remembered and that rely on structures of the associative and the formulaic rather than presenting themselves as in any sense fresh or original or as language born directly from experience. Indeed the play is made to seem even more wordy than usual by the fact that, although the dialogue in general is cut to the bone, some of it is used more than once: 'Either thou, or I, perforce must go with him' is said three times, and other lines are also repeated.

There is no question that Luhrmann here has picked up on something that deeply concerns the play itself. For a play by a young man, at the beginning of his career, writing about spontaneous young people in a still relatively uncodified and flexible genre, *Romeo and Juliet* is surprisingly self-conscious about its modes of representation. Above all, with its puns, its inset sonnets and its numerous instances of intertextuality with Shakespeare's own sonnets, it delights in the possibilities of wordplay and of multiplicities of meaning. But language is revealed as not merely playful; amongst the educated urban élite of Verona, it is also fundamentally constitutive of human identity. Discussing this play, Catherine Belsey asks 'Is the human body outside or inside culture? Is it an organism, subject only to nature and independent of history? Or alternatively is it an effect of the signifier, no more than an ensemble of the meanings ascribed to it in different cultures, and thus historically discontinuous?' (Belsey 2001: 47) and effectively answers her own question when she goes on to speak of 'the degree to which the letter invades the flesh, and the body necessarily inhabits the symbolic' (Belsey 2001: 54), while Edward Snow suggests that 'The play is full of tricks ... that make Romeo and Juliet's language seem like a medium in which their relationship takes form as well as an instrument for bringing it about' (Snow 1985: 169). Although passions may be strongly felt, they are not the primal emanations of the emotions, but are shaped and mediated by the structures of feeling obtaining in Verona, and those are primarily created by and disseminated through language.

This is revealed above all by the frequency with which passions are referred to specifically in terms of words. Tybalt exclaims, 'What, drawn, and talk of peace? I hate the word' (I.i.69). Escalus orders, 'hear the sentence of your moved prince. / Three civil brawls, bred of an airy word...' (I.i.88–9), and Romeo tells Benvolio, 'Bid a sick man in sadness make his will. / Ah, word ill urged to one that is so ill!' (I.i.202–3). In each of these three cases, attention is explicitly drawn to the word which expresses the emotion rather than the idea or emotion *per se*. And though Romeo defines love as in opposition to letters – 'Love goes toward love as schoolboys from their books' (II.ii.156) – Juliet tells him, 'You kiss by th'book' (I.v.110), and their consciously Petrarchan exchanges clearly reveal the extent to which they too are conditioned by their written culture, as does Mercutio's comment about the clichéd language of love: 'Speak but one rhyme, and I am satisfied. / Cry but "Ay me!" Pronounce but "love" and "dove" ' (II.i.9–10). Later, both Juliet and Romeo explicitly and repeatedly declare that it is the *word* 'banished' which causes them such grief: 'That "banished", that one word "banished", / Hath slain ten thousand Tybalts' (III.ii.113–14), while Jonathan Goldberg proposes that 'The circuit of desire moves through the letter R' (Goldberg 2001: 205).

There is also a general insistence throughout the play on the importance of literacy and the pervasiveness of writing in urban culture. Kiernan Ryan argues that 'Romeo's Petrarchan bondage to his mistress is matched by the projected binding of Juliet to "the golden story" of her husband's destiny' (Ryan 2001: 120), and the Servant laments, 'But I am sent to find those persons whose names are here writ, and can never find what names the writing person hath here writ' (I.ii.41–3); what differentiates the servants from their betters is, it seems, their lack of the empowering ability to read and write. An exchange shortly afterwards makes the point even more clearly:

SERVANT: I pray, sir, can you read?
ROMEO: Ay, mine own fortune in my misery.
SERVANT: Perhaps you have learned it without book. But I pray, can you read anything you see?
ROMEO: Ay, if I know the letters and the language.
SERVANT: Ye say honestly. Rest you merry.
ROMEO: Stay, fellow. I can read.

(I.ii.58–63)

Romeo can afford to play sophisticated games with the concept of reading, but the Servant cannot even understand his wit. The exchange, then, reveals how crucial literacy is to proper functioning within an urban culture.

Both the book metaphor and the idea of emotion as something culturally mediated and second-hand recur in Lady Capulet's description of Paris:

What say you? Can you love the gentleman?
This night you shall behold him at our feast.
Read o'er the volume of young Paris' face,
And find delight writ there with beauty's pen.

Examine every married lineament,
And see how one another lends content.
And what obscured in this fair volume lies
Find written in the margent of his eyes.
This precious book of love, this unbound lover,
To beautify him only lacks a cover.
The fish lives in the sea, and 'tis much pride
For fair without the fair within to hide.
That book in many's eyes doth share the glory,
That in gold clasps locks in the golden story.
So shall you share all that he doth possess,
By having him making yourself no less.

(I.iii.80–95)

For Lady Capulet, Paris is radically the subject of inscription, and this is indeed supported by the tame and uninspired nature of Paris's actions throughout the play, which collectively work to suggest that he is running through a series of pre-existing possible rôles rather than inhabiting one and personally reacting in it.

If language is all-important in *Romeo and Juliet*, though, we are equally aware that it is essentially arbitrary. Juliet sighs:

'Tis but thy name that is my enemy.
Thou art thyself, though not a Montague.
What's Montague? It is nor hand nor foot
Nor arm nor face nor any other part
Belonging to a man. O, be some other name!
What's in a name? That which we call a rose
By any other word would smell as sweet.
So Romeo would, were he not Romeo called,
Retain that dear perfection which he owes
Without that title.

(II.ii.38–47)

As Catherine Belsey has it, 'In recognising that the name of the rose is arbitrary, Juliet shows herself a Saussurean *avant la lettre*' (Belsey 2001: 54). And rapturous though their emotion is, Juliet worries about whether the expression of it in language may prove tainting to it:

Dost thou love me? I know thou wilt say 'Ay'.
And I will take thy word. Yet, if thou swearest,

> Thou mayst prove false. At lovers' perjuries,
> They say, Jove laughs. O gentle Romeo,
> If thou dost love, pronounce it faithfully.
>
> (II.ii.90–4)

The same consciousness of literacy and language is evident again when Juliet cries:

> Hath Romeo slain himself? Say thou but 'Ay',
> And that bare vowel 'I' shall poison more
> Than the death-darting eye of cockatrice.
> I am not I, if there be such an 'I'
> Or those eyes shut that makes thee answer 'Ay'.
> If he be slain, say 'Ay'; or if not, 'No'.
> Brief sounds determine of my weal or woe.
>
> (III.ii.45–51)

Learning that he has killed Tybalt, she herself falls back onto audibly second-hand language as she echoes her mother (as she will also seem to do later in the scene when she pretends to concur in the poisoning plot) when she exclaims, 'Was ever book containing such vile matter / So fairly bound?' (III.ii.83–4). It is notable that there is some suggestive use of wax imagery in this play, as when the Friar tells Romeo, 'Thy noble shape is but a form of wax' (III.iii.126), and what we see is that the characters are indeed like wax tablets on which their culture has indelibly written. It is wholly appropriate that Romeo at the end should speak of Paris as 'One writ with me in sour misfortune's book' (V.iii.82), for the characters are indeed circumscribed by the concepts of literacy, and 'whiles Verona by that name is known' (V.iii.300) they can never escape from the dominant ideologies of Verona as inscribed in its literary culture.

In an analogue to the play's games with words, names and literacy, the film, too, focuses on words (Ford 1998: 64–5 and Daileader 1998: 126). Phrases from the opening chorus glare out from the screen or appear as banner headlines in newspapers; advertising hoardings blaze 'Retail'd by posterity to Montague', 'Such stuff as dreams are made on', 'Shoot forth thunder', 'The Merchant of Verona Beach', 'L'amour' or 'Shoot forth themselves'; car number plates read 'MERCUTIO', 'MON' or 'CAP', followed by numbers that may well, we could presume, indicate their owners' place in their gang's hierarchy; guns bear the legend 'Sword' or 'Longsword'; badges say 'Montague' or 'Capulet'; Captain

Prince sits below the emblem 'In God We Trust', the word 'Haste' is written beneath a clock, Mercutio brandishes his invitation to the Capulets' party and captions flash across real and inset screens, while the name of the 'Phoenix mart' suggestively reminds us of the ways in which American English usage can sometimes come closer to Elizabethan patterns than contemporary British English does (as with the use of the past participle 'gotten'), a sharp little instance of this risky and experimental film with lead actors untried in the classics being prepared to register its own credibility and the validity of its ethos. Subsequently, Paris is first introduced both to us and, later, to Juliet, via the cover of *Time* magazine, where he appears as 'Bachelor of the Year', a neat lead-in to Lady Capulet's figuring of him as a book. Soon afterwards, while Romeo withholds Rosaline's name from Benvolio, someone else chalks it up on a board and when the cousins then move across to the counter, the man behind it does not even bother to talk, but just points to the tatty hand-written sign bearing the words 'No ticket, no gun'. Even Romeo's first speech is as much written as spoken, since we see him jot down the words in his notebook as he says them, and this scene may also alert us to a persistent pattern in the film's depiction of writing: apart from when it appears on an inset TV screen, writing is habitually seen outdoors, as though it is indeed as much a part of the external fabric of city life as the buildings. The only names which we never see written, apart from in the title of the film, are those of Romeo and Juliet themselves; even when they are first introduced, no identifying caption appears across them as it does at the first sight of other characters. They thus escape inscription just as they rise above the values of those around them, something which will be further underlined, as I shall explore later, by the persistent association of both lovers with water, the film's prime signifier of the natural as opposed to the cultural.

In this insistence on the pervasiveness and indeed the materiality of words, the forces and ideas that have shaped the characters' lives are thus vividly emblematised, especially when those words take the openly persuasive guise of adverts. Moreover, there is another suggestive implied comment about the nature of life in the city when Juliet's father appears at the fancy-dress ball he is throwing as a beglittered and betogaed Roman of more than usually decadent appearance (presumably the Antony to Lady Capulet's Cleopatra); the headier moments of Rome would indeed (as Romeo's own name suggests) provide an appropriate analogue for rich, urbane and violent Verona Beach, in which Romeo and Juliet present two isolated examples of purity and innocence.

There is also, though, a counter-emphasis in the film, and it is in this respect that it does indeed become auteurial in its own right as opposed to merely an adaptation, because Luhrmann's creative intervention has allowed Shakespeare's text to address issues of which it could not originally have had knowledge, and yet to which it proves able to speak loudly and clearly. As Judith Buchanan points out, 'Strikingly, for a film with such a celebrated word-based heritage, the main theatrical trailer for Luhrmann's *Romeo+Juliet* included no dialogue at all' (Buchanan 2005: 15). This is, I think, because while Verona Beach provides an apt linguistic alternative to the play's original setting of Verona, it also brings with it additional connotations, for words, as *Romeo and Juliet* is so abundantly aware, take on a life of their own. The beach itself may belong to the city, but a beach is also by definition a wilder, more natural space, bordering on the sea, from which wild weather will sweep in: in *From Here to Eternity* (dir. Fred Zinnemann, 1953), the beach was the site for dangerous and unlicensed passion; in *Clueless*, is the location of a disaster of unspecified nature for whose victims Cher donates possessions. In *William Shakespeare's Romeo + Juliet*, the beach is where the young men of the film are most at home, participating in a kind of counter-culture, and it also alerts us to a sustained pattern of oppositions between images of water and images of fire in the film. In one way, this can be read as simply a pattern of oppositions entirely appropriate to an adaptation of a play structured around two opposing families; however, it also has other resonances, because it speaks of a conflict pertinent not to Shakespeare's world but to our own.

As the Prologue is spoken for the second time at the beginning of the film, we see a newsreel shot of raging flames. It is clear that this represents the devastation wreaked by the quarrels between the Montagues and the Capulets, and indeed the first confrontation we see between them, in a characteristically free adaptation of the first scene of the play, leads to just such a conflagration. This scene is rich in resonances. Like the robbery at a petrol station in *Clueless* the year before, it gestures at the centrality of cars – and hence oil – to US culture, five years after the first Gulf War gave the first really clear indication of this dependency's potential for global destabilisation. In *Clueless*, this connotation is underlined when Cher's father asks her where she is – 'Kuwait?' – to which Cher replies, 'Is that in the Valley?'; funny, but in the light of subsequent events in Iraq, not as funny as all that. In *William Shakespeare's Romeo + Juliet* the idea of conflict over oil in the Middle East is not openly suggested, but in the context of conflict between two groups characterised as ethnically different it is impossible not to think of it now even if not then, and to see that, whether the film is aware of it or not, a savage irony plays over this scene and colours the background as subsequent events unfold and followers of the Montagues and the Capulets hurl obscenities at each other out of speeding cars – with the viewer thus drawn into the action again, as with the initial image of the television screen, since our point of view appears to locate us in the following car and thus to constitute us as the direct target of the abuse. Both groups then pull into a petrol station, where the literal as well as the metaphorical flammability of the situation is deftly underlined for us by the advertising caption which reads 'Add more fuel to your fire'.

As soon as the camera has finished tracing these words, moreover, it moves to the entrance of Tybalt, thus making clear their direct applicability to him, which is instantly confirmed as we see him throw a lighted match to the ground. Shortly afterwards he does it again, and, as was almost inevitable in a petrol station, fire immediately blazes. This inaugurates a sustained association of Tybalt with a motif of flammability: not only is he central to the flashpoint at the petrol station, but at the Capulets' ball, he appears as the Devil, wearing red and crowned with horns, and when he finally dies his body plunges backwards into water, suggesting that he has at last been doused, and a torrential storm breaks immediately afterwards, completing the effect. Juliet's Capulet heritage and her kinship to Tybalt are also signalled by a muted version of the same (literal) leitmotif: as Michael Anderegg observes, 'The final setting in the film, the Capulet tomb, may be the most theatrical of all, a set illuminated by hundreds of candles and dozens of neon crosses, a wedding of sixteenth- and twentieth-century light sources, self-consciously decorated as no church or tomb has ever been' (Anderegg 2004: 75).

Romeo, by contrast, is first seen by water. As Courtney Lehmann notes, 'Lurhmann explains that water serves as his motif of choice for escape' (Lehmann 2002: 149), and 'the volume of water steadily increases in Luhrmann's film, from establishing shots of Romeo and Juliet through the domestic waters of bath tubs and sinks, to their courtship by way of an aquarium and, finally, to Luhrmann's brilliant inversion of the balcony-as-swimming pool' (Lehmann 2002: 152). Various other critics have also glossed the meanings of the water imagery: James N. Loehlin, commenting on the film's aquatic nature, points out that the words of the *Liebestod* from Wagner's *Tristan und Isolde*, which we hear in the film, translate as 'To drown, to sink – unconscious – highest pleasure!' (Loehlin 2000: 129–30), while Lehmann suggests that 'the film's ubiquitous water imagery and cross iconography are inextricably linked through the rite of baptism' (Lehmann 2002: 149), and Maurice Hindle too suggests that the water imagery derives from Romeo's offer to be 'new baptiz'd' (II.ii.50) (Hindle 2007: 181).

Certainly the use of water imagery is central to the film, and creates a growing sense of the natural world as both a source of respite and a potential danger. Although Benvolio says that Romeo was last observed 'underneath a grove of sycamores', what we see is the sea (although Mercutio does later deliver the Queen Mab speech in a location captioned as Sycamore Grove). Fittingly, Juliet too is first seen in connection with water, this time by an underwater camera as her face is thrust into a full basin; moreover, even before we see her, the association has already been established, because the first time we hear her name is when Lady Capulet shrieks it while standing in front of a fountain. Both hero and heroine are, therefore, seen, even within this urban environment, primarily in terms of the elemental and the natural, and, moreover, as fit matches for one another. (Ironically, what Luhrmann could presumably not have foreseen was that Leonardo di Caprio would shortly become even more insistently connected with water as the star of the hugely successful *Titanic* [dir. James Cameron, 1997].) The lovers' strong association with water is sharply contrasted with the use made of it by others. Old Capulet and Paris are first seen in a sauna, in which Old Capulet imitates the action of his nephew Tybalt, albeit to less drastic effect, by producing steam. Lady Capulet uses water only to wash down her pills, and, with really splendid irony, dresses for the fancy-dress party as Cleopatra, Shakespeare's serpent of old Nile – both a suggestive relation for Juliet and a character who, in her grand entrance in *Antony and Cleopatra*, makes use of the water but is never part of it.

Given this pattern of imagery, it is unsurprising that the initial encounters of the lovers are fundamentally structured by water. While fireworks light up the air and a cross-dressed Mercutio does a spectacular staircase performance of 'Young hearts run free', Romeo turns disgusted from such vulgarity and excess, and douses his head in water. Then, through a tank full of ornamental fish, he sees the eye of Juliet, who is looking in on the other side. Edging along it, they gaze and smile at each other, as we see both them and their reflections. The water thus bonds them, but it also splits and separates them, looming between them like a miniature version of the Hellespont which divided Marlowe's famous lovers Hero and Leander (this, along with the ambiguous sexuality of Mercutio, may even be seen as providing a 'Marlovian moment' analogous to the singing of 'Come live with me' in Loncraine's 1995 *Richard III*). Water in *Hero and Leander* becomes the prime medium for an erotic encounter, when the god Neptune becomes enamoured of Leander's beauty, and fish are frequently an erotic symbol in Renaissance literature, as for instance in Donne's poem 'The Bait' (itself a variation on a Marlovian original); moreover, the blue/green palette of the fish tank forms such a strong contrast with the vibrant reds and purples favoured by Juliet's Latina nurse and family that it immediately serves as a way of marking her as separate from them, as well as of firmly establishing her as a suitable heroine for a love story as a figure associated with the natural.

Since the lovers have thus met through water, it becomes richly appropriate that the 'balcony scene' should not actually be played on a balcony, but in the swimming pool. Since Romeo is there illicitly, he twice has to hold his breath and remain under water while Juliet allows herself to be seen, suggesting that although water may be the couple's natural element, it may also pose a danger to them; Romeo is *not* a fish, and cannot survive in the element that is natural to fish. (Again, the later knowledge that in *Titanic*, water will kill Di Caprio's character gives the scene an added layer of extradiegetic irony.) A similar idea may also be seen playing round Juliet's introduction to Paris, who, young, handsome, rich and all-American, wears the appropriately aspirational attire of an astronaut to the fancy-dress ball – and yet, in a film released ten years after the *Challenger* disaster, the image of an astronaut may well connote failure and stress as much as soaring achievement. Juliet, however, is dressed as an angel, with a particularly splendid pair of wings, suggesting that she is native to an element in which Paris could survive only artificially and precariously.

After the powerful initial statement of the fire-water patterning, the theme continues to be strongly developed. Romeo and Juliet themselves are insistently associated with candles, suggesting that their relationship, although passionate, is purer and more controlled than the hatred that is symbolised by the raging flames; indeed throughout the film their love has a marked innocence, with no nudity (although this was presumably partly to make the film acceptable for its important target audience of American teenagers) (see Hatchuel 2004: 28), and Romeo at the ball is suggestively disguised as a knight in shining armour, a fitting partner to Juliet's angel. When Romeo asks Friar Lawrence to marry him to Juliet, the Friar is initially appalled at the rapidity with which he has transferred his affections from Rosaline; then into his mind's eye comes a vision of the fires caused by the strife between the Montagues and the Capulets, and he agrees, while the innocence of Romeo and Juliet's love is once again suggested by the voices of the choirboys in the background. Water, too, continues to be prominent. The Nurse finds Romeo at the beach, where he arranges with her for his marriage to Juliet; but it is also at the beach that Mercutio and Tybalt fight, and the pathetic fallacy comes into play as Mercutio's death is immediately followed by a sudden darkening of the sky and, moments afterwards, torrential rain. Water, it seems, can damage as well as attract, and an even more telling juxtaposition comes when Romeo falls from Juliet's window into the swimming pool, before fleeing to banishment, which he spends in this film not at Mantua or any equivalent city, but in the desert. But if the absence of love is a desert, love itself may leave you close to drowning and may also have far-reaching consequences, as we see when bubbles and ripples spread out above Romeo's head.

'Verona Beach' can, then, be split into two elements: Verona, which mimics and develops the ingredients of the urban environment depicted by Shakespeare, and the beach, an environment simultaneously natural and threatening. To some extent, the beach is analogous to the salvific 'green world' of Shakespearean comedy, and certainly the part of it which Romeo and Juliet themselves keep in their minds seems to have helped them to retain an interest in spiritual values in a violent, decadent environment. It is because the community as a whole has cut itself off from the beach, and has no use for its values or what it represents, that the urban wasteland remains a spiritual desert; but it is also because the two are so radically divorced that the beach can become a place of danger as well as refuge for those who frequent it and also a powerful emblem of the way that the natural world can encroach on and threaten urban life as well as provide a source of relief from it. In both the play and the film, there is no real escape from the city, something which is emblematised in the pervasiveness of the literary culture that has been so radically constitutive of the characters' lives and loves. That culture may now be ruined – Judith Buchanan observes that 'The theatrical ruin is first introduced approximately ten minutes into the film' (Buchanan 2005: 231), and indeed sees the film's project as being 'to narrate the waning of a public performance space as the enduring site for presenting Shakespeare' (Buchanan 2005: 230) – or seen primarily as cheapened and debased: Modenessi remarks of the Church of the Sacred Heart of Mary that 'most of us now refer to it as "The Church of Concrete," or, more interestingly, we call the statue "Our Lady of Traffic"' (Modenessi 2002: 82). Nevertheless it is a ruin which still bulks large. For both Shakespeare's lovers and Luhrmann's, then, urban life is fragile, imperilled and stressful, but it is all there is, and accommodation must be made with it.

For all its ostensible brashness, modernity and blatant disregard of Shakespeare's original setting, then, Luhrmann's film has in fact made very sensitive use of its dislocation to surroundings that, even if not conclusively identifiable as geographically on the West Coast, are, I have suggested, conditioned by the cultural products and ambience of the West Coast. Moving his picture in this way has enabled Luhrmann not only to tap into but also significantly to develop the play's sustained engagement with its own unease about language and its part in humans' implication in society, and to play to the full extent of what film can do by supplementing that verbal debate with a rich strand of visual imagery. On both the verbal and visual fronts, Luhrmann's greatest asset is in fact his American setting, for in the first instance America stands so strongly for a culture dominated by the media and advertising discourses of which Luhrmann makes such brilliant use, and in the second because its climate, geography and always potentially inflammatory international relations and domestic ethnic and class politics constitute it as so extreme a case of the interface between civic culture and the natural world. In *Clueless*, the next film to which I turn, this will become even clearer, as a burgeoning environmentalism begins to inflect the idea of the natural alongside, as we have already seen, a clear if understated sense of the lengths to which America may have to go to maintain its civic culture.

Clueless

In *Jane Austen in Manhattan* (dir. James Ivory, 1980), which I shall discuss in the next chapter, we are told that the performance of Victor Charlton in his hit show 'takes frivolity to an art form'. *Clueless* does the same. This is a film which luxuriates in its own frothiness: Cher, even vaguer than Bridget Jones on the subject of Chechnya, thinks that Bosnia is in the Middle East, and Heckerling herself observes, 'how heavy can you get without ruining the lightness of the movie? ... So I made up that arbitrary Pismo Beach disaster. We don't imply that anybody died. But they need things. So the feeling is there without the heaviness' (Heckerling 1995). If Jane Austen herself ultimately came to conclude of *Pride and Prejudice* that 'The work is rather too light & bright & sparkling' (Austen 2004: 138), one might well suppose that Heckerling could feel the same about her take on *Emma* – except that, however 'arbitrary' the Pismo Beach disaster may be, it is no accident that this film too, like *William Shakespeare's Romeo + Juliet*, instantiates the beach as a site of liminality and danger, for it is even more sharply aware of the potential magnitude of the clash between nature and culture.

Los Angeles and its cultural associations are central to the meaning of *Clueless*. Maureen Turim suggests that 'The fact that Cher's comic driving catastrophes take place in Los Angeles reminds us of the heritage of "The Keystone Cops"' (Turim 2003: 41), while Deidre Lynch observes more pertinently that Los Angeles, 'notoriously, is the first place that Fredric Jameson goes to describe "an age that has forgotten how to think historically in the first place"' (Lynch 2003: 74): she suggests that

> When Los Angeles and the postmodern are at issue, the classic as a site of value that deserves to endure is often represented as betrayed or disappearing. It is often the trigger for melancholy and nostalgia. (Think of the place of ruins in the futuristic Los Angeles of *Blade Runner* or of 'classic' Hollywood cinema in *L.A. Confidential*.) (Lynch 2003: 84)

As Lesley Stern remarks, though,

> The kind of image of LA that is summonsed up here is framed by the postmodern, but *Clueless* gives us a very different postmodern LA than that evoked by a film such as *Blade Runner*, in which the family romance, photography, and memory are in the service of a metaphysical thematic dedicated to loss and nostalgia. The fatigued irony of *Blade Runner*'s "I think Sebastian; therefore, I am" is replaced by the tongue-in-cheek "I shop; therefore I am" of *Clueless*. (Stern 2000: 229)

What *Clueless* gives us, one could say, is a kind of LA-as-icon-of-postmodernism lite, in which the troubling ontological and epistemological questions posed by *Blade Runner* are defused and displaced with the same irony and lightness of touch as Austen herself characteristically deploys. In *Clueless*, LA is above all an overgrown village – Cher's father says 'Everywhere in LA takes 20 minutes' – and even the mugger is polite, instructing Cher to 'Count to a hundred. Thank you'; indeed his brief appearance in the film not only provides the necessary structural parallel for the episode in *Emma* in which Harriet Smith is frightened by gypsies but also provides a suggestion of menace, only to defuse it, creating the impression that Los Angeles is a city so rich in possibility and potential that even apparent danger can be reconceived as harm-less. Not everything, though, is quite so light-hearted.

One particularly notable aspect of LA in the film is its weather. This may seem a trivial and superficial concern, but it is an emphasis that is not only sympathetic to Austen's original novel but also, I shall sug-gest, one that the film presents as not trivial at all but actually urgent and important, since it is viewed through the lens of a nascent but bur-geoning environmental sensibility. Ostensibly, the weather is the point in which the film differs perhaps most markedly from its Austenian original: David Monaghan scoffs at 'The constant sunshine that lights outdoor scenes' in McGrath's *Emma* (1996), but declares that the 'per-petual sunshine' of California makes the light and bright atmosphere of *Clueless* perfectly credible (Monaghan 2003: 221, 213). This makes *Clueless* very different from most Jane Austen adaptations – in the Joe Wright *Pride and Prejudice* (2005), for instance, Darcy's first proposal to Elizabeth takes place out of doors during rain – and indeed from the original novels, where the changing seasons structure the pace and rhythm of the film. In *Pride and Prejudice*, for instance, Jane Bennet catches cold because she goes riding in the rain; in *Sense and Sensibility*, Marianne nearly dies when she too is caught in the rain. In *Northanger Abbey*, it rains on the way to Blaize Castle and it rains again when Henry and Catherine go to see Woodston, both episodes that are much stressed in the most recent TV adaptation (dir. Jon Jones, 2007), and in *Mansfield Park* the changing cycle of the seasons underpins Fanny's maturation: the main events of the novel take 'about a twelvemonth' (343) and we are repeatedly made aware of the weather and the characters' response to it, as when the narrator notes that 'It was sad to Fanny to lose all the pleasures of spring. She had never known before what pleasures she *had* to lose, in passing March and April in a town' (421). The fact that Jane Austen herself seems to have been able to write only in the country, falling silent during her unhappy middle years in Bath, further suggests the importance she attached to the seasonal cycle.

In the original novel of *Emma* itself, we certainly hear a great deal about the weather and its effect on people's moods and lives: indeed as John McAleer observes, 'In *Emma* no physical detail is discussed as much as the weather' (McAleer 1991). At the start of the novel, Emma is extremely apprehensive about the social isolation threatened by the coming winter, even though she is thankful for 'Mr Weston's dispos-ition and circumstances, which would make the approaching season no hindrance to their spending half the evenings in the week together' (49). As the winter sets in, difficulties grow: first 'Isabella, the usual doer of all commissions, could not be applied to, because it was December, and Mr Woodhouse could not bear the idea of her stirring out of her house in the fogs of December' (76), and then there is the Christmas Eve dinner party at Randalls, when Emma worries that 'It is so cold, so very cold – and looks and feels so very much like snow, that if it were to any other place or with any other party, I should really not try to go out today' (131); later, when the snow begins to fall, Mr John Knightley gloomily prognosticates that 'we are two carriages; if *one* is blown over in the bleak part of the common field there will be the other at hand' (146). Even when spring comes, things do not noticeably improve when we find ourselves on 'the evening of a cold sleety April day' (302). Indeed *Emma* is well aware that summer in England may well not be so very different from winter: 'nothing of July appeared but in the trees and shrubs, which the wind was despoiling, and the length of the day, which made such cruel sights the longer visible' (410). Even when summer is warm, it brings problems as well as pleasures, as Emma warns Jane Fairfax that the fact that she is soon to become a governess 'can be no reason for your being exposed to danger now. The heat even would be danger' (357).

There have been films that have relished the engagement with the Austenian ethos of emphasising the variability and potential menace of the weather. The Joe Wright *Pride and Prejudice* certainly does so, and in Rajiv Menon's Tamil-language adaptation of *Sense and Sensibility*, *Kandukondain Kandukondain* (2000), Minu (the Marianne character), walking heedlessly through the monsoon, is sucked down a manhole, but Bala (the Brandon character) saves her; this not only responds to but significantly develops the analogous scene in the novel in which Marianne stays out in the rain and Brandon fetches her back, since the danger posed by the actual weather itself is more direct and extreme. In *Clueless*, however, there are no seasons, as is so sharply demonstrated by the fact that here, as in *William Shakespeare's Romeo + Juliet*, we see outdoor pools – Cher has one, and there is one at the party in the Valley.

There is a notable difference here not only from *Emma* but also from Heckerling's own earlier films. The *Look Who's Talking* films are set in New York, which is where Heckerling herself is from (she was born in the Bronx and then moved to Queens), and it is a New York that is represented as a strange, dangerous, and alienating landscape: in *Look Who's Talking Too* (1990), Mikey picks up a discarded crack pipe in the park, in a far cry from the village-like feel of *Clueless*'s LA setting. Moreover, New York, unlike LA, has weather that is not only bad but at times positively dangerous: in *Look Who's Talking Too* it not only rains torrentially but also later snows and blows, Mollie says 'Every year there's 20,000 fatalities related to the rain' and the climax comes when she dissuades James from taking off in his plane in adverse weather; similarly in *Look Who's Talking Now* (dir. Tom Ropelewski, 1993) there is not only hostile weather again, but also wolves. For Heckerling, then, the East Coast is a place of storms, snow and danger.

There are also instructive similarities and differences between *Clueless* and Heckerling's earlier teen culture film *Fast Times at Ridgemont High* (1982), where the school which the lead characters attend very closely resembles the school in *Clueless* (although there is presumably an inevitable generic resemblance to be expected). *Fast Times at Ridgemont High* shares with *Clueless* the mall culture, the sharing of wisdom (or not) about sex, worries about dating, the pop soundtrack, the emphasis on cars and the importance of the outdoor swimming pool. *Fast Times at Ridgemont High* also shares *Clueless*'s concern with mobility – Stacy has to get a lift from her brother – and has some similar characters: Spicol is like Travis, and *Clueless*'s Mr Hall is *Fast Times*' Mr Hand lite. However, in both *Look Who's Talking* and *Fast Times at Ridgemont High*, pregnancy, both wanted and unwanted, is a crucial issue. This is a concern notable by its absence in *Clueless*, principally, as we have seen, because of the youth of the characters. If *Clueless* is different from both *Look Who's Talking* (1989) and *Fast Times at Ridgemont High* in its lack of interest in discussing women's fertility, though, it is not so very different from *Emma*, where Emma does not immediately tell her father about her marriage plans because 'She had resolved to defer the disclosure till Mrs Weston were safe and well' (436), and where the fact of a baby's arrival is conveyed by the oblique 'Mrs Weston's friends were all made happy by her safety' (444). Emma's concern for Mrs Weston clearly reminds us that there could well have been genuine danger in giving birth (two of Jane Austen's own sisters-in-law, the wife of her brother Edward and the first wife of her brother Charles, died in childbirth, so Austen was well aware of the risks); this is, though, the only set of references to a pregnancy that clearly began shortly after the start of the novel itself, and has been developing throughout it, even though Jon Spence has recently argued that Jane Austen was more aware of pregnancy when writing *Emma* than ever before because both her sister-in-law Mary, wife of her brother Frank, and her niece Anna were pregnant and living close by for the first time (Spence 2003: 212). In *Clueless*, too, issues of female fertility are discussed only briefly, and through the sanitising slant of metaphor: Murray's 'Is it that time of the month again?' is clearly designed solely to provoke the outraged gasp it duly gets, and Cher's reference to 'surfing the crimson wave' is a strategic move designed to embarrass and wrong-foot Mr Hall and help bump up her grade.

If the rhythms of the human body are dealt with only perfunctorily in both texts, though, both are acutely sensitive to the natural world and its rhythms, and here too the Californian setting plays a crucial part in Heckerling's transposing and updating of her source text. As we have already seen, the legendary climate of California means that there can be no direct equivalence between *Emma*'s careful charting of the changing seasons and Heckerling's film, however useful the glorious sunshine may be as an analogue of the sunny mood and providential structure of *Emma*'s narrative. However, Heckerling is able to draw instead on the liberal tradition and burgeoning environmentalism of California to provide a well-fitting equivalent. Thus Josh is going to a Tree People meeting and wants to investigate the possibility of specialising in environmental law, while Miss Geist has a 'Protect coral reefs – Greenpeace' poster and is won over by Cher's promise to write to her congressman about the Clean Air Act; later she asks 'Hi girls, did you sign up for the environmental fair?'. The reference to the Pismo Beach disaster presumably gestures in the same direction, in that the only thing likely to cause a disaster on a beach is a freak wave or weather. (This is a general concern of Heckerling's: in *Look Who's Talking Too* Stuart has a gun in expectation of 'Earthquakes – flash floods – mudslides', while Mollie is worried about her mother barbecuing all the time because it's bad for the environment.) Such allusions never chart any direct equivalent to the ways in which *Emma* itself represents the importance of the natural world, but they are interestingly analogous to them.

These correspondences reveal the extent to which *Clueless*, like *William Shakespeare's Romeo + Juliet*, is centrally aware of being conditioned by the literary culture it inherits. *Clueless* is unmistakably a version of *Emma*, and borrows extensively from the plot structure of the novel in particular. This was perhaps not wholly a matter of choice or of *hommage*: plot is not Heckerling's forte – that of *Look Who's Talking Too* in particular is wafer-thin, and that of *Look Who's Talking Now* even more exiguous (though Heckerling merely co-produced this third and weakest of the films). It is certainly the clear implication of Heckerling's own remarks about *Clueless* that she was very grateful to borrow from a pre-existing structure which Austen provided: 'I had this character in my head, the girl, and the kind of things she was doing, saying and the journey I wanted to take her through. But I needed a strong plot and I had read *Emma* in college' (Heckerling 1995).

In many ways the correspondences between novel and film are striking. One notable point of similarity is Cher's struggle with her driving lessons, because mobility is a serious issue for Emma too, as when
she is forced to go home alone in the carriage with Mr Elton, or when
'Mrs Elton was growing impatient to name the day, and settle with
Mr Weston as to pigeon-pies and cold lamb, when a lame carriage-horse
threw everything into uncertainty' (349): for all their affluence and
ease, these people are dependent on the availability of carriages and
horses to transport them to the social engagements on which their happiness depends. In *Clueless*, Cher has to go home in Elton's car just as
Emma must go in a carriage with him, and the centrality of cars to US
culture is ironically illustrated in Christian's question 'Where should I
park?' when he enters the classroom. This is also an emphasis shared
with Heckerling's earlier film *Look Who's Talking*, where James is a taxi-
driver who takes Mollie to hospital when she goes into labour and gives
the baby a driving lesson. Later, we learn that he also flies planes, confirming his status as figure of mobility. (It is a mark of the insensitivity
of *Look Who's Talking Now* to the logic of the earlier films that in it,
Mollie can drive.)

Clueless is also, though, willing to take liberties with the texts that
underlie it, and to play sophisticated games with its own status as adaptation: when Elton asks Cher 'Don't you even know who my father is?',
we hear a sly joke about the whole issue of authorship and parentage.
These are indeed central concerns of this text, which is itself an adaptation but which never openly acknowledges its own parentage except in
the most delicate and oblique of ways, as for instance if we notice that
when Cher watches a news item about Bosnia, the unmistakable tones of
a BBC announcer point fairly clearly to the other side of the Atlantic, and
the film finds a neat analogue for its own insouciant commandeering
of its source text in its characters' attitude towards their parents. Mock-
menacing groups of parents and children are everywhere in *Clueless*: the
ultimate threat of Dionne to Murray is 'I'm calling your mom', and so
crucial is the concept of parenthood to the film that it even insinuates
Mr Hall into the structural position of Frank Churchill's father. However,
like the truly free adaptation that it is, *Clueless* is interested in parents
primarily in order to debunk their authority and debase their rôle, while
the couple whom Cher brings together are, in a notable contrast to their
originals in *Emma*, clearly unlikely ever to become parents. Cher even
acts as her own narrator, and we note the widespread absence of any real
parental influence amongst the teenagers on whom the novel centres:
Christian (Frank Churchill) is a tug-of-love child; Josh hides from his

multiply divorced mother; Cher's brusque, widowed father is openly dismissive of his own parents; Dionne and Tai might as well be orphans for all we ever hear of their families.

A notable example of this cheerful disregard of antecedents is that as in *Emma* itself, where we hear first that 'The course of true love never did run smooth – A Hartfield edition of Shakespeare would have a long note on that passage' (100) and then later the misquoted 'one may almost say, that "the world is not their's, nor the world's law"' (391), Shakespeare is used, but inevitably, he is also, in typically postmodern fashion, robbed of his authority. The wager at the end of the film clearly recalls *The Taming of the Shrew*, but to Cher 'Rough winds do shake the darling buds of May' is a famous quotation from Cliff's Notes rather than a line from one of Shakespeare's sonnets. Shakespeare is also used later, but again it is an icon of popular culture rather than Shakespeare himself who has made the greater impression on Cher's mind: 'I think that I remember Mel Gibson accurately'. For Cher, 'classic' is a cheap adjective rather than an accurate term: Miss Geist looks happy when she reads the sonnet lines and Cher says 'Classic', Tai looks 'classic' with a rose, and when Cher uses the classical tag 'Carpe diem' to Christian, it is with reference to a wardrobe choice.

However, the whole point of such moments is also of course radically dependent on Heckerling's confidence that a sizeable portion of her audience have *not* forgotten Shakespeare and so can register the joke, just as they will be well aware of another, more 'classic' sense of the word 'classic' against which they can measure Cher's use of it. Heckerling's auteurial attitude is in this respect similar to Austen's authorial one, in that misapplications and misquotations on the part of the characters are almost never highlighted by the author, who instead engages in a knowing and understated conspiracy of shared overhearing with the reader / spectator. The film's attitude towards the classics is crystallised in its playful and irreverent use of the scene from *Spartacus* in which Tony Curtis remarks that his function was to teach the classics to the children of his master, since here the scene has been entirely suborned from its original meanings and purposes to frame Curtis as primarily a gay icon and secondarily a signifier of Christian's own sexuality: as Maureen Turim points out, 'The film has tremendous fun with elaborating Christian through a series of visual references to 1940s and 1950s suave masculinity, unrecognized by many at the time as queer' (Turim 2003: 49), just as Murray's description of Christian as an 'Oscar-Wilde-reading friend of Dorothy' marks him as firmly aware of the histories and genealogies of the cultural construction of homosexuality. True to form, *Clueless* is also not afraid to mix the 'classic' with the modern. Cher watches *Ren & Stimpy* and the initial spark between Tai and Travis comes from her drawing of Marvin the Martian. Tai sings along to adverts and when Cher introduces her with 'Hi Daddy, this is my friend Tai', the response 'Get out of my chair!' inevitably evokes the story of the *Goldilocks and the Three Bears*. The result is a joyously eclectic assortment of references old, modern, and in between.

Most crucially, the characters' dialogue is, as one would indeed expect from characters living in the homeland of Hollywood itself, fundamentally conditioned by their awareness of cinematic techniques and terminology and their language is saturated in metaphors and allusions drawn from the world of cinema. Cher says 'Looks like we're going to have to make a cameo at the Vall party', and tells Tai that 'Dionne's buckin' for best dramatic actress at a Vall party'; similarly she assures us that 'Searching for a boy in High School is as useless as searching for meaning in a Pauly Shore movie', and laments that 'My enjoyment was put on pause when I saw how unhappy Tai was', while Tai herself is asked 'Was it like a montage of all the scenes in your life?'. For those who spot them, the film is also laced through with references to Heckerling's own previous work: Deidre Lynch observes that 'Movie fans who remember *Fast Times at Ridgemont High* (1982) will know that for Heckerling this represents a repeat engagement with the history classroom and the question of how the public idiom of history becomes personal and so memorable' (Lynch 2003: 78), while Laura Carroll suggests that 'It is usual to describe Heckerling's mastery of the teen flick with reference to her justly-admired earlier work on *Fast Times at Ridgemont High*, but the fluent and assured use of voice-over in *Clueless* has an antecedent in the director's two *Look Who's Talking* films that ought to be better recognized' (Carroll 2003: 173): for instance, both *Clueless* and the two *Look Who's Talking* films play games with narrators, with the baby providing the voice-over in *Look Who's Talking* just as Cher does in *Clueless*. At other times the references are more diverse, particularly in the film's eclectic and allusive soundtrack (see Turim 2003: 42–3 and Fullbrook 2003: 188–9 and 200–1). The ways in which Heckerling's film is informed by and engages with earlier work are also, of course, typically Austenian, since Austen's own aesthetic is so radically bound up with the protocols and practices of her contemporaries and predecessors.

However, *Clueless* is a very free adaptation of Austen's novel, and it is so not only in more ways than the obvious, but also specifically in ways that are conditioned by the transposition to America in general and to California in particular. For one thing, *Clueless* mentions topics that *Emma* never could have done. In keeping with the state's traditional image of experimentation and self-expression, drugs are openly discussed, and so too is psychology, of whose modern terminology Jane Austen was perforce wholly ignorant: Josh says 'You've never had a Mom, so you're acting on out that poor girl as if she was a Barbie doll', to which Cher pertly responds 'Freshman Psych rears its ugly head'. Equally appropriate to the setting are the changes in the characters' occupations. It is perhaps not surprising that Elton is secularised, since this is a common strategy with Jane Austen's clergymen in modernising adaptations, most notably in *Kandukondain Kandukondain* and *Bride and Prejudice* (dir. Gurinder Chadha, 2004), where neither the Edward Ferrars nor the Mr Collins characters are in a clerical position or in anything which could be considered remotely analogous to one, and in each case it is clear why this decision has been taken: to have a high school student who was a clergyman would be both impossible and wholly at odds with the tone of the film, and such a character would if anything make even less sense in the context of Indian culture than in a high school. It is, however, perhaps less predictable that Cher's father should work in law, but it is an interesting choice, because Mark Darcy in *Bridget Jones's Diary* (dir. Sharon Maguire, 2001) does so, too, similarly without warrant from the original novel. In *Emma*, Mr Woodhouse remarks 'Poor Mr John Knightley's being a lawyer is very inconvenient' (104), and the status of lawyers in general is decidedly low in the novel: musing on possible husbands for Harriet, Emma thinks to herself 'Oh! no, I could not endure William Coxe – a pert young lawyer' (156), while the narrator tells us of Mrs Elton's uncle that 'nothing more distinctly honourable was hazarded of him, than that he was in the law line' (196). Ironically, though, the law as a profession in *Clueless* is neither inconvenient nor a social liability; as in the case of Mark Darcy, to be a lawyer is apparently the closest equivalent in the modern world to having a large private fortune, as was the case for both the original Mr Darcy and Mr Woodhouse. Heckerling's updating, despite its apparent difference from the novel, therefore provides both a deft and economical transposition of the original with minimal disruption to its structure and a wry joke about the position of lawyers in American society.

Even closer to *Emma* is the way in which *Clueless* deals with the question of Cher's relationship with those around her, particularly in the light of both novel and film's representation of servants (see for instance Forde 1997: 16–17 and Greenfield 1997), and there is an instructive contrast here with later film adaptations of the novel that again reveals what the Californian setting has to offer to Heckerling in her project of updating. The Californian setting of *Clueless* is presumably chosen not only as the obvious home for a film so interested in references to cinematic culture and history, but also as a place of safety that will provide a congenial home for the comic spirit which animates *Emma* itself; ironically, if for Luhrmann what a West Coast sensibility delivers is the threat and oppression of the civic, for Heckerling it proves rather a direct equivalent for the village values and rural ambience of Austen's Highbury and the reason it can do so can be seen most clearly in the ways in which it is *not* New York, at least as Heckerling's earlier films have understood New York.

The move to the legendarily classless society of America also inevitably impacts on the complex question of class in *Emma*. On the face of it, *Emma* may seem to be the quintessential story of the English upper classes, and indeed 'A screening of *Emma* was slotted into the television schedule sensitively reorganized on the day of the funeral of Diana, Princess of Wales' (Higson 2003: 21). This seeming icon of the continuity of the hierarchy does, however, range much more widely across the class spectrum than this royal appropriation might seem to suggest. In the novel, one of the clearest markers of Emma's class and status difference is the sense that a number of those who surround her are her social inferiors, as when she muses of Frank Churchill that 'his indifference to a confusion of rank, bordered too much on inelegance of mind' (210). This is most obviously true in the case of Harriet Smith, but it also applies, in different ways and with different degrees of emphasis, in the cases of the Eltons, the Bateses, the Westons, the Coles, Jane Fairfax, Mr Perry and, of course, the Martins. Only Mr Knightley, and potentially Frank Churchill, are of a rank and fortune equal to Emma's own, and the latter is, for most of the novel, only very precariously so. Moreover, we are also intermittently aware of the presence of the Woodhouse servants, not to mention the all-important William Larkins, as well as of the gypsies and poultry-thieves who beset the margins of Highbury's wealth and ease.

In the two recent 'straight' adaptations of *Emma*, markedly varying attention has been paid to the registering of these differences. To some extent, this can be attributed to the fact that it is hard to convey the smaller distinctions and nuances of social standing within the confines of a film, where there is no omniscient narrator to fill in background information; thus in Diarmuid Lawrence's 1996 TV film, although we will presumably see that Donwell Abbey is significantly larger and more magnificent than Hartfield, especially given that Harriet observes that she would never have believed that one man could own so much, we may well not observe any real distinction between Hartfield and Randalls, so we are unlikely to deduce that Mr Weston's social station was ever any lower than that of Mr Woodhouse. Moreover, since Emma's remark on the smallness of Mr Elton's house is visually undercut by the camera panning across its not inconsiderable frontage, our sense of the relative size of houses and of their reliability as indicators of class has already been destabilised. We are left in no doubt, then, that these characters are privileged, and that they do not question the extent to which they are so, but we are unlikely if we do not already know the book to register the precise degrees of the pecking order.

Douglas McGrath's 1996 film makes even less of an effort with questions of class and status. Its Jane Fairfax is never threatened with governessing, and it is an altogether prettier, glossier affair than the Lawrence version, with romantic touches like Mr Knightley actually kissing Emma's hand (in both the novel and the Lawrence film, he merely contemplates doing so). Mr Knightley also says to Emma, 'I see you've been hard at work – making Mr Elton comfortable'; the Mr Knightley of both the Lawrence film and of Austen's original novel would, one feels, have a far clearer grasp of the fact that this is *not* real work. In McGrath's film, though, real work is in general invisible: although we do just catch a glimpse of a servant moving at the wedding and hear a male voice announcing 'Dinner is served' after the arrival of the John Knightleys, during the archery scene Emma simply remarks, 'Ah, I see the tea is ready', without there being any indication of who got it ready. There is no reference to James's daughter at Randalls and on many occasions, presumably for reasons of dramatic economy and clarity of focus, there are several scenes where servants are dimly visible in the background but the gentry themselves perform actions which would in fact have been carried out by servants: Mrs Weston pours the tea, Emma drives a carriage and sorts the post and Frank seems to imply that Mrs Elton herself has made the sandwiches when he compliments her on them. Class distinctions are made even more invisible when, after acting with notable compassion to the sick Mrs Clark, Emma refers to her as 'that poor lady', a term which it would have been quite impossible for Austen's Emma to have used of a cottager.

Most of all, it is difficult for any film aimed at audiences on both sides of the Atlantic to convey class by means of that favourite British indicator, accent. In Ang Lee's film of *Sense and Sensibility* (1995), there are, unusually for a major film, no American actors at all, and Emma

Thompson, the scriptwriter and star, is thus enabled to avoid the experiences of her former husband Kenneth Branagh, whose otherwise acclaimed film of *Much Ado About Nothing* (1993) was generally felt to have been marred by the presence of Keanu Reeves as Don John and Michael Keaton as a virtually incoherent Dogberry; both class positions and indeed character can be indicated by intonation, with Harriet Walter's Fanny Dashwood, for instance, speaking in noticeably more cut-glass tones than the unaffected standard English of her brother and her sisters-in-law. Similarly, in Diarmuid Lawrence's version of *Emma*, Juliet Stevenson's Mrs Elton has a give-away West Country accent that significantly undermines her pretensions to gentility, while the extremely upper-class pronunciation of Miss Bates (played by Sophie Thompson, sister of Emma), coupled with the careful preservation of Mr Knightley's comment that Miss Bates's notice was once an honour, reminds us of the perilously fragile and contingent nature of class position and its uneasy relationship to money. However this is a strategy not without its risks: preparing to direct *Persuasion*, 'Roger Michell ... declared in *The Daily Telegraph*, "I was repulsed by the idea of people in Jane Austen speaking in the same voice. It seemed absolutely absurd so I've tried to get as many varieties as possible"' (Hudelet 2005: 178), but Ariane Hudelet, noting this, complains that Corin Redgrave's Sir Walter in particular was not easy to understand, an observation seconded by Elsa Solender: 'I recall plaintive whispers of "What did he say?" in the first 25 minutes of the BBC's 1995 *Persuasion*' (Solender 2002: 104). In the Douglas McGrath version of *Emma*, that accents were felt to be a sensitive issue is clearly evidenced by the immaculate English tones carefully studied and adopted by Gwyneth Paltrow as Emma; but these function primarily to indicate Englishness *per se*, rather than any particular social stratum of it. Though, as with Meryl Streep or later with Renée Zellweger and Anne Hathway, one cannot but marvel at Paltrow's ability so to disguise her natural pronunciation, and although the effect is infinitely preferable to the discordance created by Keaton and Reeves in *Much Ado*, it is, nevertheless, a thinner one than that provided by the rich texture of subtly different Englishes being played off against each other that we hear in *Sense and Sensibility*.

In *Clueless*, though, the problem is cleverly solved by the fact that the Hispanic maid's accent and diction so clearly mark her status, and Cher can mortally affront her by calling her Mexican when, as Josh points out, she is actually from El Salvador. (The same effect is created in Baz Luhrmann's *William Shakespeare's Romeo + Juliet*, where the Hispanic nurse always speaks of 'Huliet'.) In Heckerling's hands, then, the apparently alien climes of late twentieth-century California provide a strikingly accurate analogue for both the ambience and the ethos of Jane Austen's early nineteenth-century Highbury; in California, both Shakespeare and Austen can find a happy home, and both, too, can be made to speak, albeit mutedly, to a developing agenda, which we would now term ecocritical and which the Californian setting has proved uniquely successful in liberating in them.

2
The East Coast: *Jane Austen in Manhattan* and *Hamlet* (dir. Michael Almereyda, 2000)

In this chapter I want to discuss two films which not only situate Austen and Shakespeare on the East Coast of America, specifically in New York, but also invoke a number of cultural issues and cinematic tropes which have become associated or in some cases arguably even identified with New York: James Ivory's *Jane Austen in Manhattan* (1980) and Michael Almereyda's *Hamlet* (2000). Although made twenty years apart and focusing on different authors, these are not as dissimilar as they might appear: the line 'We're learning to be' in *Jane Austen in Manhattan* takes us close to the meditation on interbeing in *Hamlet*, and *Jane Austen in Manhattan* prominently references *The Cherry Orchard*, in which Arkadina quotes from *Hamlet*. Both films also constitute careful and detailed engagement with a Shakespearean or Austenian ethos even if sometimes only obliquely with an original text. Though John Wiltshire declares of *Jane Austen in Manhattan* that 'This Merchant Ivory production is ... dealing not with Jane Austen's texts, but with a vague cultural notion of "Jane Austen" – an Austen which might stand for any canonical work of the past' (Wiltshire 2001: 42–3), this is a film that actually engages closely with the ethos of Jane Austen as well as with that of New York theatre; indeed one might be tempted to observe that it is oddly fitting that a director named Ivory should tackle the work of a writer who described her own art as 'the little bit (two Inches wide) of Ivory on which I work with so fine a brush, as produces little effect after much labour' (Austen 2004: 198). Moreover, Austen's own interest in adaptation is central to the film, for not only is it based on her own juvenile adaptation of *Sir Charles Grandison*, her favourite novel, as a short script for home theatrical performance, but also, as John Wiltshire points out, 'Like the novel and the playlet, the film is concerned with abduction' (Wiltshire 2001: 42), which in turn functions as something of a metaphor for adaptation. When a character in the film protests that Pierre's production lacks credibility because 'Austen was never aware', Pierre interrupts with 'But that's what we're here for, to make her aware – to bring her up to date'; for Wiltshire, however,

> the irony is that it was Jane Austen who herself who performed the original abduction. It was she who took a solemn and authoritative patriarchal text and turned it into a comic skit for family entertainment ... Austen's burlesque of the original is in effect far closer in spirit to the adventurous and irresponsible Pierre than to the heritage theatre style that seems to be demanded by his backers. (Wiltshire 2001: 43)

Together, Austen's and the Merchant Ivory team's collective musings on the processes and protocols of adaptation make for a fascinating and explosive mixture, and it is with *Jane Austen in Manhattan* that I begin.

Jane Austen in Manhattan

Early in both *Jane Austen in Manhattan* and the Merchant Ivory team's earlier *Shakespeare Wallah*, which I discuss in Chapter 4, there is a scene of highly stylised acting that takes place by a lake and has something of the same effect as a play-within-a-play. The suggestion might seem to be that the following film itself is going to offer the same limpid, oblique process of quasi-reflection of the 'original' material on which it overtly bases itself as that implied by the lake. In the case of *Jane Austen in Manhattan*, though, this is complicated by the fact that the scene is located in front of a low but wide cataract, which creates an obvious disturbance to the mirroring effect that would otherwise be provided by the water; this may be taken as gesturing at the outcrops of unruly emotion – Katya's and Victor's genuine pain, George's baffled nostalgia – that periodically threaten the comedy-of-manners structure and effect of the film, but it also indicates that the film's relationship with its source text is not a wholly smooth and untroubled one. The shot might also additionally alert us to the extent to which this film is invested in the city: later, we will see the Twin Towers and the New York skyline, and will be told with delicious irony that the money-collector's idea of escape from Pierre and what he represents was going to Los Angeles to do the *Oresteia*. In this quintessentially urban environment, the natural landscape shown here represents not a welcome excursus to the pastoral but rather a source of threat, and in this respect *Jane Austen in Manhattan*, with its resolutely metropolitan sensibility, could hardly have found a more appropriate source text than *Sir Charles Grandison*, for Richardson's novel, too, fears the natural and rural landscape and regards it as a place of menace. When Mr Reeves recounts the circumstances of the heroine Harriet Byron's abduction, he explains that

> The fellow blustered at the chairmen, and bid them stop. She [Harriet] asked for Grosvenor-street. She was to be carried, she said, to Grosvenor-street.
>
> She was just there, that fellow said – It can't be Sir! It can't be! – Don't I see fields all about me? – I am in the midst of fields, Sir. (Richardson 1986: 125)

Harriet is of course quite right to be nervous: the chairmen have deliberately taken her in the wrong direction, and they have done so because their employer, the villainous Sir Hargrave Pollexfen, expects to find a rural environment more conducive to his designs on her than an urban one. Later, Mr Reeves makes a suggestive leap of logic when he muses 'O this damn'd Sir Hargrave! He has a house upon the forest. I have no doubt but he is the villain' (128). Amidst the polite society of London, fields and forests still lurk as Gothicised sources of threat and danger almost as ominously as they do in an overtly Gothic text such as Ann Radcliffe's *The Romance of the Forest*.

This is not the only respect in which the aesthetic of the Richardsonian/Austenian original is congenial to the film; as I shall discuss, it finds its eighteenth-century avatar in other ways, too, to be a powerful key for unlocking the various topics on which it wants to touch. *Jane Austen in Manhattan* is spot on in its identification of the *Grandison* skit, however trivial it may appear, as actually offering an important insight into Jane Austen's *oeuvre*. Jane Austen's nephew reported that 'Every circumstance narrated in Sir Charles Grandison, all that was ever said or done in the cedar parlour, was familiar to her; and the wedding days of Lady L. and Lady G. were as well remembered as if they had been living friends' (Southam 1980: 9); thus writing to her sister Cassandra about a new cap, Austen observed that 'It will be white sattin and lace, and a little white flower perking out of the left ear, like Harriot [sic] Byron's feather'

(Austen 2004: 150; Austen invariably spells 'Harriet' as 'Harriot', whether she is referring to Richardson's heroine or to friends and acquaintances). Here she is referring to Harriet Byron's own description of the masquerade costume in which she will be abducted:

> They call it the dress of an Arcadian Princess: But it falls not in with any of my notions of the Pastoral dress of Arcadia.
>
> A white Paris net sort of cap, glittering with spangles, and incircled by a chaplet of artificial flowers, with a little white feather perking from the left ear, is to be my head-dress. (Richardson 1986: 115)

That Austen should recall this particular costume in such detail is suggestive of the degree of her familiarity and indeed her emotional engagement with the novel, as well as providing another telling signal of the dangers which in this text are associated with what in others would be merely the *locus amoenus* of pastoral, since it is in this costume that Harriet will fall prey to Sir Hargrave Pollexfen. Nevertheless, Austen herself did not write like Richardson in *Grandison*, and her own adaptation of that text is radically irreverent. It is therefore ironically appropriate that *Jane Austen in Manhattan*'s attitude to its own 'source' text is similarly ambivalent, opportunistic and predatory. For *Jane Austen in Manhattan*, Austen represents both what it values as paradigmatic and authorisatory and also that which it suspects to have become outmoded and unsustainable in the face of the forces of cultural change.

This becomes particularly clear when one compares *Jane Austen in Manhattan* with the other film that takes Jane Austen to New York, Whit Stillman's *Metropolitan* (1990). This features open discussion of *Mansfield Park* and Joseph Alulis (2001: 70) points to the importance for it of *Persuasion*, too. Superficially, *Metropolitan* aligns itself with *Jane Austen in Manhattan* by apparently inhabiting much the same time period: as Madeleine Dobie observes, despite the 1990 date of *Jane Austen in Manhattan*, 'The scene in fact seems to be set in the 1980s, though as the subtitle implies, the mores of the preppies that it portrays are so anchored in tradition that it could just as well be the 1950s' (Dobie 2003: 254). Like *Jane Austen in Manhattan*, *Metropolitan* conducts a debate over the value of its characters' lifestyle, and again like *Jane Austen in Manhattan*, it shows competition among its modern characters for the original Austenian rôles: Madeleine Dobie reads Audrey as Fanny (Dobie 2003: 254), as does R.V. Young, who also explicitly identifies Tom as Edmund (Young 2001: 53), but in fact the naïve and impecunious Tom, who starts the film as a figure completely outside the main group, seems an equally likely candidate for the rôle of Fanny, as Elsa Solender suggests (Solender 2002: 111); Solender sees Audrey as in fact 'possibly the Edmund Bertram of the piece' (Solender 2002: 112). Unlike *Jane Austen in Manhattan*, though, *Metropolitan* concentrates entirely on the perspective of the young – R.V. Young points out that 'Fathers make no appearance in the film ... *Metropolitan* thus presents a world ... where youthful figures are left on their own without visible adult guidance or influence' (Young 2001: 50) – and while Audrey may observe to Tom that 'Today, looked at from Jane Austen's perspective, would look even worse', the youth of all those involved means we can never forget that there is also tomorrow, and the future in general, to consider (not least because it seems apparent that these characters' tomorrow is in fact our own today). For the characters in *Jane Austen in Manhattan*, though, like the characters in *Shakespeare Wallah*, there is no real sense of a future. At best, they are creatures of the present; at worst, they are trapped in their pasts, and it is this for which their shared in interest in Austen proves so powerful a metaphor.

Above all, though, what Jane Austen as a figure offers this group of rather raggle-taggle theatre people is an unmistakable icon of old Englishness through which to negotiate their own uneasy and various relationships to the coast of America that started out its life as a new England, in a city whose name of New York points so firmly to English origins. It is not clear whether the Eastern European surname Liliana acquired from her husband has extended its influence to her first name, but perhaps it has, and perhaps she was born plain Lilian, as her accent would seem to suggest; if so, though, she would be one of the few characters able to lay claim to anything resembling a possibly WASP heritage. Pierre's accent is English, but his name points to France just as surely as Ariadne's does to Greece; Victor Charlton's high-cheekboned good looks would seem to suggest an origin in Eastern Europe, as would the names of Katya and Fritz, and that is certainly where George came from: he is Romanian, and his uncle Farkasz lived in Morocco, apparently leading the life of a classic remittance man. (A caption at the beginning of the film announces 'Workshop sequence staged by Andrei Serban', a Romanian-born director who was brought to the States by a grant from the Ford Foundation, so this may have been an influence on the choice of George's country of origin.) Nor is this the end of the cocktail of exotic locations and origins gestured at: the Indian-domiciled Ruth Prawer Jhabvala wrote the script and the Indian-born Ismail Merchant produced the film, Ariadne goes to explore when she hears Sufi chanting, Liliana dresses as a babushka to cook and almost as soon as the film starts we see a board displaying different currencies and translating the bidding as the Austen manuscript is being auctioned. The whole effect is the exact opposite of the typical Jane Austen community of families with deep roots in a small village or country town: rather, we see a group of first- or second-generation immigrants in a huge, anonymous city, connected by complicated threads to a very much wider world.

The tenuousness of the way these characters inhabit their adopted city and rôles is indicated symbolically through the snapping of Liliana's pearls and above all by the film's recurrent motif of fragile buildings, from the cardboard theatre to the sandcastle of George's youth, demolished day after day, which suggest the paper-thinness of the setting in which the characters act out their lives and cling to their self-selected identities. It is therefore not surprising that for each of them, in their different ways, Jane Austen proves to offer a firmer foundation than any they currently have for the rôles they wish to act. Like the obviously painted flats of Liliana's production, the sense of the stability of the surroundings is further destabilised by the film's games with scale. At one level, *Jane Austen in Manhattan* is all about the struggle for possession of a receding signifier: just as Pierre sings 'Give me your hand' when he is demanding marriage, so by a similar process of synecdoche Ariadne symbolises the manuscript symbolises Austen symbolises belonging/real art/cultural capital. A similar sliding is effected when the toy theatre opens out into a big one, but the process is ironically inverted when Pierre steals small valuable items from Liliana and a silver jug from George, because, ironically in this big city, it is what is small that is really valuable. Pierre's thefts also illustrate another concern of the film, which is to depict this society as one in which the traditional bonds of a gift culture have failed: Jenny never does give Jamie the gloves she intended to, and the lace he buys her is abandoned and apparently forgotten, another victim of Pierre's suborning of apparent charity to actual exploitation.

Austen helps these fragmented characters to form into the nearest they can ever approach to a group. In the opening rehearsal scene Pierre ventriloquises all the speaking parts, while Jamie speaks aloud all the stage directions. The homogenisation produced here could be either benign or alarming, but there can be no doubt that benignity predominates when after the rehearsal the actors jog four abreast and arm-in-arm along a New York pavement (foreshadowing the final shot when we see four people side by side on the stage). Next, as Katya kisses and tucks up Ariadne, we hear a siren wail outside, offering a clear juxtaposition between camaraderie and safety inside and threat and alarm in the big city outside. The genuine community-building function of Pierre's Manhattan Encounter Theater Laboratory is especially clear in the case of the obviously disturbed Billy (Charles McCaughan), who has apparently emerged from an institution and seems to be living on the streets, but is able to become a functioning member of the acting community. Groupness is most comprehensively underlined by the closing shot. Jane Austen's novels and indeed her whole 'brand' are predicated on the importance of heterosexual relations, but in this film these are tested and found to be fragile, and indeed both the film and the play of *Sir Charles Grandison* itself emphatically refuse heterosexual union; however, the closing shot of a group of four suggests that a larger ensemble will work well. (The extent to which the Austenian ethos lends itself to this sense of 'groupness' is also evidenced by the importance of Bridget Jones's three friends in Sharon Maguire's 2001 *Bridget Jones's Diary*.)

The film's interest in Austen is by no means wholly instrumental, though. As in Karen Joy Fowler's novel *The Jane Austen Book Club* (itself now a film), and as in its own slyly drawn parallel between cab drivers and abductors, *Jane Austen in Manhattan* deals principally in delicately drawn but nevertheless sharply focused parallels between modern characters and those of the long-dead author on whom their energies are focused, and in the construction of this relationship Austen's *oeuvre* is a fully functional and richly resonant partner rather than a passive means to an end. Most obviously, Pierre, one of the two rival theatre directors with dramatically opposed styles who are seeking to stage Jane Austen's script, is a classic untrustworthy Austenian charmer, with fortune-hunting motives and a dubious past – was he in a cave in the Himalayas or in Los Angeles working as a stuntman? When Ariadne is interrupted in the middle of asking 'And where is this brother of yours to whom ...', those of us familiar with the source text are irresistibly invited to supply and, by implication, apply to Pierre the answer which Miss Grandison gives us of Sir Charles: 'he is constantly going about from one place to another. But what for, we cannot tell. And we have such a high respect for him that we never interfere with his affairs' (Southam 1980: 46). For us, Pierre is a figure of mystery, and we are repeatedly reminded that he has a life outside the setting in which we see him of which we know nothing.

To some extent, we seem to be offered an obvious paradigm for understanding him in that Pierre is of course like the villainous Sir Hargrave Pollexfen, as whom he is cast in Liliana's ideal production (although it is notable that Pierre does not cast himself as Sir Hargrave, suggesting that his own self-image is rather different). When Harriet Byron first describes Sir Hargrave in Richardson's novel, she says,

> Sir Hargrave, it seems, has travelled: But he must have carried abroad with him a great number of follies, and a great deal of affectation, if he has left any of them behind him.
>
> But with all his foibles, he is said to be a man of enterprize and courage; and young ladies, it seems, must take care how they laugh with him: For he makes ungenerous constructions to the disadvantage of a woman whom he can bring to seem pleas'd with his jests. (45)

Later, she muses 'I remember, that *mischievous* is one of the bad qualities Sir John attributed to [Sir Hargrave]: And *revengeful* another' (88). Pierre fits these descriptions in a number of respects. Although we are never explicitly told reliably that he has travelled, he certainly has the air of one who has done so, and he could very fairly be called affected. His courage we can only doubt, given his rather pitiful behaviour when Victor Charlton attacks him, but mischievous, resentful and ungenerous to women he most certainly is. However, Pierre is in fact far more Austenian than Richardsonian. Like the typical Jane Austen villain, he is immensely charismatic, with Robert Powell making good use of the fact that he arrives in the film trailing his Jesus persona from Zeffirelli's 1977 *Jesus of Nazareth*. Like Willoughby reading Shakespeare's sonnets to Marianne in *Sense and Sensibility*, Pierre uses artistic sensitivity as social currency; like Wickham in *Pride and Prejudice*, he transfers his affections to wherever there is money to be had, though perhaps the parallel with Willoughby is the closer, because we do seem to be invited to suppose that both could have been different, and both seem genuinely to love the art they also make use of.

There are also other parallels between Austen characters and those of the film. The Victor / Ariadne and Jamie / Jenny relationships mirror and inflect each other in something of the same way as the Jane / Bingley and Elizabeth / Darcy ones do, with one presented as a debased, more sexualised version of the other, although Victor Charlton himself is more of a Brandon or Tilney, worthy but not compelling. Most of all, of course, Victor is like Sir Charles Grandison himself, who is above all a decent man, but a man in whom the reader will struggle to be interested. As for Liliana, what is notable both here and in *The Jane Austen Book Club* is that both go where Jane Austen herself never really did, into the dreams and psyche of the older woman. This is partly because *Jane Austen in Manhattan* is a rare exception among Jane Austen films: although the classic break-up song 'All by myself' is heard in both *Clueless* (dir. Amy Heckerling, 1995) and *Bridget Jones's Diary*, *Jane Austen in Manhattan* was essentially the only Austen adaptation or tribute film before *Miss Austen Regrets* (2008) that was prepared to contemplate the fact that Jane Austen herself was single throughout her life, and moreover looked at the single state with sharp and clear eyes, as in *Emma* where we are told that Miss Bates 'enjoyed a most uncommon degree of popularity for a woman neither young, handsome, rich, nor married' (Austen 1966: 51–2). (It is true that *Becoming Jane* ends with Jane single, but its *raison d'être* is to see her primarily as a participant in a love story.)

In *Jane Austen in Manhattan*, however, it is the ageing, loveless Liliana who alone of all the characters has the strength to be alone and draw boundaries, and although she is suggestively counterpoised with the extremely youthful Jane Austen who wrote the Grandison adaptation on which the film centres, she does nevertheless claim to speak for the author – 'Let me do the play the way Jane herself would have wanted it' – and her claim is not a wholly ludicrous one, in that the production she stages would certainly have been more comprehensible and recognisable to Austen than Pierre's would. It is, for instance, notable that Liliana's production has something of the look and feel of a Mozart opera, and Mozart not only provided a very appropriate paradigm in *Die Entführung aus dem Serail*, which matches Austen's skit both in topic and tone, but has become something of a classic signifier for Austen's own period, as evidenced by his use in the 1995 BBC/A&E *Pride and Prejudice*, where Elizabeth sings a version of Cherubino's aria from *The Marriage of Figaro*, in the 2007 *Northanger Abbey*, where Catherine and the Tilneys are seen at the opera listening to the Queen of the Night's aria from *The Magic Flute*, and in Andrew Black's 2003 Utah-set *Pride and Prejudice* in which Bingley makes his money selling Mozart for dogs. We are also drawn into Liliana's proposed production in a way that we are not drawn into Pierre's, for we see it from an impossible viewpoint – from inside the cupboard into which Harriet is trying to 'escape' – as if we were sharing Liliana's own vision of it. Pierre's, though, we see only from the perspective of a very firmly posited fourth wall, with cuts to the reaction of the audience. Later, we see Liliana's as if we were hovering slightly above the stage, very close to Sir Hargrave Pollexfen and Harriet, underlining the sense that this is not a real experience but a fantasy, and one which we are structurally forced to share with Liliana.

Moreover, despite her age, Liliana has no real rival for the rôle of Austenian heroine. Ariadne is certainly not in any sense Austenian: although the character is said to have appeared in *'Tis Pity She's a*

Whore and the actress, Sean Young, was later to become famous as Rachael in *Blade Runner* (dir. Ridley Scott, 1982), Ariadne herself is a blank, and certainly has nothing of the personality or firm sense of moral values of an Austen heroine. There is a faint touch of the Richardsons about her in that Harriet Byron, too, is occasionally helpless – when she is abducted by Sir Hargrave Pollexfen she keeps falling into fits – but for Richardson this is merely a sign of her virtue rather than one of weakness, and Harriet also has far more clearly defined values and standards than Ariadne. Most of all, though, Ariadne is overwhelmingly like a Chekhov character, drifting from predicament to predicament. The Chekhovian resonances are certainly sharply underlined when Pierre and Liliana do a scene from *The Seagull* while Liliana is cooking – a telling choice because *The Seagull* too is a text saturated with reference to another one, with the set dominated by a stage erected for the production of Kostya's play, and the scene from which Liliana and Pierre quote comes just after it has become obvious that Trigorin is likely to 'abduct' Nina from Kostya, after which Nina drifts and is destroyed, as Ariadne too presumably will be (not least since the mythological character after whom she is named was taken from her home by Theseus, who later abandoned her on the island of Naxos).

For all the overt reference to Chekhov, though, an even more salient text to consider in the context of *Jane Austen in Manhattan*'s depiction of East Coast theatre is Mel Brooks's classic comedy *The Producers* (1968), which satirises New York theatre, and indeed the excesses and eccentricities of New York cultural life in general – Lorenzo Saint DuBois ludicrously wears a Campbell's soup tin round his neck, and we meet a splendidly camp theatre director (Christopher Hewitt) and his wildly mannered black-clad assistant (Andreas Voutsinas) and watch as the film plays complex games with the relationship between rôle and reality. Like *Jane Austen in Manhattan*, *The Producers* in its audition scene offers ironic comment on preferred performance styles, and it is linked to *Jane Austen in Manhattan* by the fact that both stress the importance of theatre producers of eastern European origin: Liliana observes of her late husband that 'Everyone said I married him for his Polish name ... couldn't have been for anything else', and says to Ariadne 'You know how I see you? As one of those Russian girls who have dreams – dreams of love', while Max Bialystock in *The Producers* is clearly also of eastern European origin. In both films, too, it is the older, widowed woman who wields social and financial power: Bialystock must court the little old ladies (in ways which make explicit the deep connection between theatre and sex, since they hinge on erotic rôle play) because they have the power to fund his productions, and the widowed Liliana too is free and her own mistress. It is therefore particularly notable that *The Producers* brings on the author only first to mock and then subsequently to knock him unconscious, with Bialystock resolving that 'Next time I produce a play – no author'.

Jane Austen in Manhattan does not openly mock its author and certainly does not knock her unconscious, but it does instantiate her, like one of Bialystock's little old ladies, as not only a representative of capital, both cultural and concrete, but also as a figure possessed of a not fully explained and rather sinister-seeming power. It does so by insistently associating her with Liliana, and with the archetypally old-world East Coast theatrical sensibility which Liliana is presented as embodying, and by covertly but insistently suggesting that both Austen and Liliana sponsor an art which works to contain and diminish men. When Pierre sings (or rather lip-synchs, something that in itself suggests the degree to which he is being manipulated and ventriloquised here) the rôle of Sir Hargrave Pollexfen in Liliana's ideal production (it is unclear whether the staging of this that we see is her fantasy or the film's own, or perhaps both) his repeated, insistently delivered lines 'You shall be mine! You shall be mine!', belted out in full bass virility, seem addressed simultaneously to both Austen's manuscript and also his erstwhile lover Liliana as well as retaining their intradiegetic application to Ariadne's Harriet Byron. His aria takes a number of remarks that are indeed all uttered by Richardson's Sir Hargrave Pollexfen, but at widely scattered points in the text. Firstly Richardson's Sir Hargrave assures Harriet that 'I will not cease pursuing you till you are mine, or till you are the wife of some other man' (86); it is not until considerably later that he declares 'Miss Byron, you *shall* be mine' (157), and a little later still he says first that 'Your fate is *determined*, Miss Byron' (161) and then 'All your struggles will not *avail* you – Will not *avail* you' (165).

The aria, however, collapses these separated moments into one sustained burst of passion, and the effect is to fashion Pierre as a Sir Hargrave who purely and solely embodies desire. As he stomps around the stage, his variously explained and inexplicable limp (which Jamie attributes to 'a split hoof') becomes all too easily readable as a female romance author's fantasy of castration, like Charlotte Brontë's blinding of Mr Rochester or Mrs Gaskell's diminution and taming of her hero in *North and South*: in the woman's art, it suggests, the too-powerful male must be contained and domesticated, as Pierre is made to pace like a caged animal around the stage of a picture-perfect eighteenth-century theatre, which we are never quite sure whether to read as a real building or as a wish-fulfilment projection of the toy theatre that we see Liliana gloating over with the unmistakably emasculated George. (Unlike with Pierre's production, we never see the response of an actual audience to Liliana's, and we cannot be clear about the status of the claps we think we hear). It is notable that in his own proposed production, Pierre never appears on stage, possibly because he is reluctant to display his limp (his lack of physical confidence is certainly stressed when he tamely submits to Victor Charlton's assault); Liliana's, though, puts him centre stage, and makes the display of his corralled body and apparently impassioned soul central to its effect.

The Pierre of Liliana's fantasy version could in fact be seen as realis-ing the ultimate fantasy of several notable film adaptations of female-authored art, the construction of the male as desiring subject. The logic of this is most clearly demonstrated in the BBC/A&E *Pride and Prejudice*. In Laura Mulvey's influential proposition, it is, traditionally, men who are possessors of the gaze when viewing on screen and film (Mulvey 1989: 25–6). This *Pride and Prejudice* adaptation, however, is unashamed about appealing to women – and in particular about fetish-ising and framing Darcy and offering him up to the female gaze. What the camerawork of this adaptation insistently picks out, apart from one brief scene in which Elizabeth assesses herself in her bedroom mirror, is primarily how men are seen. Most notably, of course, this is the under-lying logic of the interpolated scenes in which Darcy is seen in the bath and diving into the lake, the latter of which has become the iconic image of the production and one much quoted in later Austen adapta-tions (in *Lost in Austen*, Amanda's first thought when Darcy declares his love is to get him to emerge from the lake).

It is, however, not a simple act of ogling that is solicited by the visual emphases of these adaptations, and nor would such a strat-egy have been likely to succeed, as was evidenced by the poor for-tunes of a rather different adaptation, the BBC's version of Conrad's *Nostromo* (dir. Alastair Reid, 1997). Although the presence of Colin Firth might have been thought to add to the visual appeal of this, the *Observer*'s Media Editor, Richard Brooks, nevertheless wondered whether *Nostromo* 'might suffer from the *Rhodes* syndrome – lack of women. Firth's character, Charles Gould, cares more for his gold mine than his gorgeous wife' (*Observer*, 2 February 1997). This comment actually implies more than it overtly states: not only do there need to be women on screen, it seems, but the men must be interested in them. What we want to see, I think, is not just a Darcy in the abstract: it is a Darcy looking – particularly at Elizabeth, but also, on other occasions, at images which have been contextualised as being poignantly redolent of her absence, because these looks too can signify his need (this is a distinct advance on the novel, where '[i]t was an earnest, steadfast gaze, but she sometimes doubted whether there were much admiration in it, and sometimes it seemed nothing but absence of mind' [215].) And we look back in a silent collusion, because it is in that need that we most want to believe. The emphasis on the hero's face and body is designed, in the end, to assert the existence of a soul, or at least a subjectivity; thus as Cheryl Nixon suggests, 'Darcy's dive is not a revelation of his physical abilities ... rather, it is a revelation of his emotional capabilities' (Nixon 1998: 24).

Men certainly have a soul in *Jane Austen in Manhattan*. One might, though, wonder in this film whether *women* have souls, for women (in *Man*hattan?) are too simply flighty or controlling; it is the men – Pierre, Victor and Jamie – who are needed to inject vision or sense respectively. Both Jamie's cab and his resistance to Pierre establish him as a figure of mobility and potential, but George's mother didn't notice his sandcastle being destroyed because she was reading Henry James, and Billy says 'They're all the same. Just like my mother'; when asked 'Where is she?' he replies 'Dead', with the clear implication that her absence and/or previous behaviour is responsible for his fragile mental state. In this respect the adaptation is very different from *Sir Charles Grandison*, of which Brian Southam justly observes 'What sinks the novel ... is its hero' (Southam calls Sir Charles's sister, Charlotte, 'the novel's undisputed triumph' [Southam 1980: 20]), and in which Harriet Byron writes 'But one word, by the bye, Lucy – Don't you think it is very happy for us foolish women, that the generality of the lords of *creation* are not much wiser than ourselves?' (47). It is notable, too, that for all the attention it nominally pays to her, the film does not in fact take Austen's art seriously, as is indeed indicated by the very fact that its source for the words of Pierre's aria is not in fact Austen at all, where none of this material appears, but the Richardsonian original.

Moreover, whatever other contrasts there may be between them, this willingness to violate and appropriate the Austenian original is common to both proposed productions: if in Pierre's version the words are swamped by mannerisms, in Liliana's they are so by the aggressively scored music. Neither of the two approaches conveys anything at all of the essential spirit and animus of the original, which is above all a skit, a burlesque on a much-loved but long, flagging and over-earnest novel, and although the film ostensibly works to stress the differences between Liliana's production and Pierre's, they do in fact have something in common. Although the line 'Is the book burnt?' in Pierre's production is followed directly by 'How could you, George?', in fact George is ultimately the man who facilitates *both* productions, and to some extent both are tarred with the same brush. It is true that Liliana's version is closer to the 'original' that we see at the opening, but for all her determination to do the play 'as Jane herself would have wanted', her production includes a telling moment which neatly crystallises the violence she in fact does to the text, when her Harriet dashes the book into the fire with the words 'No Dearly Beloveds here!'. In the manuscript, the words are 'I see no Dearly Beloveds here, & I will not have any' (Southam 1980: 77), which cleverly develops the original's

> I stamp'd, and threw myself to the length of my arm, as he held my hand. *No dearly beloved's*, said I. I was just beside myself. What to say, what to do, I knew not. (155)

However, a line has been scored through the words in the manuscript of Austen's adaptation; as Brian Southam observes, 'some of the most amusing lines of the play – in the middle of the marriage ceremony, on page sixteen of the manuscript – were crossed out, apparently by Jane Austen' (Southam 1980: 2). Liliana's version is thus true to neither the pungent economy of Jane Austen's first thought nor the prudence of her second, and not even to the original Richardson, any more than the words of Pierre's aria are. Instead, Liliana's version is a hybrid, an opportunistic form exactly revealing the predatory attitude of adaptation towards original, and in this it provides a microcosm of the film as a whole, for Ivory's take on 'Jane Austen in Manhattan' in fact proves to direct its satire and animus as much – if indeed not more than – towards Jane Austen as towards Manhattan. For Ivory, then, East Coast theatre and its traditions and conventions prove the ideal frame for an American male film director's sly attack on the art and ethos of a female European novelist-turned-dramatist, since it enables him to showcase his own art and minimise hers. In the narrative of the film itself, Liliana may triumph over Pierre, but in the extradiegetic interplay between adaptation and source, it is its own medium and aesthetic that Ivory's film finally endorses rather than that of its Austenian original. Nevertheless, he has found in Austen's skit the perfect text for his metatextual enquiry.

Hamlet (dir. Michael Almereyda, 2000)

For Michael Almereyda, too, an English classic provides an ideal vehicle for an enquiry into modes of representation, and also to address other issues as well. Where Almereyda's *Hamlet* apparently differs from *Jane Austen in Manhattan* is in its representation of ethnicity. Here names are no guide, since all are taken from Shakespeare, but the characters generally seem to form a strikingly homogenous group in terms of appearance and accent. Nevertheless, an African-American security guard replaces the Bernardo character of the original, and there are also a number of significant references to Ireland, as Mark Thornton Burnett observes:

> The protagonist's connection with Ireland is initially suggested in the casting of Horatio (Karl Geary). His strong Dublin accent and dominant role work to formulate Ireland – as opposed to New York – as an exceptional landmass where loyalty, support, friendship and integrity are still valued. The corresponding linkage of the University of Wittenberg and the city of Dublin confirms Ireland as the repository of traditions of books, learning and poetry and implies Hamlet's preference for this latter territory ... A map of Ireland hangs on Hamlet's wall, its presence in the *mise-en-scène* continually pointing up a geographical entity that is at one and the same time inspirational and aspirational. (Burnett 2007: 54)

Moreover, Hamlet himself is interested in Eastern philosophy, and when he enters the Blockbuster store the film being played stars an actor of Asian origin. Together, these tiny details work to suggest a cultural complexity and potential fragmentation to which Shakespeare supplies a reassuringly massive and monolithic counterweight; in this manic city, teeming with so many different lives and their competing narratives, here at least is a strong story with a simple, recognisable, overarching shape – a strength to which the most eloquent testimony is the number of liberties which Almereyda has felt able to take with the traditional appearance of *Hamlet*, knowing that it will still be recognisable. Here too, then, Shakespeare's status as icon of Englishness comes into play, just as Austen's does in *Jane Austen in Manhattan*.

Moreover, the two films share something else. In Almereyda's *Hamlet*, too, men are king, and that is because, for Almereyda even more than for Ivory, Manhattan is a jungle in which only the fittest can survive and one which is all the more terrifying for being made out of concrete. As Barbara Hodgdon notes, 'Almereyda establishes locale with a low-angle shot of Manhattan's canyon of skyscrapers at deep twilight' (Hodgdon 2003: 200), and like Baz Luhrmann's 1996 *William Shakespeare's Romeo + Juliet*, this is a film whose sensibility is radically conditioned by the pressures of urban living, but in this case with a distinctively East Coast inflection. The first stage direction in the screenplay reads '*A near-hallucinatory spectacle: traffic, neon, noise*' (Almereyda 2000: 5), and we are told that when Claudius speaks of 'above' '*He presses a button. The limo's overhead window slides back; skyscrapers float overhead*' (Almereyda 2000: 75): for Shakespeare's Claudius, what looms above is heaven, but for Almereyda's it is the city. In the film, the first title is 'New York City, 2000', and images of the city dominate throughout: during the scene in the Guggenheim the architecture dwarfs and traps the humans and the little photographs Ophelia strews echo the big windows of the buildings around, framing the humans they depict within the architecture they resemble. Mark Thornton Burnett compares *Hamlet* in this respect with Greg Lombardo's *Macbeth in Manhattan* (1999) and also with Kenneth Branagh's projected *Macbeth*, which

> will 'centre on the control of a global media empire ... the murders take place on Wall Street'. In writing New York as a soulless centre, the films avail themselves of one resonant strand of cinematic narrative: Martin Scorsese's *Taxi Driver* (1976), John Carpenter's *Escape from New York* (1981) and Mary Harron's *American Psycho* (2000) establish New York as both a metaphorical gaol and a breeding ground for neuroses and acquisitiveness. (Burnett 2007: 52)

Adding that '[a]ll three films draw on New York's postmodern connections to melancholia and mental illness' (Burnett 2007: 52), Burnett argues that

> As the film understands it, Hamlet is dislocated in direct relation to the *faux* historical nature of his urban contexts. Imitative Chippendale markers on skyscrapers, the pseudo-real South Street Seaport and ersatz architectural symbols in New York have resulted in a fragmentary landscape in which the inhabitant can only be *angst*-ridden and isolated. (Burnett 2007: 52–3)

Heights in particular are frightening, with the ghost appearing in a high place and the final duel taking place on a rooftop, and this final scene is prefaced by a shot of a Gothic, church-like structure silhouetted against a skyscraper whose top we cannot see. This is the only sign of anything that might even conceivably be a religious structure – there is none at the cemetery, and the scene in Claudius's chapel has been transferred to a taxi, reinforcing the image of the city as icon of material power. It is richly appropriate that after failing to kill Claudius, Hamlet runs into a cinema showing *The Lion King*, a narrative with no buildings in which nature and the stars are important and which thus constitutes the ideal escape for him, while at the same time *The Lion King*'s own indebtedness to *Hamlet* underlines the extent to which there is in fact no escape for him, since he is merely running from one version of his own story to another.

In this stress on the struggle of the individual against the civic and the corporate, Almereyda's film directly recalls an earlier take on *Hamlet*, Akira Kurosawa's *The Bad Sleep Well* (1960). Although the only overt acknowledgement of Shakespeare in Kurosawa's film is the fact that we hear the march from Mendelssohn's *A Midsummer Night's Dream* at the ill-fated opening wedding, the echoes of *Hamlet* are clear. The lame bride limps in on one high shoe and one low, recalling Claudius's 'an auspicious and a dropping eye' (I.ii.11) as well as, conceivably, the etymological derivation of his name from the Latin *claudus*, meaning lame. One of the pressmen calls the wedding 'The best one-act play I ever saw', irresistibly recalling the importance of the play-within-the-play in *Hamlet*, which also centres on a marriage; later, the supposed Nishi (Toshiro Mifune) and his friend the supposed Itakura, the Horatio figure (Takeshi Kato), watch Mr Iwabuchi and conclude that 'It's hard to believe he's bad', recalling Hamlet's view of Claudius that 'one may smile, and smile, and be a villain' (I.v.108). Iwabuchi himself (Masayuki Mori) combines elements of Polonius and Claudius, although Shirai (Kô Nishimura) also has elements of Polonius since he is the supposed Nishi's first kill, and in an obvious echo of the many psychoanalysing readings of Hamlet, Iwabuchi and Moriyama wonder whether Shirai has a persecution complex. The supposed Nishi says 'I'll be the dynamite', echoing Hamlet's 'I will delve one yard below their mines / And blow them at the moon' (III.iv.210–11), and his wife Yoshiko inadvertently betrays him to her father just as the exchange between Hamlet and Ophelia is spied on by Polonius and Claudius. Although there is no ghost as such, Wada (Kamatari Fujiwari) goes to his own funeral and thereafter functions like a ghost, and he certainly scares Shirai as much and in the same way as if he were one. At the end, the supposed Itakura confirms his rôle as a Horatio figure when he says to Yoshiko and her brother Tatsuo 'Listen to my story', echoing Horatio's closing promise that 'All this can I / Truly deliver' (V.ii.390–1).

There are differences between the two stories, however, and some of these interpretative choices too have a bearing on Almereyda's *Hamlet*. *The Bad Sleeps Well* entirely lacks a Gertrude figure, and has no suggestion of the Oedipal. Indeed the supposed Nishi's real mother is dead; only his father's widow is still alive, and laments his status as 'A son without a father's name'. This is an emphasis found too in Almereyda's *Hamlet*, where Hamlet's angst is unequivocally existential rather than Oedipal. Instead, the primary focus of both narratives is on the father-son relationship. In *The Bad Sleep Well*, the supposed Nishi hated his father, although ironically Yoshiko loves hers, and equally in *Hamlet* there is no great sense of closeness between Ethan Hawke's tormented young man and the cynical-looking figure of Sam Shepard's Ghost: indeed Douglas Lanier observes that 'It is a metacinematic masterstroke to have cast Sam Shepard as Hamlet's father, since he is so closely identified with the modern American theater and with critique of the media myth of the happy American family' (Lanier 2002: 171), and the number of different families at the beginning of 'The Mousetrap' suggests both that Hamlet has no ready image of his own happy family to hand (Hawke certainly privately conceived of Hamlet's relationship with his father as a troubled one, as we shall see) and also that this is a tragedy emblematic of (American) family life in general rather than a private and individual one.

This emphasis on the general rather than the individual is something also found in *The Bad Sleep Well*. Above all, Kurosawa's film is centrally concerned with the pernicious effects of the corporate ethos: this is, after all, a film in which personal identity is comprehensively riddled by the fact that two of the characters go throughout by false names, and the supposed Nishi explicitly depersonalises his own story when he says that he sees himself as campaigning for justice in general rather than just avenging his father. This is the world of big business, wholly focused on the material and impersonal: successful Japanese in the film think only of owning American cars (the film was made not long after the Americans had left Japan, having presided over its postwar reconstruction), and there is palpable unease when Tatsuo Iwabuchi, the Laertes figure (Tatsuya Mihashi) gives a markedly personal and very edgy speech at the wedding, laying bare dark things by explaining that he loves his sister and threatening to kill the supposed Nishi if he doesn't make her happy. Corporate loyalty is most tellingly evidenced by the fact that the President's message to Miura that he has complete faith in him is effectively an order to commit suicide, which Miura immediately does, and Wada too goes off to die out of loyalty to the firm. Equally revealing is the moment when 'Itakura' exclaims to Wada 'Stop it! You can't move Nishi with such stories. He's no petty official', and later he says to 'Nishi' of Wada 'He's not a man. He's an official'.

Throughout the narrative, moreover, we are never allowed to forget that the company whose affairs we are following is a building company, which has radically conditioned the environment in which this society lives. As 'Nishi', 'Itakura' and Wada stand on the site of a factory bombed in the war, we recall the devastation of Japan by American B29 bombers, and the extent to which it had subsequently to be rebuilt; at such a historical moment, the kind of fraud in the securing of building contracts on which the film focuses was a particularly burning issue. The importance of buildings is most sharply emblematised by the wedding cake, which is saturated in several layers of meaning: most obviously, the fact that the cake is in the shape of a building and has a red rose marking the room Furuya jumped from makes it the spectre at the feast, but it also ironically echoes the wedding cake in Billy Wilder's *Some Like It Hot* (1959), which brought death to those present. We discover later that the cake also functioned in the same way as 'The Mousetrap', since Shirai's reaction to it convinced 'Nishi' of his guilt.

Almereyda's film recalls Kurosawa's in a number of ways. In the photograph which betrays the supposed Nishi's real identity, Furuya's widow identifies him to Moriyama as 'The man standing apart, by the telegraph pole', prefiguring the importance of technologies of communication in Almereyda, as does the fact that the film proudly announces at the outset that it is shot in Tohoscope, a technology that was at the time only a very few years old. Both *Hamlet* and *The Bad Sleep Well* open with a wedding or the aftermath of one, and in both the bridal couple are greeted by a barrage of photographers with cameras. In *The Bad Sleep Well*, Furuya died by jumping from a window and 'Nishi' tries to throw Shirai from one, but is unable to go through with it, berating himself that 'I'm not tough enough ... I don't hate enough' and that 'It's hard to hate evil', after which Shirai goes mad; in Almereyda's film, Hamlet first sees his father's ghost at a high window through which the ghost then exits. In *The Bad Sleep Well*, the big men in the company are illicitly tape-recorded, as Hamlet is in Almereyda's film.

There are also some similarities with another Kurosawa take on Shakespeare, *Throne of Blood* (1957). This pits a very schematic forest against a looming castle for possession of which Washizu (Toshiro Mifune) strives; as both the forest spirit and Washizu's wife Lady Asaji (Isuzu Yamada) say, 'Every samurai longs to be the master of a castle'. Here, Cobweb Castle is the seat of a sinister, inscrutable leadership that operates in ways not dissimilar to corporate power. For much of the time we see the castle only from the outside, as we will later so often see buildings in Almereyda's *Hamlet*, and when it shakes during a storm one of the inhabitants observes that 'Its foundations have been rotten for many months'. At the close, the starkly constructed polarity of the natural versus the constructed finds its strongest statement as the wood advances on the castle, and a shot of the lone pillar which marks the site of the once-powerful castle opens and closes the film. Here, too, the room in which a man committed suicide remains tainted. The importance of rooms and buildings is thus insistently underlined both here and in *The Bad Sleep Well*, and so it is too in *Hamlet*: when Hamlet takes a last lingering look at his room before leaving for the duel, we receive final confirmation of what Almereyda's film has so often suggested, that it, like Kurosawa's, is interested in buildings as much as and sometimes more than in people.

This is because in the hands of Almereyda, *Hamlet* is not about Elsinore, but about New York. Exterior architectural detail or interior design is a crucial component of almost every shot: Almereyda himself notes that

> I managed to enlist Jem Cohen to roam around town with me for a couple days, equipped with a tripod and a rented Bolex. From this we harvested a half-dozen crucial shots featuring jet trails, statues, turreted skyscrapers, a baleful urban waterfall. What's the point of these images, apart from simple punctuation? Something to do with architecture and mortality, time travel, ghosts. New Yorkers, Jem might tell you, are surrounded at every turn by radiant ephemera, ruins and things that will outlast us – distinctions that begin to blur if your view happens to be filtered through (and transformed by) a camera. (Almereyda 2000: 136)

Almereyda is also quoted as observing that

> The DP [John de Borman] is British and was a bit amazed by the city, he hadn't spent much time there, so I think he was alert to it as a spectacle. A lot of it is a kind of document of what's available to the eye. It's a key thing in any movie that the locations are a manifestation of the way your characters are feeling. (Fuchs)

This is, moreover, a New York whose already iconic landscape is even more saturated in resonance by the fact that Almereyda's city is also clearly identified as New York as an icon of power, as in *King Kong* when the violation of the Empire State Building becomes the emblem of the assault of savagery on civilisation. As in *King Kong*, too (and also as in *Jane Austen in Manhattan* where the toy theatre is teasingly poised as half-real and half-fantasy), scale is insistently played with here. As well as minimisation in the form of the ubiquitous technology (even the fencing, which might seem one of the film's few nods to the historical period of its original text, is electronically monitored), there is the fact that the similarity between the red backgrounds of the film itself and of *The Mousetrap* suggests *mise en abîme*, a potentially infinite regression of size and distance. (The allusion to *The Lion King* also creates something of the same effect.) Most notable is the miniaturisation of humans: all of the pictures on Hamlet's wall are postcard-sized; as Laertes warns Ophelia we see behind her row upon row of small glass objects, as if we were watching *The Glass Menagerie*, something which prepares us for the way in which her madness leads her increasingly to be dwarfed and confined by physical structures that loom over and around her; and everyone ends reduced to flickering, low-resolution images, something which is underlined by the clearly focused close-up on the face of Horatio. Even the closing words, 'our ends none of our own', are reduced to a screen after being spoken.

Most notably, this is a New York that insistently recalls the urban nightmare of *Batman*'s Gotham City. Though W.B. Worthen compares Luhrmann's *William Shakespeare's Romeo + Juliet* with 'the 1960s *Batman* series' (Worthen 2006: 301), there is in fact a far closer set of parallels between Almereyda's *Hamlet* and Tim Burton's *Batman* (1989). Early in *Batman*, we see the murder of a father, and the film sets up throughout an implicit contrast between the individual and the civic and corporate by the way in which it constantly emphasises the height of New York buildings not only in their own right but also as a clear and potent metaphor for the structures which condition life in the city. As in *Hamlet* and *The Bad Sleep Well*, the only means of escape from the life bounded by such buildings is through the window: although we do not see it, we hear afterwards that Alicia has thrown herself out of a window. We are told early that 'The words Gotham City are synonymous with crime', and the city is bedevilled with civic corruption and bought police officers; as Jack Napier says, 'Decent people shouldn't live here. They'd be happier some place else'.

There are a number of correspondences between *Batman* and *Hamlet*. In *Batman*, we see *Time* and *Vogue*; in *Hamlet*, Kyle MacLachlan's Claudius holds up *USA Today*. In both, there is mayhem in a museum and, as in

Batman, Ethan Hawke's Hamlet is dwarfed by buildings for Claudius's 'My cousin Hamlet' speech. In *Batman*, the camera shoots up to the top of a building for a discussion between Jack Napier and Grissom; in *Hamlet*, we are always on high floors, and the final duel takes place on a roof. Bruce Wayne has a huge mirror in his hall of armour, while in *Hamlet* there is mirrored glass in the limousine windows, Gertrude has mirrored wardrobe doors which Hamlet shoots through, and 'Except my life' is delivered next to a mirror. Indeed mirror effects both literal and metaphorical were originally intended to be a structuring device of the film, although financial considerations made it impossible to realise the proposed schema fully: Almereyda tells us that in the original screenplay there was to have been a Fortinbras, who was envisaged as '*a scruffy young man wearing a sharp suit, a hat with earflaps, a bag slung on one shoulder*' (Almereyda 2000: 128). This figure would have offered a double for Hamlet and also for Almereyda himself:

> In the original shooting script the multiple deaths were followed by the entrance of Fortinbras, described as 'a scruffy young man ... a bit like a young Bob Dylan,' strongly resembling Almereyda himself. Like Hamlet, Fortinbras turns out to be a young film-maker, and his final act is to pull out his videocam and photograph the scene of carnage and the audience that has witnessed it, in the final shot 'aiming his camera straight into ours' and muttering, in a brilliant recoding of the play's final line, 'Go, bid the soldiers *shoot*'. (Lanier 2002: 177)

The gravedigger was also intended as a mirror for Hamlet but similarly had to be cut (Almereyda 2000: 140). One double does, though, remain, and suggestively he, like in *The Bad Sleep Well*, is of visibly Asian rather than American origin: Yu Jin Ko points out that the film playing in the Blockbusters store is *The Crow II*, starring Brandon Lee, son of Bruce (Ko 2005: 26), another son burdened with the heritage of a famous father, while an avatar of Almereyda himself can also be seen as hovering over the film: 'The figure of the newscaster that bookends *Romeo + Juliet* as the uninvolved voice of narration and commentary was, in effect, to stage a come-back four years later as the voice of summation ... at the end of Michael Almereyda's *Hamlet*' (Buchanan 2005: 236). The parallel between Luhrmann's film and Almereyda's is further confirmed by the fact that Ophelia is seen by a water feature, recalling the prominence of water imagery in Luhrmann's film.

Such doubling effects are of course already prominent in *Hamlet* itself, where Laertes and Fortinbras both provide strongly marked parallels to

Hamlet, but they are also a well-established generic marker of the super-hero genre to which *Batman* belongs; even in such a clean and sanitised version of it as *Raiders of the Lost Ark* (dir. Steven Spielberg, 1981), Belloc can tell Indiana that they are like each other, just as in *Indiana Jones and the Last Crusade* (dir. Steven Spielberg, 1989) we learn that Indiana gets his hat and his general visual style from the bad guy who steals the cross of Coronado, and the sense of a dark mirror is often much more strongly developed than that in films of this genre. This recurrent feature of superhero narratives is particularly well demonstrated in the hugely savvy *The Incredibles* (dir. Brad Bird, 2004), which combines every superhero film cliché going – the tall buildings, the corruption and pettiness of institutional America – with a sharply focused interest in doubles, as the would-be Incrediboy haunts, duplicates and almost destroys Mr Incredible. The parallels lay bare a crucial aspect of *Hamlet* as conceived by Almereyda, the extent to which it draws on the paradigm of the lone American hero struggling against institutionalised corruption, emblematised above all by the cityscape and the corporate world which it bespeaks.

To a certain extent the parallels between Almereyda's film and Burton's are already present in the source narratives on which each draws. Like Hamlet, Bruce Wayne is seeking revenge for the murder of his parents, and Jack Napier 'comes back' as the Joker saying rather as the ghost of Hamlet's father might, 'You set me up over a woman ... I've been dead once already'. There is also, though, a more subtle parallel in the two directors' conceptions of their characters. It is notable that Batman is something of an oddity amongst superheroes in that he does not have super powers or extraterrestrial origins, only money for equipment, making him in one way the most ordinary and recognisable of the group. In other respects, though, *Batman* is perhaps the extreme case of the superhero genre, in ways which Hamlet doubles: in the case of each, a mild-mannered appearance belies a potential for danger, and both are simultaneously expected to right wrongs and at are the same time felt as an awkward encumbrance to the community they inhabit.

To some extent the emphasis on the cityscape encouraged by the parallels with the Kurosawa and Burton films is in fact appropriate for *Hamlet*. As we saw in the last chapter, Shakespearean comedies typically include an excursus to the green world, but this changes in the problem plays and tragedies, giving rise to a sensibility which has sometimes been classified as 'city tragedy'. In *Hamlet* the green world is evoked only ironically, as in Hamlet's reference to the unweeded garden and Ophelia's to the grass-green turf marking her father's grave, and although what *Hamlet* offers us may not be a cityscape, it is a castlescape, and within are secrets, as Vermandero says in Thomas Middleton and William Rowley's play *The Changeling*:

> We use not to give survey
> Of our chief strengths to strangers: our citadels
> Are placed conspicuous to outward view
> On promonts' tops, but within are secrets.
>
> (I.i.161–4)

For such a conception of the castle as both stronghold and Gothicised site of a tormented and repressed interiority, the bastions of corporate America provide an eerily appropriate metaphor.

This sense of the overriding power of the corporate, though, is constantly counterpoised by an insistence on the reality and vibrancy of a personal sensibility, which operates on both an intradiegetic and also an extradiegetic level. Throughout the published screenplay, Almereyda stresses the involvement of the cast in creative decisions: 'Ethan's contributions were essential. Fortified by Harold Goddard's excellent critical study, *The Meaning of Shakespeare* ... he made a case for Hamlet as someone whose hesitation to kill Claudius is justified' (Almereyda 2000: ix). Hawke himself is quoted as saying that 'I think you could build a good case that that Ghost breathed nothing but evil into his son's ear' (Almereyda 2000: xiv), and Hawke's personal scepticism about the ghost is clearly reflected in the film's shooting direction '*Hamlet looks heartsick, amazed and appalled. His father, we might sense, never spoke to him so directly while alive*' (Almereyda 2000: 31). Almereyda is also careful in the published screenplay to stress his own distance from corporate America: 'From what I can tell, global corporate power is as smoothly treacherous and absolute as anything going on in a well-oiled feudal kingdom, and the notion of an omnipresent Denmark Corp. provided an easy vehicle for Claudius's smiling villainy' (Almereyda 2000: x). It is well worth noting the sense of exclusion implied here by 'from what I can tell', and also how often in this film we are outside buildings, usually for the simple reason that Almereyda could not in fact afford the costs of filming inside them: he recounts that 'we had dire, ongoing trouble securing locations. It was especially difficult, on our budget, to find and lock high-end corporate spaces' (Almereyda 2000: 139), and at one point recalls that 'we were shooting from an open van without permits or lights' when Gwyneth Paltrow and Ben Affleck recognised Ethan Hawke and strolled over for a chat (Almereyda 2000: 138), not realising that they were interrupting the shooting of a scene. Almereyda also registers the importance of an actor's own personal experience and the ways in which it can impact on a performance when he notes that Bill Murray 'had never taken on a film in which he was obliged to die. Whereas Ethan Hawke had always resisted roles requiring his character to kill someone' (Almereyda 2000: xii) and that 'When the camera was ready Julia [Stiles] quietly removed her headphones, stood and moved into frame, and in the guise of "acting" some desperate grieving part of herself came swimming up in her eyes' (Almereyda 2000: 138). Perhaps most tellingly of all, Yu Jin Ko observes that 'Interspliced throughout the film are the video diaries that Almereyda encouraged Ethan Hawke to produce on his own with a Pixelvision 2000 camera' (Ko 2005: 22).

It is this use of video diary that brings us to the heart of the film's project, because this *Hamlet* has throughout an added layer of significance in that it is constantly conscious not only of what we see but of how we are shown it, and its use of the classic device of the mirror, beloved of *film noir*, the Gothic and the superhero narrative alike, is insistently inflected by the added complication of the visible camera lens. In this film, technology of all sorts is important: as Alessandro Abbate neatly puts it, 'Trying to catch the conscience of the King in his *Mousetrap*, Hamlet finds himself caught in the solipsistic *trap* of his own computer *mouse*' (Abbate 2004: 86). Above all, though, the film is obsessed with the technologies of image reproduction. Carolyn Jess observes that 'the tools and techniques of film production that are showcased here display those elements of cinematic apparatus that are available to the consumer for individual use' (Jess 2004: 91), and quotes Barthes: 'All those young photographers who are at work in the world, determined upon the capture of actuality, do not know that they are agents of Death' (Jess 2004: 92). The lens is certainly a master image for this film: Abbate observes that

> In *Hamlet*, the glassy world of Manhattan – with all its transparent and reflecting surfaces of monitors, camera lenses, smooth metals, marbles, and windows – points to a problem of extensive social and personal blindness and impossible communication. This is a transparency through which one cannot see, which allows no possibility of contact beyond the surface. Hamlet's hotel suite has a wide window over the city skyline, in which he can only catch glimpses of his own reflection. (Abbate 2004: 83)

Almereyda himself notes that 'Nearly every scene in the script features a photograph, a TV monitor, an electronic recording device of some kind' (Almereyda 2000: x), that *'The limo door opens and Gertrude and Claudius get out, greeted by photographers and onlookers crowded behind velvet ropes. We're at a major movie premiere'* (Almereyda 2000: 28), and that 'the characters in the film are never exposed to a real landscape until they arrive, *en masse*, at Ophelia's funeral – the graveyard being the only respite from the city's hard surfaces, mirrors, screens and signs' (Almereyda 2000: xi).

Death, though, is not the only answer the film itself has to offer, because although the characters may be trapped in this landscape, the constant emphasis on the power and prominence of individual subjectivity means that they are not seen as simply powerless in it. Although Almereyda's film has often been compared to *film noir*, it is in fact ultimately much more optimistic, for it does allow for the possibility that individual agency can make a real difference. To make its desired point, it draws, like *Jane Austen in Manhattan*, less on its source text than on earlier filmic incarnations and representations of New York, but it uses these not to box in or critique its source text, but rather to liberate it and allow it to speak in an arena into which on the face of things it could never hope to enter. *Hamlet* has obviously nothing to do with Japanese construction companies, superhero narratives or technologies of reproduction, yet in Almereyda's extraordinary fusion of all these discourses, he does indeed show that actually *Hamlet* speaks to all of these things, because all are merely different but equally potent ways of expressing one core problematic, of the individual against the corporate, for which the image of one lone young man against the New York skyline stands as so powerful a metaphor.

3
Across the Pond: The Real Presence in *In the Bleak Midwinter* and 'Mr Darcy *is* an actor': Repetition in *Bridget Jones's Diary*

In this chapter I want to look at two films, Kenneth Branagh's *In the Bleak Midwinter* (1995) and Sharon Maguire's *Bridget Jones's Diary* (2001), which may seem to be very different from each other. However, the underlying kinship between them is neatly emblematised in *Beginner's Luck* (dir. James Callis and Nick Cohen, 2001) which could indeed be described as *In the Bleak Midwinter* meets *Bridget Jones's Diary*. In this, James Callis (Bridget Jones's friend Tom) is seen looking straight into the camera reflecting on the production as in *In the Bleak Midwinter*, and there is also much the same format of an advert in *The Stage* followed by selection of the cast. Again, as in *In the Bleak Midwinter*, there are only a few minutes of actual performance, which is dire; Andrew Fontaine (Christopher Cazenove) is this film's equivalent of *Galaxy Terminus*, and Mark takes them to Paris, as in *Bridget Jones's Diary*. Nevertheless, although *Bridget Jones's Diary* and *In the Bleak Midwinter* have more in common than might appear, they may nevertheless seem anomalies in my project because not only is neither a direct adaptation of an Austen or Shakespeare text, but neither has been uprooted from England. *Bridget Jones's Diary* is set entirely in London and the Home Counties and *In the Bleak Midwinter* in an English village emblematically named Hope. Ironically, however, these two films represent in some ways an even greater cultural shift than those which have been transported to new locations.

In the first place, *Bridget Jones's Diary* makes no secret of its relation to *Pride and Prejudice*, while *In the Bleak Midwinter* centres on a production of *Hamlet* that, although apparently initially quite separate from the normal lives of the actors, gradually reaches out to permeate every aspect of them. In the second place, what both of these films show is an England that can now be understood only in relation to America, not least because of the importance of US funding and bankable US stars for the international film market. In both cases, America is the lure that threatens to entice the hero away from a British job and a British girl, who is represented as unable to follow him because in both films flying represents danger for the heroine: Nina's husband died in a mid-air collision, giving a terrible poignancy to Henry's injunction to think of Joe 'up there in his lonely aeroplane', and by the time the film of *Bridget Jones's Diary* was released fans had already been able to read the next novel, in which a trip to Thailand leads to Bridget's arrest and imprisonment, so that a similar irony plays around the shot of Darcy landing in a snowy US. Both of these women need to keep their feet on the ground literally as well as metaphorically; if their men are lured to America, it is unthinkable that they could follow. Both of these films, then, are set not simply in the England in which their 'base texts' were originally conceived but in an England-which-is-not-America, and in which sophisticated games with reality and fiction can be generated by the extent to which, in both films, England is identified with reality and America with illusion, which in turn sets to work a nicely structured analogy with the truth/fiction duality underpinning both films' comic structures.

The Real Presence in *In the Bleak Midwinter*

In the case of *In the Bleak Midwinter*, the distinction between America/illusion and England/reality is significantly inflected by a third equation, cinema/illusion versus theatre/reality. *In the Bleak Midwinter* is a film that is sacramental in its attitude to theatre. Set in a church at Christmas in a village called Hope and taking its title from Christina Rossetti's popular Victorian Christmas carol, it includes two characters called Joe and Molly, whose full names are presumably Joseph and Mary. Partly this may be a homage to Ernst Lubitsch's 1942 black comedy *To Be or Not to Be*, which John C. Tibbetts sees as linked with *In the Bleak Midwinter* as part of a tradition of films that 'employ Shakespearean allusions as "mousetraps" that "capture the conscience," as it were, of the action and the characters' (Tibbetts 2001: 147), and in which the hero and heroine are called Josef and Maria Tura. Certainly *To Be or Not to Be* is like *In the Bleak Midwinter* in that it too focuses on actors performing *Hamlet*, with a latent pun on ham acting implicit throughout, and here too the performance of theatrical rôles proves to be a way of addressing real-life problems.

Equally, however, the names of Branagh's central characters clearly recall the Christmas story, and Joe openly draws the analogy when he says, 'Churches close and theatres close every week because finally people don't want them'. Moreover, Emma Smith points out that 'Like Branagh, when he played a full-text Hamlet for the Royal Shakespeare Company, the actor-director Joe is thirty-three years old'. Smith suggests that 'this correspondence identifies Joe's production of *Hamlet* with Branagh's stage experiences rather than with his contemporaneous work on the play for the big screen' (Smith 2000: 143). At the same time, though, it also does something else – it makes Joe the same age as Christ when he died, reinforcing the sacramental echoes. When, against all the odds, the performance of *Hamlet* actually proves a success, garnering not only an appreciative audience but a review in *The Times*, it is a miracle of the same kind if not the same magnitude as the Christmas story itself, and suggests that, whether they know it or not, people *do* need theatre, which can offer a communal spiritual experience in a way which churches once might have done but do not any longer seem able to do. As Douglas Lanier observes, 'Given its Christmas setting, the performance in an abandoned church, and the pointed allusion to Christina Rossetti's carol, it is not too much to see Shakespearean theater emerging from this film as a secular substitute for the salvific holy family and the lost communion of religious congregation' (Lanier 2002: 155), while Danièle Berton remarks that 'A la fin, définitivement guéris comme dans l'évangile selon Saint Marc, le bègue parle ouvertement et la très myope Nell [sic] voit' ('at the end, definitively cured as in the Gospel according to St Mark, the stammerer speaks clearly and the very shortsighted [Nina] sees') (Berton 1998: 230).

In this instantiation of theatre as the site of miracle, Branagh's film closely prefigures John Madden's *Shakespeare in Love* (1998). Indeed the parallels between the two are striking, down to the fact that, as Emma French notes of the trailer for *In the Bleak Midwinter*: 'theatrical clichés appear in the trailer that also appear in *Shakespeare in Love*: a lead actor complaining about coughing in the audience, as Will Shakespeare does, and a sign says "the show must go on!"' (French 2006: 84). In each a supposedly creative artist (Shakespeare, Fadge) is reduced to creative impotence. In each an actor thought not to be available to take a part (Joe, Viola) appears at the crucial moment and another actor is plucked off (Molly, Sam). In each the 'plucked' actor is playing against gender: Sam had been cast as Juliet and Molly as Hamlet, so that their replacement in each case becomes not only a triumph of superior acting but an affirmation of innate gender rôles (a precisely similar effect will be achieved at the close of another film that celebrates theatre, Richard Eyre's *Stage Beauty* [2004] – indeed Richard Burt calls *Stage Beauty* 'a direct reply' to *Shakespeare in Love* [Burt 2006: 53] – in which the 'woman actor' Ned Kynaston, once famous for his Desdemona, finally finds his true métier when he plays Othello). This is not wholly positive in its ideological implications: Shakespearean scholars including Stephen Greenblatt, who advised on the film, spoke out against *Shakespeare in Love*'s resolute refusal to engage with the idea of the bisexuality that might seem to be suggested by the sonnets. The insistence on the 'norm' in matters of both gender and sexuality is, however, an emphasis wholly characteristic of the loosely linked group of films that I will be discussing in this chapter, because it is in the end the ideology that underpins their romcom roots. As Stephen M. Buhler points out, 'As both Joe and Branagh recall their "first times" with *Hamlet*, the sexuality of the story and the heterosexuality of the recollecting actor are emphasized', and a rather aggressive heterosexuality is also underlined by the fact that 'Branagh offers a fair number of Benny Hill-style gags on female anatomy' (Buhler 1997: 50), while in the published screenplay Branagh permits himself the Frankie Howerd-like stage direction 'HENRY and TERRY's dorm. Two camp beds (ooo er, vicar)' (Branagh 1995: 62). Thus even Terry, whom the shooting script calls 'a man for whom the word camp was invented' (Branagh 1995: 10), has strayed sufficiently from his apparently confirmed homosexual identity to father a son, which proves to be the only thing which can bring him Christmas comfort, and Fadge's very name evokes *Twelfth Night*, in which Viola, contemplating her disguise as a boy, is confident that all will 'fadge' and that time will restore her to her proper gender (II.ii.33).

The similarities between *In the Bleak Midwinter* and *Shakespeare in Love* do not end with the two films' treatment of gender, however. In both *In the Bleak Midwinter* and *Shakespeare in Love* an actor who also appears in the BBC/A&E *Pride and Prejudice* (first shown in 1995, the same year as *In the Bleak Midwinter* was released) plays against type: Colin Firth (Mr Darcy) becomes the villainous Earl of Wessex in *Shakespeare in Love*, while Julia Sawalha (the silly and flirtatious Lydia) is the heroine in *In the Bleak Midwinter*. Both are films praising theatre, which is cast as a 'real presence' in implicit or explicit contrast to the showiness and make-believe of film; both focus on the performance of a tragedy to tell a comic story; and in each case there is an old theatrical hand who is a noted curmudgeon (Tom Wilkinson's Henslowe and Richard Briers's

Henry). In both, parallels are suggested between the events of the plays and the lives of the actors, as Shakespeare's scripting of *Romeo and Juliet* melds with his real-life love story in *Shakespeare in Love* and as each character in turn in *In the Bleak Midwinter* reveals something about their life which resonates with the part they play. (Notably, Joe's own crisis occurs towards the end of Act II, just as 'To be or not to be' does, and like 'To be or not to be', it provokes only an interruption, not the resolution that is allowed to the others.) In each case, too, there is an extradiegetic suggestion that something is being concealed or withheld from the audience: as Courtney Lehmann points out, 'for the first time in Branagh's directorial career, he is not "in" the film as a character' (Lehmann 2001: 57), while there has been a steadfast refusal on the part of those involved in *Shakespeare in Love* to clarify the precise nature of Tom Stoppard's involvement with the script. In this respect, it is not only the theatre that is the site of mystery, but the films themselves.

Most notably, in both films the biggest threat is of enforced departure to the New World: Viola must go to Virginia (indeed the closing shot originally intended for *Shakespeare in Love* was to have shown the Manhattan skyline visible in the distance as she landed), while Joe's ostensible departure for America structurally replaces Hamlet going to England. Although *Shakespeare in Love* postdates *In the Bleak Midwinter* by three years, and so was not in any sense part of the film's original set of meanings, the strongly marked parallels between the two films serve to highlight the extent to which *In the Bleak Midwinter* focuses not just on the difference between theatre and film but on the degree to which it marks theatre as both English and also as fully real, and grounded in attested experience: as John C. Tibbetts comments,

> Much of the film is frankly autobiographical, both of the adventures Branagh himself has experienced on the road, and of his childhood delight in watching Hollywood backstage musicals. In particular Branagh wanted to emulate the cycle of backstage movies that teamed up director Busby Berkeley with Judy Garland and Mickey Rooney. (Tibbetts 2001: 156)

Moreover, Courtney Lehmann points out that Joe's surname is Harper, the maiden name of Branagh's mother, and that for some time Branagh was linked to the part of the young Obi-Wan Kenobi in *The Phantom Menace* (dir. George Lucas, 1999) ultimately played by Ewan McGregor, which clearly lies behind the *Galaxy Terminus* film to which Joe is so nearly lured, but feared that if he took it he would be too old to play Hamlet by the time it was finished (Lehmann 2001: 57–8). Branagh also lost the lead in *Amadeus* (dir. Milos Forman, 1984) to Tom Hulce as Joe nearly loses a part to Dylan Judd, and it is therefore perhaps worth noting that in *Amadeus* too art is born from a direct relationship with life – the bitter and disappointed Leopold Mozart feeds straight into the vengeful figure of the Commendatore in *Don Giovanni* and the shrill tones of Mozart's nagging mother-in-law are directly transcribed as the aria of the Queen of the Night. Although Branagh did not in the end appear in *Amadeus*, the relationship that it posits between art and life is clearly apparent in *In the Bleak Midwinter*.

In the Bleak Midwinter is certainly not afraid to make us aware of parallels between the intradiegetic and the extradiegetic worlds, and this stress on correspondences with both real life and Englishness places its vision of theatre in sharp contrast with its vision of film, which is consistently associated with unreality and above all with America,[1] as embodied in Jennifer Saunders' monstrous Hollywood producer. (It is notable that the film by which Joe might have been lured away belongs to the wildly unrealistic genre of sci-fi, which is also used in another of the films I shall be discussing in this chapter, *Notting Hill* (dir. Roger Michell, 1999), as a symbol of the shallowness and triviality of mainstream cinema, while Molly laments that *Hamlet* can never compete with *Mighty Morphin Power Rangers*, which is, as Mark Thornton Burnett notes, 'an American television action show that, modelled on a syndicated Japanese series and internationally exported, implicitly mocks philosophical Shakespearean heroes' [Burnett 2007: 14].) By contrast, although in the documentary shown on UK TV to coincide with the release of Branagh's *Hamlet* there was 'A version of *Hamlet* in the style of American soap opera called "Dane-Nasty"' (Smith 2000: 145), the film is quite innocent of any knowledge of Joan Collins's appearance in the actual *Dynasty*, and instead resolutely marks her as English: indeed Courtney Lehmann suggests that 'The beautiful and sophisticated Margaretta D'Arville ... offers an unmistakable portrait of Branagh's consummately cosmopolitan agent, Pat Marmont' (Lehmann 2001: 58–9). The film producer and the theatrical agent are thus set up as polar opposites, with the representative of film designated as American and the representative of theatre designated as English, even if the film itself knows at some level that extradiegetically these alignments are by no means so clear-cut, not least because Jennifer Saunders herself is course British. Moreover, though Lehmann hears the name of Joe's agent as 'D'Arville', and the shooting script does indeed call her that (Branagh 1995: 2), the Internet Movie Database names her as Margaretta

D'Arcy, as do a considerable number of reviews and websites including the *Encyclopaedia Britannica Guide to Shakespeare*, and that certainly seems to be what Joe is saying when he introduces her. Even if this is the result simply of a collective mishearing, this possible identification is well worth pausing over, for Margaretta D'Arcy (b. 1934), wife and collaborator of the playwright John Arden, shares Branagh's Irish background, was first a member of Sinn Fein and then expelled from it, and has served time in Armagh jail as a political prisoner. To present her as an icon of Englishness would thus be, to say the least, ironic.

In this insistence on the distinction between America/illusion and England/reality, *In the Bleak Midwinter* is not only like *Shakespeare in Love*, but also draws on an earlier Branagh film. The opening sequence of Branagh's *Peter's Friends* (1992) shows the group of friends who go on to feature in the film ten years previously, taking part in the 1982 Footlights Revue at the ADC Theatre in Cambridge (as many of the real-life actors did indeed do), thus clearly identifying all its lead characters as one-time theatre performers even if some of them are so no longer. *Peter's Friends*, unlike *In the Bleak Midwinter*, is a post-Christmas narrative rather than one which climaxes at Christmas, and consequently more downbeat than its feelgood friends, but the family relationship with Branagh's other films, and indeed with other works in its cast's careers, is unmistakable. Hetta Charnley (Molly from *In the Bleak Midwinter*) has a walk-on part. Emma Thompson sings a Christmas carol, prefiguring *In the Bleak Midwinter*, and Stephen Fry and Hugh Laurie make sheep noises at each other, reprising their rôles in the quintessentially English *Blackadder Goes Forth*, where Fry's General Melchett enters baaing like a sheep. When Peter asks 'Do you remember that cabaret we did in Bradford?' there is an obvious allusion to Bradford's iconic status in English theatre as the place where Henry Irving died immediately after appearing on stage, and this is underlined by the fact that Richard Briers, who is himself a member of the Irving Society and whose character expresses his admiration for him in *In the Bleak Midwinter*, has a cameo here as Peter's father. Finally, when the bookcase door swings open, we glimpse a motif famously to be reprised in Branagh's 1996 *Hamlet*.

Peter's Friends also prefigures *In the Bleak Midwinter* in that it fears and despises America in more or less equal measure. Andrew says dismissively of his weight-obsessed American wife Carol – who despite her name definitely does not contribute to any kind of Christmas spirit – 'She's fine when she's asleep'; the equation of America with a shallow diet culture is underlined later when he is told that 'It's called a pot belly, Andrew – we have those in England, along with culture'. Here too America is characterised primarily as unreal – 'Do you have wood in Los Angeles?' 'We have Hollywood' – and as understanding English culture only in terms of clichés: Carol demands of Peter's insufficiently servile housekeeper, 'Did you never see *Upstairs, Downstairs*?'. (The housekeeper is played by Phyllida Law, mother of Emma and Sophie Thompson and then mother-in-law of Branagh as well as a very well established actress in her own right, making this doubly ironic.) Above all, America stands as the clear antithesis to this troubled but still functional friendship group: as Peter ironically remarks, 'I was interested to hear you describe Hollywood as a community, Carol'. Nevertheless, America still lures people: Andrew may have 'felt like a slimy bastard running off to the States like that', but he went nevertheless, and he will doubtless go back there at the end of the film, since this story, unlike *In the Bleak Midwinter*, does not deal in miracles.

Even in *In the Bleak Midwinter*, though, we are aware of the improbability and fragility of miracle: what we are offered is, as Emma Smith says, 'only a momentary victory in the middle of winter: the lights and warmth of Christmas as a fleeting reprieve from the dark and cold' (Smith 2000: 141). Moreover, at the same time as it sends up a paean to reality, *In the Bleak Midwinter* paradoxically foregrounds its own artificiality. Indeed Douglas Lanier notes that Branagh 'underscores *Midwinter*'s debts to a particular film genre, the backstage melodrama, which both idealizes the theater and puts its institutional mechanics before the viewer', foregrounding the artificiality (Lanier 2002: 157). And as Courtney Lehmann observes, 'Joe's production and Branagh's film smack rather oddly of a Hollywood ending' (Lehmann 2001: 73): for all their shared scorn of American values as superficial and unreal, they themselves are both glad to participate in and borrow from American cinematic convention. It is perhaps unkind to note that the audience which Branagh seems to value most is in some respects also the audience which is most easily deceived; in the screenplay, one of the markers of the final production's success is that we see a 'Close-up of riveted children's faces' (Branagh 1995: 103). Any audience more sophisticated would be only too liable to see the contradictions and paradoxes by which the theatre's instantiation of its own reality is fissured.

One of the most troubling and far-reaching of these is that even the techniques used to authorise theatre are drawn from film: *In the Bleak Midwinter*'s logic of moving from a relatively three-dimensional London to the static church set, to which the cast is thereafter confined, directly inverts that of Olivier's 1944 film of *Henry V*, where at the end of the first act the Globe set melts away and gives place to the 'real world'. In its use of this motif, *In the Bleak Midwinter* insists that the confined space of a theatre *can* be anywhere, and at the same time echoes the shooting set of the Olivier *Richard III* (1955), which had its church space directly contiguous to the living quarters – but in both cases, it can make its point about theatre only by quoting film. Nor are these isolated instances. As Kathy Howlett points out, the film makes a number of references to Olivier (Howlett 1999: 116), and although these are complicated by the repeated allusions to Irving, with Henry Wakefield's self-association with Irving being ironically confirmed when he is paired up with a 'Terry', they do nevertheless serve to constantly remind us of the extent to which this film, like all Branagh's, is nervously aware of the earlier filmic *oeuvre* of Olivier hovering over its shoulder.

The distinction between theatre and film is further blurred by the fact that, unlike *Shakespeare in Love* with its catchphrase 'it's a mystery' or Branagh's own *Henry V,* where the mechanics of film are laid bare in the opening scene, it is film rather than theatre that is invested with mystique here: Emma Smith observes that 'It is the film of *Hamlet* which maintains the mystery, with its use of special effects and trick photography, and with its period of rehearsal carefully tucked away behind the scenes' (Smith 2000: 142), and the same is of course true of the film of *In the Bleak Midwinter* itself, which is presented as a solid, seamless performance all the while that it is apparently showing us the elaborate preparations behind the scenes of theatre. It is also noticeable that, in flat contradiction of the usual and necessary logic of theatre, only one performance of Joe's *Hamlet* is seriously envisaged, and even of that we see only a swift montage of selected scenes; moreover, *In the Bleak Midwinter* has only three acts, as opposed to the five of *Hamlet,* and Emma French notes that 'Although based on *Hamlet, In the Bleak Midwinter* is not marketed with Shakespearian quotations. The marketing team instead emphasises the film's status as a thespian farce: "The drama. The passion. The intrigue. And the rehearsals haven't even started"' (French 2006: 58). Most particularly, as Danièle Berton notes with wry understatement, 'Certains puristes eux aussi, ont pu considérer comme fâcheuse l'absence du célèbre monologue "to be or not to be"' ('some purists might well have been irritated by the absence of the famous soliloquy 'To be or not to be') (Berton 1998: 224). So they might, and this glaring omission draws attention to the fact that, for all its ostensible fetishisation of theatre and instantiation of theatrical performance as source of truth, the film is in fact distinctly wary of giving us too much of it.

It is also notable that Branagh seems to posit an audience that has been fed on the experience and knowledge of films rather than of theatrical performances. *In the Bleak Midwinter* deliberately locates itself as a film amongst films, and asserts membership of a number of separate filmic peer groups for itself. Most notably, there are similarities with Branagh's other movies, both those which he had already shot and those which then were still only at the planning stage: Ramona Wray remarks of his later *Love's Labour's Lost* (2000), for instance, that 'the ensemble numbers and general camaraderie evoke the spirit of *In the Bleak Midwinter* ... with its "show must go on" philosophy' (Wray 2002: 175). Branagh himself is clearly aware of a group mentality both intradiegetically and extradiegetically, since he deliberately seeks to position his film as one of a class, remarking in the introduction to the shooting script that 'The theatre as a metaphor for life's madness is hardly new. And movies that use the stories of particular productions to provide a microcosmic view of human nature abound' (Branagh 1995: v). Ironically, the only place where this film about companionship in the theatre can find its own sense of companionship is with other films (there is, for example, a clear sense of kinship with the use of *Troilus and Cressida* in the 1987 TV series of *Fortunes of War* [dir. James Cellan Jones], in which Branagh played Guy Pringle).

It is a mark of its complicity with this slightly uncomfortable compromise between film and theatre that *In the Bleak Midwinter* also foreshadows what I shall argue is *Bridget Jones's Diary's* interest in the public sphere, particularly as it is embodied in the star system. This is made particularly clear by a comparison of *In the Bleak Midwinter* and Branagh's *Hamlet*, for which *In the Bleak Midwinter* served as deck-clearing, dry run and, Emma Smith suggests, 'scapegoat, diverting what is potentially ridiculous and laughable about the play itself' (Smith 2000: 137) – or as Sarah Hatchuel has it, '*In the Bleak Midwinter* seems ... to be a way to purge Branagh's film of *Hamlet* from every parodical and metadramatical element, in order to insist even more on diegetic illusion in the latter' (Hatchuel 2004: 74–5). As John C. Tibbetts points out, 'There's a private joke in *A Midwinter's Tale* ... when the director reassures his troupe they'll perform the play with cuts' (Tibbetts 2001: 158), since his actual *Hamlet* is famously uncut, and the link between the two films was confirmed when *Hamlet* opened in America on Christmas Day 1996 (it is in any case, as Kathy Howlett points out, a play often associated with Christmas) (Howlett 1999: 121). In *Hamlet* we are always aware of the massive impact of star-spotting, with Charlton Heston's Player King; but *In the Bleak Midwinter* too cannot afford to be indifferent to such considerations, as we see in the casting of Joan Collins and Jennifer Saunders. Branagh learned to his cost when making *Much Ado About Nothing* both the indispensability and the potential limitations of bankable American stars, because though Robert Sean Leonard as Claudio and Denzel Washington as the Prince acquitted themselves admirably, Keanu Reeves's Don John, and Michael Keaton's Dogberry even more so, were universally pilloried and identified as the weakest links in an otherwise strong film. In *In the Bleak Midwinter*, where he is not governed by commercial imperatives, Branagh is so determined to see jobs go to British actors that even his American, Nancy Crawford, is played by a Brit, Jennifer Saunders; but when it came to the real *Hamlet* which he went on to make later he is only too well aware that he cannot cast Michael Maloney, who is a fine actor but, as is knowingly glanced at in *In the Bleak Midwinter*, 'too short' (the first thing the shooting script says about him is 'Mid-shot on JOE who speaks directly to camera. He is of medium height' (Branagh 1995: 1). Instead Branagh had to cast himself, uncomfortable as he visibly is with some aspects of the rôle. Equally, his supporting players could not be drawn just from old-school British actors who admired Irving, but had to include Jack Lemmon as an execrable Marcellus and Charlton Heston as a Player King made memorable precisely by the fact that his acting style is deliberately posited as a contrast to that which the film itself offers.

It is perhaps partly in order to register the extent of the threat posed by America and the virtually annual tribute paid to it by British theatre that the one actor who does eventually leave for America, Tom, is potentially the most interesting and complex character in the film. Douglas Lanier comments that

> As several reviewers observed, [Joe] clearly stands in for Branagh the idealist, the populist Shakespearean director whose despair mirrors Branagh's personal crisis on the heels of the public breakup of his self-mythologized marriage and romance with Emma Thompson and the critical failure of his 1994 *Mary Shelley's Frankenstein*. Yet Branagh complicates the scenario with a second alter-ego, the humble, enterprising Vernon. It is Vernon who voices the bond of love between actors in its purest form ... And early on it is Vernon who worries about "tickets, box-office, the cash-advance, advertising".
> (Lanier 2002: 156–7)

However, Tom too is an obvious comparator for Joe, much as Fortinbras and Laertes both offer doubles for Hamlet. Tom certainly merits the longest introductory description in the normally laconic screenplay: 'The face of an intense young actor, TOM NEWMAN. Vegetarian, Planet-saving, Whale-rescuing, Trade-papers reading and, finally and conclusively, self-absorbed. He is in earnest flow, despite being intellectually challenged' (Branagh 1995: 8). While others of the actors are cynical, Tom is whole-hearted, saying 'Everything I am as a human being is here' – that is, in rehearsal. While everyone else reveals a personal connection with *Hamlet*, he does not, not only because he wonders 'Why does everyone want to see behind the scenes nowadays?' but also because he alone commits himself to a wide variety of rôles, putting his faith in versatility and professionalism rather than personal identification. Although he hides behind accents and props, such as the hilarious book about the Eiffel Tower meant to give credibility to his Paris-bound Laertes, it is Tom who ends up the professional winner and who also gets the girl, in the shape of Fadge, becoming, in structural terms, an alternative hero-actant. Tom is also the least easy of all the motley troupe to pigeonhole: he objects to red meat, but eats it; he objects to cigarettes, but smokes them; he objects to vulgarity and innuendo, but will end up playing a character called Smegma; he has 'serious disease' but knows it. In comparison with him, Michael Maloney's upright, straightforward Joe looks two-dimensional. On one level, the opposition between the two seems simple, but just like the opposition between theatre and film, it actually proves to be rather less clear-cut than it appears.

The fact that the film invests so much energy in the creation of Tom and then dispatches him to America is, then, a marker of how seriously it takes the threat posed by Hollywood. Theatre may be able to perform miracles, but it is always in the face of a threat, and for Branagh, the biggest threat comes from America. At one point in *In the Bleak Midwinter*, Vernon cites David Lean's 1945 classic *Brief Encounter* as the thing that makes life worth living for him, and promises to buy Joe the video for Christmas. This is a richly suggestive choice because of the ways in which it does *not* seem to fit with *In the Bleak Midwinter*. Although they share black and white photography and *Brief Encounter* has a brief and rather underdeveloped series of film-within-the-film vignettes when the characters go to the cinema, it hardly seems to offer much of a celebration of traditional English culture: Laura's children are unappealing and quarrelsome, and family life is not satisfying, not least because her husband, like Carnforth, spends his time doing the crossword without having any particular aptitude for it. However, where *Brief Encounter* certainly would appeal to Branagh's sensibilities is in the fact that the film registers no knowledge whatsoever of America; indeed to get away from it all, Alec Harvey goes to Africa, as if this were the only natural destination for emigration. As Laura says, 'the British have always been nice to mad people', and this safely cosy world in which eccentricity is tolerated and, only just after the end of the war, the GIs are no longer over-sexed, over-paid and over here, is perhaps oddly like that of *In the Bleak Midwinter* after all.

Branagh's film, then, is riddled with ironies. It celebrates theatre, but it can do so only by quoting film. It celebrates Englishness too, but it can do so only by constructing an artificial and fragile opposition between that which it classes as American and that which it classes as English, which involves designating Joan Collins, star of an American soap opera, as quintessentially English, and Jennifer Saunders, British-born star of a UK sitcom, as quintessentially American. For this film, indeed, America is essentially an enabling myth, which has almost visibly had to be invented in order to throw a shadow suitably dark for England to 'like a star i'th'darkest night / Stick fiery off indeed' (*Hamlet* V.ii.253–4). In the next film to which I turn, *Bridget Jones's Diary*, America continues to work in the same way, and *Bridget Jones's Diary* too repeatedly reminds us of its affiliations with other films in order to make its points, and draws on a classic text to do so.

'Mr Darcy *is* an actor': Repetition in *Bridget Jones's Diary*

There are a number of links between *In the Bleak Midwinter* and *Bridget Jones's Diary*. Perhaps most obviously, there is the shared presence of Celia Imrie as Fadge and Bridget's mother's friend Una Alconbury, and Emma Smith's comment on *In the Bleak Midwinter* and *Hamlet* could usefully be extended to include *Bridget Jones's Diary* too: 'Both films are set in winter: the snowy winterscapes are borrowed from an earlier, more innocent age' (Smith 2000: 144). *Bridget Jones's Diary* both opens and closes in snow, and this is not an incidental detail but a fundamental part of its framing of itself as English, and thus being prepared to embrace every aspect of English life, even the weather. In staging this self-presentation, it firmly identifies itself as part of a group of films, all of them produced by the production company Working Title and all starring Hugh Grant, which includes *Four Weddings and a Funeral* (dir. Mike Newell, 1994), *Notting Hill, About a Boy* (dir. Paul Weitz, 2002) and *Love Actually* (dir. Richard Curtis, 2003). Collectively, these can be seen as offering a new mythologising of Englishness. A fundamental part of their vision is an amused affection for the weather; hence thunder, lightning and rain accompany the climax of *Four Weddings and a*

Funeral, Bridget gets her hair hopelessly dishevelled while trying to look like Grace Kelly, and in *Notting Hill* snow transforms Somerset House into a Dutch Renaissance skating scene. For these films, as for *In the Bleak Midwinter*, the winter is not a threat or even an inconvenience, but the time when English life blossoms into a collective sense of cheer, festivity and companionship.

All of these films also share with *In the Bleak Midwinter* a profound fear of America. In the case of *Bridget Jones's Diary*, this is fundamentally connected with the film's own intense anxieties about originality. *Bridget Jones's Diary* is a film based on a novel which itself recasts and reprises one of the most famous and best-loved books ever written, so this anxiety is not wholly surprising. What is perhaps less inevitable, though, is that the anxiety attaches itself firmly to a concern about repetition which is associated with an idea of a public world where things are known, recognised and shared, as opposed to a safe private one which is seen as the domain of personal fantasy and where shared resonances or memories do not need to be acknowledged except insofar as they give pleasure. Part of the point of this group of films is that they are in some ways the opposite of backstage dramas – a recurrent figure is the character who is unable to perform in public, and in *About A Boy*, the boy (Nicholas Hoult) observes that he could never be like Haley Joel Osment because he is 'crap at drama', even though he does later echo Osment's character in *The Sixth Sense* by having a vision of a figure who is on the point of death. Such explicit disavowals might well lead us to assume that there will be no metafilmic sensibility of work, but in fact there are such pronounced similarities between *Bridget Jones's Diary* and the other films in the group that, however hard it tries to project itself as private fantasy hermetically sealed from outside realities, our awareness of its extradiegetic echoes and repetitions becomes an important part of its meaning.

Such an awareness is hardly surprising because to anyone with a working knowledge of *Pride and Prejudice*, it is clear that the film of *Bridget Jones's Diary*, like Helen Fielding's original book, is fundamentally dependent for its effects both upon repetition of names and motifs from Austen's novel and also upon the audience's informed and pleasurable recognition of that repetition. Indeed in this respect the film goes even further than Fielding's book. The disparaging remarks which Mark makes about Bridget at the Turkey Curry Buffet have no source in Fielding's book, but they do clearly recall Mr Darcy's similar snub of Elizabeth Bennet on their first meeting at Netherfield; moreover, not only does the casting of Colin Firth as Mark Darcy point so obviously in the direction of the BBC/A&E *Pride and Prejudice*, but other members of the cast are also associated with other Jane Austen films, since Hugh Grant, who plays Daniel, was Edward Ferrers in Ang Lee's *Sense and Sensibility* (1995), and Gemma Jones, who plays Bridget's mother, was Mrs Dashwood in the same film.

As well as its strand of sustained allusion to *Pride and Prejudice*, the film also deploys other forms of repetition and echoing. There are, for instance, echoes of other classic serials, the most notable of which is that Celia Imrie, who played Mrs Nightingale in Metin Hüseyin's *Tom Jones* (1997), reappears here as Bridget's mother's best friend – a particularly appropriate resonance given that it is clearly from Henry Fielding's hero's mother, Bridget, that Helen Fielding's heroine takes her name, while Bridget's mother is called Pamela, the butt of Fielding's *Shamela* and *Joseph Andrews*. America is also the destination to which Lord Fellamar plots to send Tom Jones, with the Metin Hüseyin adaptation featuring the hilarious exchange 'Upon reflection, my lord, the gallows are infinitely preferable to the Americas' – 'I've heard that everywhere said, my lady'. The ITV *Emma* (dir. Diarmuid Lawrence, 1996) is also recalled: the moments when Emma imagines herself interrupting Jane and Knightley's wedding with 'But what about little Henry?' and her fantasies of Elton and Harriet at *their* wedding are both directly echoed, the first when Bridget really does interrupt the Darcys' ruby wedding festivities and the second when she imagines herself marrying Daniel. Darcy and Natasha working seriously in their boat while Bridget and Daniel are larking around in theirs recalls the early episode of *Brideshead Revisited* (dir. Michael Lindsay-Hogg and Charles Sturridge, 1981) in which Charles Ryder and his friends are having a philosophical discussion which is interrupted by Sebastian being sick through the window, and this echo is a particularly interesting one, since *Brideshead Revisited* both connotes the country-house culture so important to Austen and is also emblematic of an Englishness which is seen as essentially Arcadian and innocent, as well as having something of the same glamorised version of homosexuality as is offered by Bridget's friend Tom. Its score also bears a marked similarity to the theme music from the BBC version of *The Chronicles of Narnia* (both were composed by Geoffrey Burgon), which lends a further air of innocence.

Nor are other obviously classic serials or films the only literary or filmic texts which *Bridget Jones's Diary* repeats. In Helen Fielding's book, we read that 'Jude introduced the concept of Boy Time – as introduced in the film *Clueless*' (Fielding 1999: 68), and certainly Amy Heckerling's film, with its smart updating and dizzy heroine, does seem to be an influence on Sharon Maguire's. There is also internal repetition within *Bridget Jones's Diary* itself: the closing scene, with its falling snow and Bridget out of doors in it, echoes the first, while Daniel – who has already told Bridget three times 'same' – proves mistaken when he tries to avoid the force of repetition by saying 'I think it's about time you and I put the past behind us, don't you, Darce?' only to have to observe moments later 'Bloody hell, wait a minute, he's back'. At the close of the film, indeed, Mark (whose status as reliable is subtly boosted by the fact that his own name repeats his father's, whose wedding anniversary explicitly testifies to the longevity of his marriage) expressly invites Bridget to perform an act of repetition when he suggests that she should replay her speech at the party at bar mitzvahs and christenings, and it is also notable that both say 'Not', he when she observes that he is not in New York and she when she is asked if she is going to Paris. Repetition in these instances functions as a guarantee of legitimacy, stability and compatibility.

However, repetition is not a simple and monolithic phenomenon, because its meanings are not always positive. In the original book, there is a long conversation between Perpetua and her friends about the relationships of sources to adaptations:

> 'I have to say, I think it's disgraceful. All it means in this day and age is that a whole generation of people only get to know the great works of literature – Austen, Eliot, Dickens, Shakespeare, and so on – through the television.'
> 'Well, quite. It's absurd. Criminal.'
> 'Absolutely. They think that what they see when they're "channel hopping" between *Noel's House Party* and *Blind Date* actually *is* Austen or Eliot.' (99)

This culminates in the snooty Natasha's assertion that 'I always feel with the Classics people should be made to prove they've read the book before they're allowed to watch the television version' (101), while when Bridget first meets Mark Darcy at the Turkey Curry Buffet she writes, 'It struck me as pretty ridiculous to be called Mr Darcy and to stand on your own looking snooty at a party. It's like being called Heathcliff and insisting on spending the entire evening in the garden, shouting "Cathy" and banging your head against a tree' (285). Although these two statements work in very different ways, their ideological pull is finally the same: both suggest that repetition, particularly in its capacity as imitation and reduplication, can be dangerous as well as pleasurable. We are, moreover, always aware that what we ourselves are seeing is *not* Austen, however much it may strive to look like it. (Similarly in *Notting Hill* an analogous distinction is suggested by the fact that not only does the hero run a bookshop but the closing image shows him reading a book, while Anna is obviously not presently involved in film-making: the implication is clearly that books are real in a way that films are not.)

There is certainly a marked uneasiness hovering over some of the instances of repetition in *Bridget Jones's Diary*. The ways in which the 'smug marrieds' repeat each other, for instance, are simply absurd, as both members of each clone-like couple make the same gestures and say the same things, and repetition is also distinctly threatening when Tom quotes Darcy at the birthday party, revealing that Bridget has indiscreetly passed his comments on to her friends, and when Bridget herself 'repeats' her mother (both have an accident with eggs; Mark comments scornfully that she 'dresses like her mother'; and Bridget's mother makes an appeal to her husband just as Bridget does to Mark, with both initially seeming to fail). Indeed Bridget's echoing of her mother raises a broader issue touching on both metaphorical and actual parentage (perhaps in turn echoing Elton's anxiety-of-influence-laden question in *Clueless* (dir. Amy Heckerling 1995), 'Don't you even know who my father is?'). It is notable, for instance, that when Daniel first sees Bridget's pants he cries 'Mummy!', and that Bridget replaces her father as driver of the car on the way to the Darcys' ruby wedding, while Mark too echoes her mother, whom he parrots in the conversation over cooking. While this might suggest the greater flexibility of modern postfeminist gender rôles, it might equally serve firstly to imply that we are all compelled to imitate our parents and secondly to feminise Mark in ways that are not entirely attractive, both of which suggest that repetition can be a negative as well as a positive force.

What all this ultimately seems to suggest is that self-conscious repetition is a potentially dangerous act, and this, I think, is an idea which finds its way deep into the tonality of Sharon Maguire's film. In the book, Bridget knows perfectly well that her story has some obvious analogues with *Pride and Prejudice*; in the film she has no idea, something which is neatly imaged by the way in which she is totally wrongfooted when she catches Daniel's other woman naked in his bathroom and concealing her modesty with something published by Pemberley Press. Indeed there is generally a remarkable lack of knowingness on many scores in the film. In the book, Richard Finch refers to one particularly notorious real-life episode involving someone who was later to be a star of the film:

> 'Come on! Come on!' he was saying, holding up his fists like a boxer. 'I'm thinking Hugh Grant. I'm thinking Elizabeth Hurley. I'm thinking how come two months on they're still together. I'm thinking how come he gets away with it. That's it! How does a man with a girlfriend with looks like Elizabeth Hurley have a blow-job from a prostitute on a public highway and get away with it? What happened to hell hath no fury?' (197)

One would imagine that when Hugh Grant himself appears in the film, some kind of allusion might be made to this, but there is no hint of it: here he is simply Daniel Cleaver, as if he were not in fact Hugh Grant at all. Similarly, there are repeated references to Daniel's new girlfriend being American, but the film, like *Shakespeare in Love*, is entirely innocent of the knowledge that its own heroine is played by an American actress: Renée Zellweger has become as entirely absorbed and invisible in her rôle as Hugh Grant is in his.

There is a marked contrast here with the original book, which plays elaborate games with its own fictional status, as when Bridget notes,

> I stumbled upon a photograph in the *Standard* of Darcy and Elizabeth, hideous, dressed as modern-day luvvies, draped all over each other in a meadow: she with blonde Sloane hair, and linen trouser suit, he in striped polo neck and leather jacket with Shoestring-style moustache. Apparently they are already sleeping together. That is absolutely disgusting. Feel disorientated and worried, for surely Mr Darcy would never do anything so vain and frivolous as to be an actor and yet Mr Darcy *is* an actor. Hmmm. All v. confusing. (247–8)

In the film, Mr Darcy is, indeed, an actor; but both Colin Firth's Mark Darcy and Renée Zellweger's Bridget Jones are so utterly incapable of performing creditably in public that actor is the last profession with which we would credit either of them. It is notable, for instance, that although Mark Darcy is a barrister, we never see him in court, since that would militate against the creation of a cripplingly shy and inept public persona for him; like Fanny Price, we would suppose, Mark and Bridget cannot act, even though Mr Darcy *is* an actor. (In a similar paradox, Hugh Grant's best man speech in *Four Weddings and a Funeral* is apparently grossly inept and bumbling, but in fact does the job.)

Thus as in Austen's novel *Mansfield Park*, where *Lovers' Vows* functions not like a metatheatrical play-within-a-play but rather as an excursus into a completely different mode of being, the film of *Bridget Jones's Diary* is never self-conscious, but confines itself almost entirely to the intradiegetic realm – apart from the reference to Pemberley Press and the fact of Mark Darcy's name there is no open reference to Austen in the film, and there is no trip to the Edinburgh Festival, as there is in the book, to draw our attention to questions of literary influence and status (or, incidentally, to widen the film's frame of reference beyond England to Scotland). Salman Rushdie and Jeffrey Archer do both appear in the film when neither was mentioned in the book, but both are male writers writing predominantly about men, so this suggests difference from the literary world of the film itself rather than similarities with it, and indeed the whole point of the scene in which they appear is to show how ill at ease Bridget is in these surroundings. In fact the scene serves to cement the image of Bridget as someone who can operate only in the private sphere and for whom any attempt to enter into the public sphere is inevitably disastrous (as in the memorable moments in the sequel when her 'private' comments to Mark are caught on speaker phone or when she announces to the entire clientele of a Swiss pharmacy that she thinks she may be pregnant). In this sense, although this is in some ways as far as possible from being a 'backstage' movie, it subscribes to exactly the same aesthetic, and again this is something shared with *Notting Hill*, where private/public merge seamlessly into each other at the final press conference, which in itself further collapses the distinction between viewer and viewed by its focus on the reflected expressions of the two faces looking at each other.

The apparent incompatibility between public and private in Maguire's film enhances the impression of the screen giving us access here to a private world rather than a public one, and this is something that is also found in the film's pervasive concern with the fragmentation of public communication. In the office, for example, Perpetua, Daniel and Bridget, who are all within talking distance of one another, are instead all having private conversations on the phone, and Bridget and Daniel are emailing each other. Even when they are ostensibly communicating in the public world, it is the private one which really matters: when Bridget is pretending to be on the phone to the (dead) critic F.R. Leavis, 'fuuuuuuuck' comes up across the screen as if it were expressing her private thoughts, while a voice-over notes 'Have been seduced by informality of messaging medium'. By contrast, Bridget is utterly incapable of communicating publicly: as Mark so aptly remarks, 'You really are an appallingly bad public speaker'. Driven to the desperate remark that 'The mike's not working', she remains locked in a private world in which a sabotaging voice mutters in her head 'Tits-pervert'. The prominence of this private world is also evident in the way Bridget's weight flashes up on a public display monitor as though the screen were her dream, and the effect is very marked too in the 'first draft' of Bridget's introduction of Perpetua to Mark and Bridget's final speech, where what we apparently see happen subsequently turns out to exist only in Bridget's fantasy world. (This idea of film as dream is something which, like many other elements of *Bridget Jones's Diary*, can be traced back to *Notting Hill*, specifically the sequence in which Anna Scott persuades Will Thacker that he is having a good dream.)

The film's purpose in assuming this innocent posture is to offer a sustained exploration of the differences between public and private modes of communication, and, even though it knows that this is ultimately only a fantasy, it tries insistently to align itself with a private world which it associates with England, as opposed to a public world which it associates with the US. At the same time, however, the film knows that to sustain a private vision is ultimately impossible. Perhaps its deepest paradox is that despite her extradiegetic status as heroine of a film, and her successive jobs in a publishing house and as a television journalist, Bridget Jones actually has no sense of the importance of a public world – her speeches both at the launch of *Kafka's Motorbike* and at Mark's parents' party may have the opposite effect from the dreamlike status of *Notting Hill* in that they are in fact like a nightmare, but they both remain rooted in Bridget Jones's private world rather than being experienced as public events. Even when she is on television we have no sense of the consequences of her appearances as real because, in a witty comment on the self-absorbedness of television journalists, we never see anyone other than herself watching her. In another borrowing from *Notting Hill*, we are constantly reminded of the instability and insincerity of public communication, as with the 'telespeak' which Julian spouts when he meets Bridget (again this is a change from the original book, where Julio, the Julian figure, has nothing to do with television), and it is easy to detect the palpable clichés and insincerity of the platitudes about communication which Bridget mouths during her first two interviews for a job in TV. Conversely, Mark's successful defence of Kafir Aghani is not remotely realistic but simply the stuff of fairy tale, as indeed Daniel virtually reveals in his dismissal of the relevance of Chechnya to his own life; we have no sense of the importance or even the reality of any outside event. Perhaps most interesting of all is the marked switch in the status of Mark's compliment that he likes Bridget 'just as she is', because when Shazza repeats the phrasing as a toast at Bridget's birthday party, Bridget looks daggers at her; now that the remark has been repeated as a public communication, it has become dangerous and overly revelatory, since it clearly shows that Bridget has been talking to her friends about Mark. What was safe in private becomes perilous when it enters the public sphere.

Nor is this just a case of women keeping to the private sphere, as they did in the days of Jane Austen. In the first place, men too shirk the public arena: Mark may be a barrister, but we never see him perform; Tom entered the public sphere only briefly and only to succeed the better in the private one; and Daniel too, despite the fact that he works in a publishing firm, keeps largely to private communication. (Apart from the very vaguely characterised *Kafka's Motorbike*, there is no sense of what the publishing firm actually publishes, and when Bridget asks 'Daniel, what do we do at the office?', we might well feel that there is some point to the question.) In the second place, there is in fact no sense of the necessity or virtue of public action; it is doubtless a good thing that Mark's defence of Kafir Aghani saved him from deportation, but all of our attention is fixed purely on Bridget's artless, informal questioning of the couple about their private life. There is an interesting contrast here with another Jane Austen adaptation, Amy Heckerling's *Clueless*, where there is a notably less muted sense of the necessity for good behaviour or morality. Initially in *Clueless* what matters is primarily appearance, as when Josh says to Cher of Tai that 'under your tutelage she's exploring the challenging world of bare midriffs', but as the film unfolds Cher develops a genuine conscience and a desire to 'do good deeds'; indeed John Wiltshire argues that 'the plot of *Clueless*, like *Emma*, delivers a moral outcome, even if in *Clueless* this is presented as a "makeover of the soul"' (Wiltshire 2001: 56). In the world of Helen Fielding, though, the worse Bridget Jones behaves, the funnier we are obviously expected to find it (and probably do). In this respect, what we are offered here is Jane Austen without either the satire or the moral impulse, and the reason that this is so is that there is simply no sense of the existence of a public sphere.

Of course the film knows that to stay entirely in the private world is ultimately impossible. This is neatly imaged when Mark tells Daniel to come 'Outside' for the fight, but they inadvertently move 'inside' again, into the disturbingly 'crossover' space of a restaurant, with Bridget and her friends shouting 'no no no no' as they do so, but nevertheless watching avidly. It is impossible to stay in one place or to inhabit only one sphere, just as Bridget's speech at the Darcys' ruby wedding party hideously traverses the bounds of public and private. Moreover, the private world is seen to have dangers of its own when Mark picks up the diary and then appears to storm off as a direct result of reading it. Bridget has to assure him that 'Everyone knows diaries are just full of crap' before he in turn reassures her by saying 'I know that – that's why I've bought you a new one'. In this scene, where a private romance strays so inappropriately into the public street, we finally see that the two worlds must both be recognised as important – a fitting prelude to the end of the film and our departure from it, just as Bridget has moved on from her diary.

The reason why the private world remains preferable, though, is that it is, in this film, directly associated with England, and as in *In the Bleak Midwinter*, this is an England which is seriously threatened by America, instantiated here as the incarnation of the public world with a vengeance. In Fielding's book, the principal fear is of the European outsider Julio, 'the filthy wop'; in the film, Julian is not Portuguese but has, if anything, tones more cut glass than Bridget's mother and her friends, and instead the sense of fear which he generated in the original book has here been displaced entirely onto America. America owns the publishing firm and could apparently shut it down if it chose; America can lure English lawyers and American girls can steal men from English girls. America invented the TV format in which Julian works and extradiegetically provided the film's leading actress. In this respect, the film is quite different from the novel, in which Mark is 'just back from America' (12) where 'apparently he made a fortune' (211), but there is no question of his returning there. Instead it is Daniel who goes – 'Eventually manage to worm out of Perpetua that Daniel has gone to New York. He will clearly by now have got off with thin American cool person called Winona who puts out, carries a gun and is everything I am not' (39) – and Bridget who would not be averse: 'Think would like to move to New York' (142), a sentiment that it is impossible to imagine the Bridget of the film expressing, since these polarities and trajectories have been entirely reversed.

As I suggested earlier, this fear of America can to some extent be traced back to the fact that the film of *Bridget Jones's Diary* is both a reprise and an inversion of an earlier film produced by Working Title and starring Hugh Grant, *Notting Hill*. 'Even funnier and more romantic than *Notting Hill*' says the blurb on the UK version of the DVD of *Bridget Jones's Diary*, and the similarities are certainly strong. Both linger lovingly on shots of an improbably snowy England and of parties in London at which one finds terrible cooking but good friends (it is significant that in both *Notting Hill* and *In the Bleak Midwinter*, the paradigmatic American film is set in space, which is clearly envisaged as a sterile and unrewarding setting, as too in *Jane Austen in Manhattan* (dir James Ivory, 1980) where Pierre says sententiously 'We're not sending man into space, we're sending space into man', whereas these Hugh Grant rom-coms are having a love affair with London). Both, too, have scenes in which the occupants of a car change places before setting off in hot pursuit of an object of desire. The difference, though, is that in *Notting Hill* Grant plays not a cad but in fact the male equivalent of the Bridget Jones character, a nice, diffident, middle-class worker in a book-related business who has a difficult mother and is notably unsuccessful in romantic terms and not much more so in professional ones, and who is woefully unable to perform in public. Into his life comes not a female equivalent of Mr Darcy but an American actress, played by a Julia Roberts trailing her *Pretty Woman* persona, who, while beautiful, cannot cope with acting Henry James and is no great shakes as a thinker. The film even makes a joke of this, having Thacker at one point ask her if she ever says anything but no, and Anna's intellectual limitations are further suggested by the fact that she always chooses the identity of a cartoon character – Bambi, Flintstone, Pocahontas – as her alias when staying in hotels. We also see her struggling with learning lines, and the fact that this may be the case extradiegetically as well as intradiegetically is suggested not only by how laconic she is but also by the fact that the nudity clause of which Anna speaks intradiegetically quite clearly applies extradiegetically to Julia Roberts too, in the extremely coy bedroom scene. Indeed in the ultimate insult, Anna's face is even seen on the back of a bus, suggesting a definite animus on the part of this film towards its heroine.

The fear of Americanness adumbrated in *Notting Hill* reaches its apotheosis in *Love Actually*, Richard Curtis's 2003 rom-com again produced by Working Title and again starring Hugh Grant, which opens and closes at the arrivals gate of Heathrow Airport. The family likeness between *Notting Hill*, *Bridget Jones's Diary*, *Love Actually* and the earliest of the group, *Four Weddings and a Funeral*, is obvious. They all loudly announce their decision not to concentrate on physical perfection (Bella in *Notting Hill* is in a wheelchair, David in *Four Weddings and a Funeral* is deaf and Gareth in the same film is overweight), and they are considerably more sexually explicit than their American rom-com equivalents would be likely to be. All speak of an obsession with women's weight (Anna, Bridget and Natalie are all painfully conscious of their weight, while Henrietta in *Four Weddings and a Funeral* is delighted that

'I weigh almost nothing'). They are all interested in Christmas: Will Freeman (Hugh Grant) in *About A Boy* lives off the royalties of a feelgood Christmas song written by his father, and *Love Actually*, *About A Boy* and *Bridget Jones's Diary* all include key sequences set at Christmas, while in *Notting Hill* we see Christmas decorations on sale in Portobello Road. All use celebrity actors or indeed celebrities themselves and make game of their real identities (Julia Roberts in *Notting Hill* and Claudia Schiffer in *Love Actually*, while at one point it was rumoured that George Clooney would play Colin Firth in *Bridget Jones: The Edge of Reason*, since Colin Firth himself was already playing Mark Darcy). Most are prepared to face up the idea of death, even if they are not always entirely comfortable doing so: the first two of the deleted scenes on the DVD of *Bridget Jones's Diary* allude to death, which also of course features in *Four Weddings and a Funeral*. *Love Actually* continues the earlier films' love affair with London with some glorious shots of the Thames, and the love of cold weather also returns, as we see the ice rink at Somerset House. (This film, however, also features the countryside as well as London, just as *Bridget Jones's Diary* has the mini-break in the country.) Other similarities with *Love Actually* include the obvious casting overlaps, the reappearance of Colin Firth as a man cuckolded by someone very close to him (along with a reprise of his famous jump into water from *Pride and Prejudice*, particularly pertinent since his surname here is Bennett; the jump is also gestured at in *Bridget Jones's Diary* when Colin Firth looks longingly at Hugh Grant falling into the water), and the reuse of the line 'I am very busy and important', spoken this time by Hugh Grant's character to his sister. As with both *Bridget Jones's Diary* and *In the Bleak Midwinter*, too, this is a miracle-at-Christmas story, because 'At Christmas you tell the truth', so, in another staple of this group of films, a bevy of women offer their hearts and bodies to the men around them, just as Fiona tells Charles that she loves him in *Four Weddings and a Funeral* and Bridget appeals to Mark at his parents' ruby wedding party.

In *Love Actually*, though, America is no longer safely on the other side of the Atlantic: it has come over here, in the shape of a louche and sexually predatory US president who makes a play for Natalie, object of the prime minister's affections, who thus becomes an emblem for England as a whole – identified here as the country of Shakespeare, Churchill, David Beckham and also of Harry Potter, in a deft extradiegetic comment on the battles between J.K. Rowling and Hollywood over the film adaptations of her books. Although Wisconsin proves 'girl heaven' for Colin, because 'Stateside I am Prince William – without the weird family', Hugh Grant as Tony Blair's slyly-named successor 'David' must unhappily acknowledge that 'America is the most powerful country in the world'. By contrast, those in England may produce bad art, as seen as in the risible contents of the art gallery, Jamie's worthless novel and Billy Mack's terrible song, but it is nevertheless art that communicates: the song sells, the book helps Jamie to get the girl and the amateur wedding video through its very deficiency tells a profound emotional truth.

In the fantasy climax of the film, America is defeated on every front. The UK prime minister, not the US president, gets the girl, Joanna comes back from the States, and there is a glorious wish-fulfilment sequence of avoidance of airport security procedures for the delectation of anyone who has flown to the US recently. The emotional tone in these scenes is far more secure than that of the provisional and uneasy relationships of some of the individual love stories; love actually may be difficult to deliver, but paying off old scores, it seems, will always give satisfaction. Equally in *About A Boy* there is a sideswipe at America when Fiona tells Marcus 'I can't stop you from going to McDonalds, I'd just be disappointed if you did', while in *Four Weddings and a Funeral* a question about whether there is anyone who can just walk up and introduce themselves at such events is answered with 'If there are, they're not English', and we have a brutally frank exchange between Charles and Carrie: 'I have to go.' 'Where?' 'America.' 'That is a tragedy.' Conversely, Englishness in *Four Weddings and a Funeral* represents not only reserve but also tradition: we hear the Book of Common Prayer used in the marriage services and see the Zuccaro painting of Elizabeth I on the wall of a country house hotel.

This concept of Americanness as more glamorous but less intelligent than its English equivalent is what *Bridget Jones's Diary* takes from this group of films as strongly as it does the other elements of plot and detail which it reprises. In *Notting Hill*, we might suppose that the final question to which the closing press conference is leading up is 'Will you marry me?'; in fact, it is 'How long do you intend to stay in Britain?', and the answer 'Indefinitely' stands structurally as the same moment of triumph and release that the acceptance of a proposal might be expected to generate. Anna commits to England as much as to Will Thacker, and the final shots are not just of them together but of them together *in London*. In *Notting Hill*, to forsake America and its culture of celebrity is to be redeemed and to enter into a world marked as real rather than fake. *Bridget Jones's Diary* signals its participation in the same aesthetic by casting as its token American the model Lisa B, who signals celebrity culture perhaps even more clearly than Julia Roberts did, and by having

Darcy too, like Roberts's Anna, commit to both England and Bridget in the same breath. Here too then, just as in *In the Bleak Midwinter,* the only England we have left proves ultimately to be one definitively established not just as itself but as an England-which-is-not-America, and in which we are always aware of what looms on the other side of the pond, and although neither of these films directly adapts an Austen or a Shakespeare text, each finds in Austen or Shakespeare respectively a powerful icon of Englishness as endangered but as still deeply rooted in a sense of tradition and the past.

Note

1. There is a delicate irony for British readers in an American description of the film: 'The sword fight features Hamlet and Laertes, bare-chested in pants and suspenders' (Tibbetts 2001: 158). British viewers would be sadly disappointed when the scene totally fails to provide the provocative lingerie that this would imply to them.

4
Across the Ocean: *Shakespeare Wallah* and Shakespearean Performance; and *Bride and Prejudice* (2004)

The UK film industry has long had a love affair with India. Exotic, colourful, photogenic and profoundly resonant because of its rôle as the 'jewel in the crown' of the British Empire, the subcontinent has provided an extremely congenial location for a wide variety of films. Although the US lacks the same kind of historic relationship with India, the unique artistic team of James Ivory, Ismail Merchant and Ruth Prawer Jhabvala has nevertheless also produced a series of probing, sensitive explorations of Indian issues. Collectively, both Anglo-Indian films as a body and the *oeuvre* of the Merchant Ivory stable tend to be very aware of each other, and indeed could essentially be seen as hunting in packs: Ronald Merrick in *The Jewel in the Crown* (dir. Christopher Morahan and Jim O/Brien, 1984) offers an obvious comparison with Ronald Hislop in *A Passage to India* (dir. David Lean, 1984), for instance (and Daphne Manners with Adela Quested), while there is a Russian emigré count in *The Jewel in the Crown*, and the princess in *The Far Pavilions* (dir. Peter Duffell, 1984) has a Russian mother. In this chapter, I want to look at two films of which this is particularly true, the Merchant-Ivory team's *Shakespeare Wallah* (1965) and Gurinder Chadha's *Bride and Prejudice* (2004).

Foreshadowing the debate later to be played out in Branagh's *In the Bleak Midwinter* (1995) and Madden's *Shakespeare in Love* (1998), *Shakespeare Wallah* (dir. James Ivory, 1965) pits theatre against cinema, but it does so from a position conditioned by a radically metacinematic sensibility, as it reaches out beyond its own meanings to its rôle in a series, because its links with other Merchant Ivory films are central to its meanings. As Parama Roy points out, Madhur Jaffrey functions as a blocking figure of interracial marriages in both 1983's *Heat and Dust* (in which she plays the mother of Shashi Kapoor's maharajah, and helps procure an abortion for his white mistress) and *Shakespeare Wallah* (Roy 2002: 491), while Shashi Kapoor, who plays Sanju in *Shakespeare Wallah*, is to some extent reprising his rôle as commitment-shy, ironically named Prem (meaning love) in *The Householder* (1963) and anticipating his divorced maharajah in *Heat and Dust*. *Bride and Prejudice*, too, shows itself acutely aware of its place in a long tradition of British filmic encounters with India, but here this is supplemented and complicated by the fact that Chadha's own previous work has focused not on the old staple of the British in India, a topic which is now safely consigned to the realm of the heritage film, but on the rather edgier and less comfortable question of Indians in Britain. Furthermore, a central part of both films' effect is the way in which indigenous Indian performance styles are played off against imported British ones, to which is added, in the case of *Bride and Prejudice*, a smartly sophisticated awareness of the traditions of Bollywood and the many ways in which they differ from those of Hollywood; this is evoked when Kholi Sahib's house, which is in 'colonial style', is in the Valley, which for Jane Austen fans is now forever associated with *Clueless* (indeed Kholi actually says, 'Our girls that are born there – they've totally lost their roots. Completely clueless'), and when Mrs Bakshi cries excitedly 'He just said Hollywood'. The heading 'Kholiwood' and the fight in the cinema (for which 'The film in the background, Manoj Kumar's *Purab Aur Pachim* (1970), which translates as "East and West," was consciously chosen, Chadha explains, as one of the first Bollywood movies to depict Indians in Britain' [Wilson 2006: 330]) also foreground the importance of metacinematic references such as these, as does Lakhi's remark that 'It's what everyone's wearing in Mumbai', undisputed capital of the Bollywood industry. As a result, we are always insistently aware in both of these films not only of what we are looking at, but also of how it is being represented to us and of the implicit cultural politics of the cinematic style, and in each case, a text by Shakespeare and Austen respectively proves an ideal vehicle to address this.

Shakespeare Wallah and Shakespearean performance

The Merchant Ivory stable's *Shakespeare Wallah*, based on Geoffrey Kendal's autobiographical book *The Shakespeare Wallah*, is ostensibly a nostalgic lament for the passing of the English way of life in India, with Shakespearean performance used essentially as a convenient shorthand for the quintessence of Englishness. Certainly it is as a paean to lost English values that *Shakespeare Wallah* is received by Lubna Chaudhry and Saba Khattak in one of the relatively few critical responses to it: they argue that 'The film has the tone of a tragedy: the British characters are romanticized and the Indian characters are reduced to stereotypes, serving as foils for the idealistic leftovers of British colonial rule' (Chaudhry and Khattak 1994: 19) and conclude that

> Nationalism as a concept in *Shakespeare Wallah* emerges chiefly as a subversion of colonial norms. The influence of colonialism is equated with order, structure, and civilization; once this influence degenerates 'Things fall apart, the center does not hold.' The assertion of Indian nationalism results in chaos. In its treatment of Indian nationalism, the film participates in the heroic discourse of innovative modernism, where myths of primitivism are constructed and perpetuated in order to position Western civilization as the hallbearer of enlightenment and progress. (Chaudhry and Khattak 1994: 20–1)

For Chaudhry and Khattak, then, this is a film that incriminates its Indian characters and celebrates its British ones.

Chaudhry and Khattak's point of view would appear to gain support from some aspects of the film. One scene in particular has the British leading lady Carla Buckingham tell her Indian cast to recite the beginning of G.K. Chesterton's 'The Song of Quoodle', of which the first two stanzas run as follows:

> They haven't got no noses,
> The fallen sons of Eve;
> Even the smell of roses
> Is not what they supposes;
> But more than mind discloses
> And more than men believe.
> They haven't got no noses,
> They cannot even tell
> When door and darkness closes
> The park a Jew encloses,
> Where even the law of Moses
> Will not let you steal a smell.

Later the smells thus cut off prove to include 'The smell of Sunday morning, / God gave to us for ours'. Clearly this is racist in general and anti-Semitic in particular, and the spectacle of an Englishwoman teaching 'natives' to recite such a poem is not an edifying one; however, it seems equally clear that its presence in the film is ironic rather than intended as any kind of endorsement of the values it proposes, for *Shakespeare Wallah*, like Ivory's 1980 *Jane Austen in Manhattan*, is delicately ambivalent in its treatment of English cultural authority *per se*.

On the one hand, the film is fully responsive to the appeal of Shakespeare to Indians and English alike, and, again like *Jane Austen in Manhattan*, it is sensitive to the genuine emotional investment which tired souls make in a beloved author and the extent to which they derive sustenance from such enjoyment. Even Geoffrey Kendal himself, who is generally resistant to the film's project, recognises its resonances and the force of its appeal to nostalgia when he says that 'The Gaiety's stage [in Shimla] is the one seen in *Shakespeare Wallah*, the stage that had been trod by Rudyard Kipling, the Mountbattens, and a succession of people who came to India during the days of the Empire' (Kendal and Colvin 1987: 148): the actual stage that we see in the film is thus imbued with a century and more of British engagement with India, and has indeed something of the same iconic status as the apparent sight of the Globe stage in *Shakespeare in Love* (although that was in fact a replica in San Diego). However, Kendal's reference to the Mountbattens also alerts us to another undercurrent, because the viceregal couple had a strong association with the use of drama as a tool to promote British values, having already done much the same thing in Malta before they came to India: as Governor of the Maltese islands Lord Mountbatten had acted in the Malta Amateur Dramatic Club, and in 1964 he himself made the comparison between the two when he wrote to Ella Warren, who with her sister Kay was the driving force behind the MADC,

> Now that Malta is to get her independence you are faced to a certain extent with the situation which the famous Simla Amateur Dramatic Club faced in India in 1947.
>   My advice to them was to get as many Indians into their Club and actually acting as possible. They took my advice and the Club so far as I know has survived.
>   I urge you to go all out to get as many Maltese members as you can and to get them actively interested in taking parts in the various plays. (Mompalao de Piro 1985: 65–6)

Not only did this occur, but with it developed an active sense of ownership of the English drama, and of Shakespeare in particular; the Malta Amateur Dramatic Club's annual summer Shakespeare is still unfailingly performed. Nevertheless, what worked in Malta does not, in the film at least, work so well in India. For all of the film's registering of the status and emotional pull of Shakespeare, it is also aware that as a commodity (and the use of the occupational term 'wallah' underlines the fact that for the fictional Buckinghams, Shakespeare is above all a commodity, being the tool of their trade) he is losing his appeal. All Sanju can remember of the play he claims to have enjoyed so much is 'Romeo, Romeo, wherefore art thou?'; as he says himself, 'What words he spoke! I wish I could remember the words!' – but he cannot.

Sanju's impotent nostalgia and his sense of a deep, if not fully articulated, cultural loss is particularly important because although his inability to remember Shakespeare's words may appear to tap directly into a simple opposition of an Indian response versus an English one, this is something in which the film is in fact relatively uninterested – Sanju's race is never an issue in the Buckingham parents' growing hostility to him, merely the fact that he first fails to attend their performances and then is associated with disruption to them, and this is something firmly in line with the tradition of adapting Shakespeare in colonial India: Paromita Chakravatri notes '[t]he silence about racial issues in colonial adaptations of *Othello*' (Chakravarti 2003: 45), in which 'gender issues rather than racial matters assume importance' (Chakravarti 2003: 45). (Although the Kendals did in fact oppose their daughter Jennifer's real-life wedding to Shashi Kapoor, who plays Sanju, it was on the grounds of age rather than race [Kendal and Colvin 1987: 136], since they thought her too young.) In fact, the film's real energy is focused not on any possible tension between English and Indians, which it regards as a non-issue, but on a very different and more far-reaching debate about the nature of Shakespearean performance on camera: as John C. Tibbetts astutely remarks, 'The disasters that befall the Buckingham Players exemplify the schisms opening up between worlds old and new, between classical and popular entertainment' (Tibbetts 2001: 155), and thus to a certain extent are seen as potentially able to occur anywhere and at any time, rather than being a product of a specific history or particular location.

Ironically, this conflict between residual and emerging cultural forms is duplicated in the film itself, in the tension between the actors who are represented in the film and the actors who are doing the representing: as John Pym notes, 'Geoffrey Kendal and Laura Liddel were prevailed upon to play the Buckinghams themselves, although they took, Ivory has recorded, rather a dim view of the art of film acting' (Pym 1983: 37). Kendal and Liddel were also deeply resistant to the actual characters they were asked to portray as well as the medium in which they were asked to portray them. Declaring simply that although the screenplay was based on his diary, 'This film was not about us, but concerned some travelling hams to whom we bore no resemblance' (Kendal and Colvin 1987: 144), Geoffrey Kendal in his autobiography complained specifically that the Buckinghams' troupe was far less successful than their own, that Mrs Buckingham 'seems to have very stay-at-home ideas for a lady of the theatre' (147) and that 'The Buckingham Players had been wandering around the East longer than Somerset Maugham in a sort of miasma, and had not a clue as to what was going on in the world' (145). There certainly were discernible differences between the Buckinghams' fictional story and the Kendals' actual one: although Geoffrey Kendal noted that the character played by their younger daughter Felicity was modelled on their elder daughter Jennifer (145), so far from the Kendals' real-life son-in-law, Shashi Kapoor, having no experience of the theatre, his father, Prithviraj Kapoor, was 'the first name in Bombay Theatre' and 'a throw-back to the old-time English actor-managers' (109–10), and indeed Shashi Kapoor's own growing fame soon ensured that he was mentioned on a poster for *Othello* when Shakespeare himself was not (143). Moreover, unlike the film, where Lizzie has never visited England, Jennifer Kendal had been born there, and Felicity Kendal had spent part of her childhood there (102–3).

Ironically, Geoffrey Kendal saw the film's changes to his story as intended to make him and his troupe seem ridiculous, but Chaudhry and Khattak view them as having entirely the opposite effect, and intended rather to represent the Indians of the film as primitive for failing to respond properly to English culture (Chaudhry and Khattak 1994: 21). I want to suggest that neither of these perspectives is right. In the first place, it is important to note that the Indians of the film are by no means staging a blanket rejection of English culture, nor is English culture as a whole seen as by any means entirely outmoded. There is at least one aspect of it – cricket – that the Indians of the film have taken totally to their hearts; one of Sanju's most sympathetic moments comes when, having snatched a quiet moment to have a drink and listen to the cricket on the radio, he has to wearily rouse himself to face yet another drama in his love life. This passion for cricket would, moreover, be something readily recognisable as a wholly credible representation of Indian culture, as is also reflected in Rajiv Menon's *Kandukondain Kandukondain* (2000), for instance. In this Tamil-language version of *Sense and Sensibility*, Bala's uncle says of Srikanth's wooing of Minu 'He hits a six with laughter', and one of Soumya's colleagues doesn't want to work because 'I want to watch Sachin [Tendulkar] bat'.) Nor is cricket the only thing still beloved: as Valerie Wayne notes,

> Even Manjula, whose popularity as a film star depends upon the rise of the new India, serves Lizzie a formal English tea, using the occasion to manipulate the observance into a kind of ritualized subjugation of the English woman. (Wayne 1997: 98)

The tension is not, then, simply between English culture and Indian culture; rather it is about previously dominant versus emerging cultural forms.

This is most obviously imaged in the tension between theatrical and cinematic performance, but this in turn is further inflected by a triangulated debate between three specific Shakespeare plays, *Romeo and Juliet*, *Othello* and *Antony and Cleopatra*. These have clearly been very deliberately chosen for the specific ideological purposes of the film; although the Kendals' repertoire did indeed include *Othello*, which has traditionally been the most popular choice for Shakespearean performances in India (Trivedi 2005: 48), there is no trace here of the fact that their most popular production was in fact *The Merchant of Venice* (Kendal and Colvin 1987: 66–7). The selection of these three plays in particular appears to serve two principal purposes. In the first place, the film is able to suggest that the ways in which they represent human relationships, particularly inter-racial ones, is one reason why Shakespeare has fallen out of favour when cricket and afternoon tea have not. In the second place, *Romeo and Juliet*, *Othello* and *Antony and Cleopatra* are ironically apposite not only to the specific events of *Shakespeare Wallah* but also to the wider valencies of the debate about performance on stage and performance on screen. *Romeo and Juliet* has indeed now established itself as the favourite text for this discussion, since it lies at the centre of both *Shakespeare in Love* and Luhrmann's 1996 *William Shakespeare's Romeo + Juliet*; in *Shakespeare Wallah*, *Romeo and Juliet* also clearly functions as an ironic counter-text to a love story that is not so much star-crossed as bedevilled by deep-seated cultural misunderstandings and doomed to founder on two fundamentally opposed attitudes to art.

Romeo and Juliet were both citizens of Verona, alike in many respects and eminently suitable as marriage partners for each other on the grounds of race, class and age, except that their families were riven by a feud of which we are never told the root cause. Lizzie and Sanju, on the other hand, are kept apart by differences in tradition and attitudes that are never fully articulated and that both cultures indeed do their utmost to mask, but which are nevertheless powerfully at work. In this their story might well seem to mimic that of Antony and Cleopatra, except that the rôle of Cleopatra is so comprehensively displaced onto Manjula, in her capacity as exotic other woman who lures the hero from what thus comes to seem as the path of his duty. In a final complication, the film's allusions to *Othello* introduce the idea that a cross-cultural marriage might indeed be fatal to both partners; as Valerie Wayne notes, 'Both Othello and Manjula fear that their loved ones will turn coward and make the more conservative, white, and Western choice' (Wayne 1997: 99). This would be a message with particular resonance in India: Ania Loomba observes that 'More students probably read *Othello* in the University of Delhi every year than in all British universities combined. A large proportion of these are women' (Loomba 1992: 10), and for them the play can be made to produce a message which elides all national or racial differences in order to stress a deeply conservative and allegedly transnational gender politics: 'as undergraduates at Miranda House, Delhi (the name is not insignificant ...) who were "dissatisfied" with Desdemona's silence in the face of her husband's brutality, we were told that we did not "understand" her because we had never been "in love". *Othello* thus became a sort of universal text of love, and love implied female passivity' (Loomba 1992: 39). (This is also interestingly illustrated by Vishal Bharadwaj's *Omkara* [2006], a Hindi version of *Othello*, which I shall touch on later.) Together, then, these three plays collectively fashion our understanding of Lizzie's and Sanju's relationship in ways that ultimately work to marginalise wider differences and stress smaller, more local ones. In terms of the paradigm afforded by *Othello*, racial difference is stressed, but not only can this be downplayed, as in Loomba's experience and as in *Omkara* where it is in fact totally silenced, but it is in any case countered by the evocation of *Antony and Cleopatra*, a text that works to drive just as big a cultural wedge between Sanju and Manjula, while *Romeo and Juliet* removes the question of racial difference from the arena entirely and recasts it as a story of old versus new, in ways whose force is much greater for contemporary audiences now that *Romeo and Juliet* has become the master text for metacinematic Shakespeare.

The film's narrative, moreover, is further complicated by the fact that it is also profoundly interested not just in Shakespeare but also in the British royal family. This both reflects the cultural insecurity of an Indian elite educated in uneasy emulation of imperial culture and again foreshadows *Shakespeare in Love* with its romanticised vision of English royal power. The first person who entertains the Kendals' troupe is quick to inform them that he had been at the Queen's coronation; later, when Sanju rescues them, he takes them to the house of his uncle, perhaps reminding us of the fact that the marriage between the Queen and Prince Philip had been brokered by the latter's uncle, Lord Mountbatten, the last viceroy of India; and most pointedly of all, despite the fact that this is an essentially true story based on the experiences of the actual Kendal family, who are in fact playing themselves, the heroine's name has been changed to Lizzie Buckingham, in an obvious evocation of both Queen Elizabeth and Buckingham Palace. To some extent there could be an in-joke here: Geoffrey Kendal notes in *The Shakespeare Wallah* that the Kendals went out to India in the winter of 1946–7 on the P&O liner *Strathmore* (Kendal and Colvin 1987: 85), a ship named after the Queen's maternal grandfather, and he further adds that it was only through meeting the Queen's relatives, the Mountbattens, in Malta in the early fifties (where, amongst other plays, the Kendals performed *Othello*, and where the Queen and Prince Philip also lived after their marriage) that they were enabled to return to India in 1953 (Kendal and Colvin 1987: 105). Most notably, though, these references to the royal family turn this ostensible story of a private family into a metaphor for much larger concerns: as John C. Tibbetts notes, 'the travails of a traveling Shakespearean troupe bespeak the larger tensions of a newly liberated India' (Tibbetts 2001: 147–8). The conclusion of the story thus implies not only that Lizzie cannot marry Sanju but also that England and India must now drift apart, with India going in a new direction in which Shakespeare and what he represents will have no further part. This is an emphasis that, as we shall see, Gurinder Chadha's *Bride and Prejudice* will revisit and deliberately attempt to revise.

Bride and Prejudice (2004)

It is not easy to take Jane Austen to India, even though she did in fact have a strong family connection with the subcontinent: her father's sister Philadelphia Austen, sent out to India in search of a husband, not only married there but became a close friend of the Governor-General, Warren Hastings, who may in fact have been the father of Philadelphia's only child, Eliza. This was a piece of family history of which Jane Austen herself would have been well aware because Eliza was to become not only her first cousin but also later her sister-in-law, since Eliza's second husband was Jane Austen's favourite brother Henry (Lane 1984: 42–4). This quirk of history, like the references to slavery in *Mansfield Park*, may serve to remind us that the historical Jane Austen's quiet corner of Hampshire was not as cut off from the wider world as we might sometimes suppose, and indeed in some ways an Indian setting ought to prove particularly sympathetic to film adaptations of Jane Austen, since Indian dating and behavioural conventions, both in real life and in films, adhere to a positively Austenian sense of decorum. Thus in *Bride and Prejudice* it seems entirely appropriate that Lalita and Darcy do not kiss (indeed Aishwarya Rai, in a fate which has also befallen other Bollywood actresses, has since become the subject of an obscenity suit taken out by a private individual offended by the fact that in another film she and the actor Hrithik Roshan kissed on screen – or 'locked lips' as the *Times of India* likes to have it on these occasions). However, 'Jane Austen' the product has been so effectively constructed as the epitome of a conservative Englishness in radical opposition to all things foreign that 'Jane Austen' and 'India' now seem the most unlikely of couplings.

Nevertheless, thirty-five years after *Shakespeare Wallah*, audiences were treated to the unlikely spectacle of a Jane Austen heroine performing in total earnest precisely the kind of Indian song-and-dance sequence that gets Manjula a bad name. In Rajiv Menon's *Kandukondain Kandukondain*, former Miss World Aishwarya Rai, who was later to play the Elizabeth figure in *Bride and Prejudice*, plays Meenakshi (Minu), the Marianne figure. Minu's elder sister Soumya (played by the model Tabu) is the Elinor figure; the studious younger sister Kamala corresponds to Margaret. The plot events of *Sense and Sensibility* are replicated with surprising fidelity: the mother's brother Swami and his hideous wife Lalitha are the equivalents of the John Dashwoods and their conversation about how much to give his sister and her daughters is wholly recognisable, although the hostility between the two groups is far more naked than it could ever be in Austen, culminating with Lalitha telling the girls and their mother that they are 'refugees'. (Later, Swami is killed when the ceiling falls on his head and he proves to have left them the house.) The poetry of the Tamil writer Subramania Bharati stands in for *Sense and Sensibility*'s references to Shakespeare's sonnets, and there is a telling moment when Srikanth, the Willoughby figure, confuses Bharati (1882–1921) with Bharati Dasan, also a Tamil poet but prominent later (he was born in 1891 and lived until 1964) and storms off when Minu corrects him.

There are, however, also some significant differences between *Kandukondain Kandukondain* and *Sense and Sensibility*. Srikanth is not simply an impecunious adventurer, as Willoughby is, but a dodgy financier whose fall ruins many people, and in the same darker vein the mother and sisters' experience of poverty here is also much harsher and brings them closer to the breadline than any Austen heroine ever goes. Particularly notable is the fact that Manohar (Ajith), the Edward Ferrars figure, is not a clergyman but a would-be film director who meets the sisters when he seeks permission to use their house for location shots, leading to a sustained metafilmic strand to the narrative. Soumya wonders 'Can I trust film people?' and Major Bala (the Malayalam star Mammootty), the Brandon figure, who was a commando with the 9th Paras until he stepped on a landmine and lost his leg, tells Minu to 'keep dancing and singing', making the musical element diegetic as well as ironic. The same note of self-reflexivity is struck when Bala dismisses his own experience with 'If you made a film of it, no one would go. Better to make a love story', while later, Manohar is asked if he has made a film in English, a question with obvious resonance in this Tamil-language adaptation: a prospective actor tells him 'I walk English, talk English, dance English, do anything'. Manohar's ambition is to make a suspense film set on a train, focusing on defusing a bomb in time, but he is told that 'making a Tamil film involves emotions, songs, etc.'. In a particularly good example of the film's metacinematic sensibility, at exactly the point at which Soumya begins to claw her way up at work by helping to develop software, Manohar embraces the suggestion that his film could have an action heroine rather than a hero and casts Nandini Varma (Pooja Batra), who becomes the Lucy Steele figure. Finally, Manohar asks 'What's in a title?' after he changes the name of his film from *Speed* to *First Love*, neatly reminding us that although this film may have the very un-Austenian name of *Kandukondain Kandukondain* (loosely translatable as 'I have found it! I have found it!'), it is neverthe-less recognisable as *Sense and Sensibility*. There is even a knowing glance towards other film adaptations of Austen when Srikanth (Abbas), the Willoughby figure, swims out of a lake towards Aishwarya Rai's Minu, who falls over and hurts her ankle, and this nod towards the iconic image of Colin Firth in the lake is in turn something also echoed in *Bride and Prejudice*, Rai's later and more famous Austen film, where Wickham comes up out of the sea.

Rai's appearance in *Kandukondain Kandukondain* foreshadows and dir-ectly feeds into her later incarnation as Lalita, the Elizabeth Bennet figure of *Bride and Prejudice*. When I have mentioned *Bride and Prejudice* to Indian scholars their usual reaction has been to apologise for its existence and beg me not to believe that all Indians would treat Jane Austen with such disrespect, and indeed there are elements of the film that are clearly not Austenian: Mr Bakshi wholly lacks the spirit and indeed the detachment of Mr Bennet, and the plot and logic of *Pride and*

Prejudice are both left far behind when Kiran – the equivalent of Caroline Bingley – actually tells Lalita where Darcy is in the final sequence, as if she were giving her blessing to the relationship. It is also true that *Bride and Prejudice* is unusually daring for both an Indian film and also for an Austen one: Naveen Andrews, who plays Balraj (the Bingley figure), has been the subject of much unfavourable comment in the British press because of his colourful personal life, Chandra Lamba (the Charlotte Lucas figure) shockingly says that Jaya (Jane) should 'Seduce him before he leaves. Give him a little taste so he'll come running back for more', and perhaps most surprisingly, Lakhi, the Lydia figure, does not marry the man who appears to have seduced her, but instead returns to the family home, simultaneously flying in the face of both Indian sensibilities and Austen's plot. Moreover, a large part of the appeal of Jane Austen on screen has traditionally proved to be the films' depiction of English landscapes: as H. Elisabeth Ellington observes of the 1995 *Pride and Prejudice*, 'The majority of the film ... takes place out of doors, which is perhaps Davies's most radical rewriting of Austen's novel ... As Fay Weldon cynically, but accurately, remarks in her review ... "Experience tells [film-makers] you can sell English heritage all over the world, and get your money back"' (Ellington 1998: 94), while Mike Crang argues that 'Austen calls forth a specific type of landscape that in turn authorises a particular version of English history' (Crang 2003: 113) and James Thompson declares that in Ang Lee's *Sense and Sensibility*, for instance, 'the real actors are the great houses and the spectacular landscapes' (Thompson 2003: 24). Even the wholly Tamil-based *Kandukondain Kandukondain* offers its audience a version of this particular pleasure, with a song and dance sequence set, however improbably, in Urquhart Castle on the banks of Loch Ness, but the England that *Bride and Prejudice* shows us is almost entirely suburban, with a few shots of central London. In fact, though, the real trouble with *Bride and Prejudice* arises not from any of these causes but from the fact that just as *Shakespeare Wallah* gestures towards other films in the Merchant Ivory canon, so too it is impossible not to read *Bride and Prejudice* in the context of other filmic encounters with India, including, inevitably, some by Merchant Ivory, and this leads to a slightly less comfortable picture than that which Chadha is clearly aiming to present.

Although the visions of India offered by these films are diverse in many respects, they do tend to have a number of features in common. One particularly notable feature of what I shall call 'the India film' is that it is generally very concerned to demonstrate animus against the British in India – in the case of adaptations, often even more so than the original novels had been. In Ruth Prawer Jhabvala's novel *Heat and Dust*, for instance, the modern-day heroine Anne is the step-granddaughter of the twenties heroine Olivia: her grandfather was Douglas, Olivia's husband, and her grandmother was his second wife Tessie, who met Douglas because she was the sister of Beth Crawford, the Collector's wife. It is Grandma Tessie and Great-Aunt Beth jointly who provide much of Anne's knowledge about Olivia, who sees a fair amount of Beth and even on one occasion, after she has been to visit Mrs Saunders, thinks 'What a relief, after that, to be with bright, brisk Beth Crawford!' (Jhabvala 1975: 28). In the film, though, Anne is the granddaughter of Olivia's almost equally racy sister Marcia, and Beth Crawford is anathema: in Susan Fleetwood's magnificent performance, she is the archetypal, quite intolerable Memsahib, with cut-glass tones and no redeeming features whatsoever. Conversely, the Olivia of the book is by no means wholly admirable or innocent: when she is first invited to the palace 'She felt she had, at last in India, come to the right place' (15), and when she first meets the Nawab 'His eyes had lit up – he checked himself immediately, but she had seen it and realised that here at last was one person in India to be interested in her the way she was used to' (17). However, the Olivia of the film is entirely sympathetic, something which is indeed almost inevitable given that Greta Scacchi's Olivia constitutes a feast for the eye and is certainly the unfailing centre of visual attention.

The second salient feature of such films is that they almost invariably trope the relationship between the two countries as thwarted romance. Here above all they hunt in packs: *The Jewel in the Crown*'s Bibighar Gardens clearly echo the Marabar Caves in *A Passage to India*, and Hari Kumar has a photo of Daphne Manners just as Dr Aziz does of his wife. Perhaps the most obvious comparison for *Bride and Prejudice* in this respect is *Heat and Dust*, since Chadha's Wickham figure is very like Merchant Ivory's hippy, Chid. 'Johnny' Wickham makes himself out as being, like Chid, a stereotypically ill-equipped and starry-eyed Western traveller when he says 'I just feel like people here have got their priorities sorted', in rather the same mode as Darcy's mother later makes the impossible demand 'So tell me everything about India'. *Heat and Dust* in turn presents itself as a link in a long chain of English engagements with India since Olivia's husband, Douglas, is descended from a John Rivers (154) who inevitably recalls St John Rivers, who set out for India at the end of *Jane Eyre* (and perhaps also Jean Rhys's 1966 novel *Wide Sargasso Sea*, which explored the relationship between *Jane Eyre*'s Mr Rochester and his black first wife). Although the story of the modern-day heroine

Anne in *Heat and Dust* ends more happily than that of her great-aunt Olivia, whose baby was aborted and who died alone, it does not seem to be suggested that she will stay in India after her baby is born, or maintain any relationship with its father. India has already proved too much for Chid, forced to flee to the safety of his aunt's super-clean bathroom in the States, and Inder Lal can hardly leave his children and his ailing wife to provide any kind of meaningful presence in the lives of Anne or her baby.

Heat and Dust is by no means the only film in which this motif of blighted romance occurs. It is, as we have seen, present in *Shakespeare Wallah* too, and it is also widespread elsewhere. In *The Jewel in the Crown*, which is linked to Chadha's work by the fact that the actress who played Lily Chatterjee (Zohra Segal) also appears in *Bend it Like Beckham* (2002) and *Bhaji on the Beach* (1993), Daphne Manners' tentative romance with Hari Kumar is brutally ended by gang-rape, and her subsequent death in childbed leaves any product of Anglo-Indian entente effectively orphaned (and also of questionable parentage). It seems clear that Daphne and Hari could have been really happy, but social pressures from both sides are too great; even Aunt Lily pushes Ronald Merrick as a suitor for Daphne. Moreover, the fate of Daphne and her child, like that of Olivia, will echo ominously down to future generations, blighting romance and tainting the lives of children not yet born, while Sarah Layton and Ahmed Kassim never even get to that stage: 'Ahmed and I – we weren't in love, but we loved each other'. In *A Passage to India*, the irony is that romance is not even a possibility: although we do not know what happened in the Marabar Caves, we can be very sure that it was not the result of an attraction between Adela and Dr Aziz, whatever the film's rather cheap introduction of a scene in which Adela stumbles upon Indian erotic carvings may be thought to insinuate. Indeed the inappropriateness and intrusiveness of such an episode are smartly castigated by Santha Rama Rau, who had been consulted during the development of the screenplay:

> Although dismayed at first that she had not been more involved in the writing of the film, Santha Rama Rau later expressed relief because, she said, 'I think I would have had a fit if I had known in advance that the film was going to contain the sequence of a lonely "brave" Memsahib cycling about the Indian countryside and coming upon erotic sculptures only to be scared into flight by a pack of shrieking monkeys. This sort of vulgarity was so remote from Forster's oblique, equivocal approach to Adela's sexual malaise'. (Sinyard 2000: 156)

Only in the egregious *The Far Pavilions* are we offered an India where romance can flourish, and that is only because the India of this series is a ludicrously oversimplified one, where an Englishman can happily and unproblematically 'pass' as both Hindu and Muslim while speaking a catch-all 'Indian' which is apparently understood the length and breadth of the subcontinent. (At one point, it almost looks as if he can speak Elephant, too.) In *The Jewel in the Crown*, Hari at the outset declares that 'I don't speak Indian', but has soon learned enough to say 'I don't speak Hindi' next time he needs to; in *The Far Pavilions*, we are not invited to register any such complications, in a cultural indifference rivalling that of Robert Taylor's legendary line 'I speak no Austrian' in the 1952 *Ivanhoe*.

This well-established pattern of thwarted romance in the India film significantly troubles the waters of *Bride and Prejudice*, especially when it is viewed in the context of Chadha's own earlier work. In *Bride and Prejudice*, a deafening silence surrounds the fact that Martin Henderson's Mr Darcy is white, as if it were a topic that Chadha shies away from addressing. Yet in her two previous films, *Bhaji on the Beach* and *Bend it Like Beckham* (which is retrospectively linked to *Bride and Prejudice* by the fact that Keira Knightley was herself a future Elizabeth Bennet), the difficulties attendant on mixed-race relationships have taken centre stage: in *Bhaji on the Beach*, Sarita Khajuria's Hashida is pregnant by her black boyfriend, and in *Bend it Like Beckham*, Parminder Nagra's Jess is in love with Jonathan Rhys Meyers' white football coach, Joe. Equally, in Rajiv Menon's *Kandukondain Kandukondain* Soumya is considered unlucky because her previous fiancé committed suicide in America, and as Minu indignantly points out, 'He had a white girl's photo in his pocket, not my sister's'. In *Bride and Prejudice*, however, we tiptoe around this issue with only the barest of glances at it, as when Mrs Bakshi says of Darcy 'Shame he's not Indian though'. The question of potential tensions in this marriage is not tackled head on but in fact seems comprehensively fudged when a multiracial chorus all in blue sing 'Show them the way / Take them to love' in the fantasy sequence of Lalita and Darcy falling in love; here the uniformity of the characters' clothing is apparently intended to distract from the fact that their skins are such different colours, and to suggest the possibility of a harmony that would be unlikely to prevail in real life. As Christine Geraghty notes, 'colorful and noisy Amritsar is as much fantasy India as MGM's Meryton Village was fantasy England' (Geraghty 2008: 40).

It is certainly true that a marriage between an Indian woman and a white man would find greater social acceptance in modern India than a marriage between an Indian woman and a black man, as is gestured at in *Bhaji on the Beach*, since, uncomfortable as it may be to have to note it, there is undoubtedly a colour-based hierarchy at work, as when Jess in *Bend it Like Beckham* defines the range of possible husbands as 'White, no. Black, definitely not' and Mrs Bhamra complains 'Look how dark you've become playing in the sun'. The unease attaching to this issue is seen particularly clearly in the absolute silencing and repression of the subject of colour in both the recent Hindi version of *Othello*, *Omkara* (dir. Vishal Bharadwaj, 2006), and '*Kaliyattam*, an award-winning film by Jayaraaj (1998), in which the relocation of *Othello* becomes a means to examine the circulation of power within class and caste structures in rural Kerala' (Trivedi 2007: 151) (the same director was also responsible for *Kannaki* [2002]), a version of *Antony and Cleopatra*); Trivedi goes on to observe that 'Some of the Malayalam intelligentsia has had a somewhat lukewarm response to *Kaliyattam* holding its depiction of a romantic union between a *theyyam* personator, always a low caste, and a Brahmin's daughter as entirely implausible' (Trivedi 2007: 152). At the very beginning of *Omkara*, Langda, the Iago figure (Saif Ali Khan), says to the Roderigo figure, Rajoh (Deepak Dobriyal), 'The half-caste's abducting your bride even as we speak', adding 'If you've got what it takes, go save Dolly' (in fact, in the first of many signs of the film's thorough transplantation to the modern world, his moped gets a puncture, so he can't). After this loud and clear announcement that what is at stake is definitely not race but caste (although this in itself touches on a very thorny issue in India, the question of whether discrimination on the basis of caste in fact constitutes racism), the insistence is further underlined when Dolly's father refers to Omkara's mother as a slave girl, and Omkara himself explains 'My mother belonged to a lower caste ... That's why they call me a half-caste'. To a large extent, indeed, political disagreements take the place of racial ones, with the old woman's question 'How in the world did you get such a fair girl in these parts?' the only real gesture in the direction of a discussion of either colour or race. Omkara's patron, the lawyer Bhaisaab (Naseeruddin Shah) is a parliamentary candidate who is temporarily imprisoned and who has a faintly Gandhiesque appearance. Omkara's role is as 'General of the Party', something that not only politicises him but also scales down the sense of his achievement and impact, and this diminution in the idea of his effectiveness is accompanied by a similar reduction on other fronts too. There is no exotic, impressive speech about his travels; instead Dolly (Kareena Kapoor) reflects 'God knows how it all began ... how I lost my heart to Omkara', and we are never very much the wiser on that score, since in general Omkara (Ajay Devgan) is an unimpressive figure; he doesn't talk noticeably well and he falls back on violence much more readily than the Shakespearean original. The plot is different in other ways too: although we see the preparations for Dolly's aborted wedding to the Roderigo figure, the wedding of Dolly and Omkara is deferred and the plot is further altered when Langda's resentment of Omkara is seen considerably to predate his being passed over in favour of Kesu. What the film seems in fact to find most interesting is the tension between the India of the past and the India of the present: the handkerchief becomes a traditional decorative waistband, but this symbol of tradition sits oddly in a world in which mobile phones play a crucial part, while Kesu, the Cassio figure (Vivek Oberoi) is trendily given to speaking English and at one point is addressed as 'You Anglo shit!'. Other characters also occasionally speak English: Dolly sends Omkara a note in Hindi which finishes 'I love you. Yours forever. D.' Similarly, Langda taunting Rajoh asks him in Hindi 'Where did your guts go walking then?' and then switches to English to add sarcastically 'Company garden?', while Kesu speaks in English to Billo, the Bianca figure. It is, the film perhaps implies, anglicisation and its spread of different norms and values which have facilitated the 'deviant' relationship between Omkara and Dolly that precipitates the tragedy, because there is certainly no other visible cause or logic for such a liaison to flourish, and in many respects the most notable effect of this attempt to move *Othello* to India is to show how very uneasily it sits there.

Omkara's queasiness is powerful testimony to the extent to which interracial marriage remains a difficult issue in Indian society, as indeed is a love marriage in the first place, as the existence of Indian marriage-broking websites such as the one Mrs Bakshi is seen using abundantly testifies. In fact, the end of the film, where Darcy and Lalita appear in public as a couple to apparently universal acceptance and acclaim despite the fact that Mrs Bakshi has just said to Balraj 'Why don't you find our Lalita a nice Indian husband?', could well be read as being as much of a fantasy sequence as the multiracial chorus scene – it has the same quality, and the use of a fantasy sequence seguing seamlessly into reality is something of a Chadha hallmark, as in *Bend it Like Beckham* where Jess's imagined appearance at Old Trafford is so seamlessly integrated into real footage of a typical and familiar scene of Alan Hansen and Gary Lineker commentating. Devices such as this are dear to Chadha's heart, as we see in *Bend it Like Beckham* with the appearance of Shaznay Lewis and euphoric images such as the victorious team re-dressing Jess for the wedding, Mr Bhamra getting up and Jess sitting in his chair as if to symbolise her elevation to his position and the closing image of a plane soaring into the sky; nevertheless, it is all too obvious that this is wish-fulfilment rather than realism, as when no concern is expressed about the possible future facing the sympathetic gay character, Tony. Mr Bhamra may say 'You know how hard it is for our children over here', but actually Chadha's films after *Bhaji on the Beach* do *not* know it. It is hard not to suspect, though, that a real Sikh girl with Jess's aspirations and talents still might find it so, just as it is hard not to suspect that a marriage between a real-life Lalita and Darcy might be rather less rapturously received than it is in *Bride and Prejudice*.

Not only does placing the narrative of *Pride and Prejudice* within the context of the India film ask us to question the verisimilitude of the crowning marriage, it also asks us how much of an achievement and fulfilment such a marriage would actually represent for the heroine, because the India film also habitually stresses gender differences. This is a phenomenon that is at its clearest in perhaps the least obviously identifiable of India films, *Indiana Jones and the Temple of Doom* (dir. Steven Spielberg, 1984). This may seem to have very different concerns and tonality from the films I have been looking at so far in this chapter; in fact, though, it dates from 1984, the *annus mirabilis* of the India film, which saw the release of *A Passage to India* and the first screenings of both *The Jewel in the Crown* and, less gloriously, *The Far Pavilions*. For all its apparent gung-ho simplicity, the Indiana Jones series is in fact significantly indebted to and aware of its place in film history, as evidenced by the marked parallels between the first film in the series, *Raiders of the Lost Ark* (dir. Steven Spielberg, 1981), and the classic movie *Casablanca* (dir. Michael Curtiz, 1942): Belloc, the archaeologist, is reminiscent of Claude Rains' chief of police (why else is he French? – and such a very stereotypical Frenchman at that, who orders clothes for a woman and has a family wine label). Moreover, Indy, who wants to go to Marrakesh, walks into a bar owned by an old flame just as Ilsa Lund does, and, like her, meets Nazis there. The shot of the plane moving across a map obviously recalls *Casablanca*, as indeed does the visual style in general, and finally, as in *Casablanca*, the American and the Frenchman find common cause in the face of Germans. It is therefore notable that *Indiana Jones and The Temple of Doom* shares with *The Jewel in the Crown* the fact that several important sequences are located in Pankot, and that the opening sequence of *The Jewel in the Crown* is very similar to the shot of Jones, Willy and Short Round crossing a stream on elephants, while there is an ineffectual British officer of the kind so often found in India films, Captain Blumburtt, who serves with the 11th Poona Rifles.

Indiana Jones and The Temple of Doom may be comically disrespectful about Indian food, but it is in fact not totally ignorant about Indian history, culture and religions: the Maharajah, for instance, is clearly identified as a Sikh, and the characters show themselves aware of at least some aspects of Indian history. The film is, though, totally uncompromising in its representation of female incompetence (and, in this respect, notably different from the other two films in the series): Willy is wholly inadequate – Jones and Short Round can perform a spot of male bonding over playing cards and riding elephants and eating bugs, but she is totally unwilling or unable to join in, and while Jones understands guns and flying, she worries only about breaking nails. There is also the unmistakable point that the tunnel into which they enter is accessed by cupping the breasts of a female statue, is all red and ragged at the edges like a vagina dentata, and is dedicated to Kali. No wonder that Jones says 'Shortie, you keep an eye on her' – the boy is more reliable than the woman, who is overtly belittled and covertly comprehensively incriminated.

This should alert us to the fact that in the India film in general, women's lives and prospects are very different from men's. Even in *The Jewel in the Crown*, which has not one but two feisty female lead characters, women are vulnerable to pregnancy, rape and forced marriage in ways that men can never be. Indeed given the condition of Indian women and the film's own investment in representing the English as powerless, Lizzie Buckingham actually comes remarkably well out of her situation in *Shakespeare Wallah* (is it significant that she is called Lizzie, associating her with the resourcefulness of Austen's heroine – an association perhaps subconsciously prompted by Felicity Kendal's reference to 'daughterly pride and prejudice' in the prologue to the book?). One would have to wonder, though, what Lalita achieves: a love marriage, yes, but with a terrifying mother-in-law and a necessity to base herself from now on in a country that she doesn't want to live in. In fact, the importance of the mother-in-law in Indian marriages (seen when Jaya greets Balraj's mother) makes Darcy's aggressive mother a real threat, and far more menacing than Lady Catherine de Burgh, who is merely Darcy's aunt, not least since Darcy's mother is called by Mr Kholi 'Miz Catherine', which makes her sound for all the world like a slave-owning plantation-dweller straight out of *Gone with the Wind*. As Cheryl Wilson observes, after

> Lalita and Darcy ride off into the sunset on the back of an elephant after their traditional Indian wedding, questions about the union

remain – where will they live? How will they blend cultural values in raising children? What kind of interaction will their families have? (Darcy's family is noticeably absent from the wedding). The affinity shared by Darcy and Lalita as individuals, of course, suggests nothing but a happy marriage, but the practical aspects remain troubling – this Elizabeth cannot be welcomed to Pemberley, which in the film is an upscale Los Angeles hotel owned by Darcy's mother, nor does she particularly want to be. (Wilson 2006: 330)

In Chadha's earlier *Bend it Like Beckham*, we know very well what Jess wants to do with her life. But what will Lalita, apart from being a wife and presumably in due course a mother?

Bride and Prejudice also differs from Chadha's earlier work in being markedly less interested in what is normally her main area of concern, which is the representation of Britain and above all of the Asian (and specifically the Sikh) community within it. Though Punjabi is heard in *Bride and Prejudice*, so too is Hindi, and although they live on Fudham Singh Road, a name that irresistibly gestures towards a Sikh neighbourhood, Lalita's family are not visibly Sikh, since Mr Bakshi wears no turban (nor does Balraj). There is a marked contrast here with *Bend it Like Beckham*, in which Anupam Kher, who plays Mr Bakshi, appeared as Mr Bhamra, and *did* wear a turban, although Pinky's presumably Sikh fiancé does not. Sikh holy images are also prominent in both *Bend it Like Beckham* and *Bhaji on the Beach*, along with open mention of visits to the gurdwara. Equally notable is the fact that Mr Kholi, unlike his equivalent in the original novel, is not a clerical figure (except insofar as his profession of accountant makes him a servant of that new god, money). The representation of religious affinities may perhaps be further complicated by the fact that Aishwarya Rai herself is a Bunt (something that was extensively commented on in the Indian press when she later became engaged to Abishek Bachchan, since the Bunts are matrilineal). In Chadha's other work, then, the practicalities of Sikh worship and attendance at the gurdwara are openly mentioned, but here the subject is silently erased.

Instead of difference, similarity is stressed. Chadha herself wryly notes, that 'The only time I used to feel like an outsider was when I first went to India' (she, like Mr Bhamra, was born in Kenya, part of the substantial Sikh diaspora there). This is a line directly echoed in the film when Darcy says that it 'Reminded me of when I first arrived in India'. Though Chadha declares that 'I think the reason I have the drive I do is ultimately about racism. It's about finding ways to diminish the impact of difference' (Chadha 2007: 11), the consistent thrust of her work is in fact to downplay the existence of difference in the first place. This is, I think, because Chadha is anxious to minimise any possible barriers to marriages such as those of Lalita and Darcy and to stress an essential compatibility between the two very different communities. (It is perhaps worth noting that she herself has a Japanese-American husband.) Her earlier work is darker in this respect: in *Bhaji on the Beach*, Sikh women are abused by white yobs. The fact of the disappearance of this darkness from her later work is hardly, though, attributable to any general perception that such tensions have now vanished from British society, because her earlier, grimmer view of the colonial relationship is still to be found in another recent adaptation of a classic text to offer a view of Indians in England, Tim Supple's *Twelfth Night* (2003). Supple was shortly afterwards to become celebrated for a legendary stage production of *A Midsummer Night's Dream* performed, to tremendous effect, in seven different Indian languages (one of which was English), and his *Twelfth Night*, which flaunts its own extradiegetic resonances when Olivia's dead brother is seen playing a song from *The Magic Flute*, which Supple had directed for Opera North, can be seen as having a bearing on and indeed to some extent commenting on the Chadha *oeuvre* because of its casting of Parminder Nagra, who had come to fame in *Bend it Like Beckham* the year before and who is here cross-dressing again.

In Supple's *Twelfth Night* Sebastian, Viola and Antonio are all equally at home in English or Hindi, and the music fuses Western, African and Indian. However, for all that *Twelfth Night* is a comedy, the picture that Supple's film presents of its multicultural community is a distinctly uneasy one. This adaptation is set in England, as we see in the scene where Sebastian and Antonio meet in a street market, but although the adapter, Andrew Bannerman, called it 'the Britain we all live in today' (Greenhalgh and Shaughnessy 2006: 99), it is in fact a country that few would *want* to live in, particularly not Indian asylum seekers, and one to which the twins have come only because their father was a general who was shot. Throughout the film, darkness, insecurity and menace are the hallmarks of English life. Sir Toby's (David Troughton) remark about the death of Olivia's brother is made to seem unusually real for us by the fact that it is accompanied here by his stroking the cheek of a photo of his dead nephew (we have previously seen the crashed car), and there is an image system of bars – Sir Toby is first seen in what looks like a network of cells. This is also a surveillance culture, as we see when Sir Toby, Sir Andrew and Feste are caught singing and playing on CCTV; later, they turn the tables when they spy on Malvolio finding the letter. This, in short, is an England that is uncomfortable to live in and hostile to foreigners. In *Bend it Like Beckham*, however, a signpost shows Southall, emblem of polarisation, and Central London in different directions; this and the fact that we have already heard reference to 'Southall Sari Sisters' clearly marks integration as Chadha's preferred way forward, and Central London, not Southall, as her preferred direction, even though Chadha herself settled in Southall when she arrived from Kenya (Wilson 2006: 324).

Certainly integration is the preferred mode of *Bend it Like Beckham*. In *The Jewel in the Crown*, Hari indignantly rebuffs Daphne's suggestion that their shared status as orphans 'Makes us rather the same' with 'How the same ... I don't feel the same. It's not the same ... I'm sorry. It's not the same, for anyone'. For Hari there is 'the river ... from my side to yours', and after his encounter with Colin Lindsey, the former best friend who fails to recognise him, Hari's new Indian friends burn his solar topi, symbol of his former self-association with the British. Although Hari apparently agrees with Daphne when she says that when the rains come, 'Then everything'll be green and fresh like England', his 'Like England, yes' echoes very hollowly in the circumstances. The adaptation itself may insistently riddle and complicate difference – class in fact makes as much of a river for Merrick as race does for Hari, and in what is both a sharp irony in terms of the series itself and also a deft reversal of the habit of having Indians played by English actors in make-up, the actor who plays Colin Lindsey, emblem of the English Raj, is named Karan Kapoor, while Ahmed Kassim is played by Derrick Branche – but it nevertheless knows that for the characters it represents, difference never goes away.

In *Bend it Like Beckham*, though, things and people *are* the same. Implicit in the title is the idea that an Indian girl can be like Beckham in the first place, and indeed when Tony says 'No, Jess. I *really* like Beckham' what we are presented with is a Beckham who transcends difference by acting as a figure of appeal to both sexes: in fact the gender boundary is collapsed here, and to a lesser extent when Jules is mistaken for a boy, in the same way as the boundary between English and Indian when Jess plays alongside Paul Scholes. Time and again similarities rather than differences are stressed. Jess and Juliet are insistently paralleled at the beginning as both are taken shopping by a girly-minded female relative; Jess and Joe are bonded by both having scars on the knee; Jules says 'It ain't just an Indian thing, is it? Look how many people come out to support us'; Jules's mother hopes Jess can teach Jules Indian values and says 'Do you know, I cooked a lovely curry the other day', and later differences blur and dissolve again when Jules's mum and Jess's mum both panic simultaneously about what's happening to their daughters. Joe says to Jess 'Losing to the Jerries on penalties comes natural to you English. You're part of the tradition now', and because he is Irish he understands what it's like to be called a Paki, as if both marked equal degrees of (unimportant) difference from traditional Englishness; later, he elides both her difference and his own when he says 'I'd like to have seen you play for England one day'. In the end we can have, equally, half and half – half the wedding, half the match; football, after all, is famously 'a game of two halves'. It is particularly notable that Mr Bhamra works at Heathrow; in the hands of a different film-maker, he would be an immigration officer policing Englishness, but here he seems much more likely to function as a point of entry and facilitator to it, as he ultimately does for his daughter.

In *Bride and Prejudice*, too, difference is inverted, downplayed, or riddled. There is a sense in which, for all that the film opens and closes in India, it is India which is odd and exotic here: we see the Golden Temple, an iconic image that would need no explanation to any Indian, and then cut to a screen saying 'Amritsar – India', whose presence silently condones ignorance and legitimates a non-Indian perspective. When Balraj tells his Burberry-bikini-wearing sister to 'Stop being such a coconut', one might well feel that such a remark echoes rather disturbingly in the context of Chadha's film, with its apparently whole-hearted subscription to Western values. Certainly any ethnic or class differences between Kholi and Darcy disappear in the bond of their shared horror at Maya's cobra dance, which irresistibly works to figure her as a Cleopatra-like, exoticised cultural Other of the same stamp as Manjula in *Shakespeare Wallah*, except that Maya seems constituted much more clearly than Manjula as an Indian who reprehensibly will not subscribe to Western norms. Moreover, although the girls are strewn with flowers in a street named Gandhi Nagar and there is a dance of eunuchs (thought to bring luck at weddings), for the most part specifics of Indianness are notably not engaged with. In *The Shakespeare Wallah*, for instance, Geoffrey Kendal writes of the perils of passing through Amritsar at the time of the storming of the Golden Temple (Kendal and Colvin 1987: xii), and Amritsar was also the scene of a notorious massacre in 1919, but in *Bride and Prejudice* Wickham merely asks innocently 'Amritsar ... Is that where the Golden Temple is?' and no further comment is made. Most notably Lalita's apparently impassioned defence of India is qualified by the fact that we are so clearly asked to read it in terms of Elizabeth's reflex antagonism to Darcy.

Hers is the prejudice, after all, and it is clearly she who puts words like 'natives' into Darcy's mouth, ascribing to him racist attitudes he never actually manifests himself.

In another contrast with Chadha's own earlier work, though, Britain, too, is treated sketchily and schematically. It is true that as in *Shakespeare Wallah*, the royal family is gestured at here: Balraj lives in Windsor, near 'the queen's castle'. *Bride and Prejudice*, however, is more interested in another kind of crowned head, as is made clear when Aishwarya Rai, a former Miss World, tries on a tiara and sings 'you have to ask the queen'. ('He'll get to see her in a swimsuit' is obviously another Miss World joke.) Moreover, the global perspective inevitably implied by the presence of a Miss World is appropriate, because America looms almost as large as Britain in the film: the scene selection screen on the DVD has Hollywood in the top left hand corner and a British postbox below, while Big Ben appears in the top right with the Beverly Hills sign below, as if to suggest the equal importance of both countries, and the film is just as interested in Indians who go to America as in those who go to the UK, and indeed in the differences between them. The Bakshis had a chance to go to the US but didn't, and the contrast between Mr Bakshi's swimming pool joke and Mrs Bakshi's longing to go there clearly instantiates an equivalence between India and genuine values, and the US and false ones. For Mr Kholi (ironically the only character in the film to speak 'Indian English'), 'UK's finished, India's too corrupt' and America is the brave new world, but the film as a whole does not fully subscribe to this, for Darcy laments the lack of family feeling in the US and the Bakshis, by contrast, are seen staying at a house in London which presumably belongs to émigré relatives who have not forgotten their family ties.

Ultimately, though, it is similarities rather than differences that are stressed even in the case of America, and indeed in Kholi's pronunciation of it, 'Amrica' is clearly paralleled with Amritsar. This is, I think, because for Chadha, Jane Austen is transnational. A line like 'So she's arranging his marriage' may be fired into making new sense in an Indian context, but generally the idea is clearly that themes and motifs can be seamlessly transferred from the UK to the US to India and back again, just as the characters jet so effortlessly around the globe. In *Bend it Like Beckham*, in which the US looms as the land of opportunity, a plane is seen taking off against a sign saying 'Exit', and for the two girls, the marker of freedom is to be able to go to the US; at the same time, though, Jess looks forward to coming back at Christmas (which this Sikh family apparently celebrates) and seeing Joe again. For Chadha, movement is easy and the boundaries between countries are fluid and permeable.

This is in many ways a cheering and positive vision, but sadly the film as a whole does not convince us that it is a wholly realistic one. The initial impression of *Bride and Prejudice* may be that it is not very like Jane Austen, but in fact the relationship between India and the UK maps with surprising ease onto that between the country and the city in which Austen is so interested: Darcy's appalled question 'Jesus, Balraj, where the hell have you brought me?' might seem like a dismissal of India of the same kind as Hari's outburst in *The Jewel in the Crown* that he hates India, but it is in fact very close to the Darcy of the original novel's similarly dismissive attitude to Hertfordshire: 'In a country neighbourhood you move in a very confined and unvarying society' (*P&P* 88). Equally Cheryl Wilson points out that Lalita's remark to Darcy, 'I think you should find someone simple and traditional to teach you to dance like the natives', picks up on Darcy's comment about savages dancing (Wilson 2006: 327), and it is with justice that Wilson observes that '*Bride and Prejudice* can be viewed as a film that integrates two well-suited partners – the Bollywood form and Austen's comedy of manners – to both preserve and update the cultural critique of the original' (323). In other ways, too, the film finds easy enough equivalents for Austen's novel – even the dream sequences in the two versions of *Northanger Abbey* are not that dissimilar to the song-and-dance moments in Bollywood – but unlike *Clueless*, it is the film's vision of the modern world, rather than its vision of the source text, which viewers may well find suspect. Both *Shakespeare Wallah* and *Bride and Prejudice*, then, find in India a peculiarly rich and resonant setting for the negotiation of the interface between the Englishness of which Shakespeare and Austen stand as icons and the modern world, but while *Bride and Prejudice* may reveal, as indeed *Kandukondain Kandukondain* had done earlier, that Austen can slide with surprising ease into an Indian setting, it ironically suffers from the very fact that India had proved such fertile ground for examinations of Britishness under pressure, and therefore brings with it traditions and connotations of its own that cannot be so easily co-opted to the preferred set of meanings which Chadha wants to bring to bear on her use of it. In India, Shakespeare and Austen adaptations, like so much else, take on a life and logic of their own.

5
Modernity: *Mansfield Park* (dir. Iain B. MacDonald, 2007), *Becoming Jane* (dir. Julian Jarrold, 2007), *Pride and Prejudice* (dir. Joe Wright, 2005), *Northanger Abbey* (dir. Jon Jones, 2007) and *Shakespeare Retold*

'The past is another country; they do things differently there'. In this chapter, I want to discuss adaptations of Austen and Shakespeare that take them on the longest cultural journey of all – from their own time to what I shall term the modern world – and to ask what these can tell us about which aspects of Shakespeare and Austen make them so richly amenable to the processes of transposition and relocation, and in what ways they resist it. As I suggested in the introduction, the modernising of Austen seems to have been modelled quite closely on the modernising of Shakespeare, and certainly the two enterprises seem to be directly paralleled by the casting of Billie Piper as both Fanny Price in the ITV *Mansfield Park* (dir. Iain B. MacDonald, 2007) and as Hero in the BBC *Shakespeare Retold*'s version of *Much Ado About Nothing* (dir. Brian Percival, 2005), not to mention the clear influence of *Shakespeare in Love* (dir. John Madden, 1998) on *Becoming Jane* (dir. Julian Jarrold, 2007). There is also clear evidence of cross-fertilisation between groups of films: Ramona Wray notes that '*Much Ado*'s network of interlocking hotel rooms that permit and frustrate romantic ingress and egress is very much the territory of *Four Weddings and a Funeral* ... among other films of a similar ilk' (Wray 2006: 186) and sees Shirley Henderson's role in the Bridget Jones films as an operative part of her persona as Katherine in the BBC *Shakespeare Retold*'s *Taming of the Shrew* (Wray 2006: 187), not least because 'Petruchio's line – "I like everything about you" – mimics the central refrain of *Bridget Jones' Diary'* (Wray 2006: 197). However, Shakespeare proves notably more flexible than Austen in this respect.

It is, I think, both undeniable and initially surprising that Shakespeare works better than Austen when modernised in this sense. Shakespeare and Austen may be twin icons of Englishness, but Shakespeare proves adaptable to the modern world in ways that Austen does not; indeed Poonam Trivedi suggests that 'the more Shakespeare is cannibalised, the more he seems to flourish' (Trivedi 2003: 56). In one sense this might seem logical, in that Shakespeare clearly had a much more wide-ranging imagination: he set roughly two-thirds of his plays abroad, while Austen confined herself entirely to her own country, and, more-over, to a relatively small part of it, never venturing farther west than Lyme or farther north than Derbyshire, and indeed her advice to her niece Anna on the novel she was attempting to write was 'we think you had better not leave England. Let the Portmans go to Ireland, but as you know nothing of the manners there, you had better not go with them' (Austen 2004: 172). Nevertheless, Jane Austen, as we have seen, can be taken to California in *Clueless* (dir. Amy Heckerling, 1995) and to India in *Bride and Prejudice* (dir. Gurinder Chadha, 2004) and do well in both of these new locations; she has even been taken to Brigham Young University in one version of *Pride and Prejudice* (dir. Andrew Black, 2003), which can make some sense because Mormons are traditionally opposed to divorce and in favour of early marriage, while Elsa Solender suggests that the American-set *You've Got Mail* (dir. Nora Ephron, 1998) as 'an imitation of *P&P'* (Solender 2002: 116), since Kathleen has read the book 'about 200 times' and introduces Joe to it (his copy neatly features Colin Firth on the cover); in *Lost in Austen* (dir. Dan Zeff, 2008), she can even be comfortably postmodern. In the modern world, though – at least the modern world as conceived by some of the adaptations I shall be discussing here – she withers and dies. So why do certain aspects of modernity prove so inimical to her art, and which are they?

What characterises the modern world as I use the term here is above all a view of personal morality as either redundant or old-fashioned: as Charlotte Heywood reassures her sister in Reginald Hill's Dalziel and Pascoe novel *A Cure for All Diseases*, which offers a continuation of *Sanditon* by other means, 'hes (sic) one of those guys you know will always do the right thing – I don't mean morally – but like if your pants fell off on the dance floor – he would slip them into his pocket without missing a step!' (Hill 2008: 138). This is partly true of *Bridget Jones's Diary* (dir. Sharon Maguire, 2001) and, though to a lesser extent, of *Clueless*, and indeed of all the films I have discussed in this book, perhaps only *Metropolitan* (dir. Whit Stillman, 1990) takes personal morality really seriously: Joseph Alulis notes that 'Success, *Metropolitan* suggests, depends upon the traditional intellectual and moral virtues – preeminently, practical wisdom and temperance' (Alulis 2001: 64). For Austen, though, the social rituals and conventions which she represents are fundamentally underpinned by a set of moral principles. As a corollary of this, while Shakespeare is more interested in emotion, and primarily emotion as it is experienced by individuals, Austen's primary concern is behaviour, and above all behaviour in social groups. The classic instance of this is the Box Hill scene in *Emma*, but it is an emphasis found throughout her work and it means that her narratives can only unfold satisfactorily within a large and securely delineated society: no Jane Austen adaptation can flourish without a large cast of strong, well individuated actors.

Nevertheless, Austen's characters are also essentially homogenous. Shakespeare is typically interested in exploring difference, and tends to do so in an overtly schematising way which lends itself exceptionally well to superimposition on sets of differences other than those originally portrayed: thus his feuding Montagues and Capulets can with equal ease become the Sharks and the Jets, or Latinos and WASPs. In the case of Austen, though, any adaptation of her books requires a cast of people who, however different they may be in appearance, must all talk and walk in largely the same way. (A telling illustration of this is *Jane Austen in Manhattan* (dir. James Ivory, 1980), where the similarities generated by involvement in the theatre overlie very different cultural and social backgrounds.) As a result, it is fatal to an Austen adaptation to shoehorn a big-name actor or actress with 'popular' appeal into a cast of actors with a background in classical theatre, as is done with relative impunity in, for example, *William Shakespeare's Romeo + Juliet* (dir. Baz Luhrmann, 1996); hence in Iain B. MacDonald's *Mansfield Park*, Michelle Ryan from *Eastenders*, playing Maria Bertram, sticks out like a sore thumb in the company of actors such as James D'Arcy, who had played Mr Blifil in the highly successful *Tom Jones* (dir. Metin Hüseyin, 1997), and Douglas Hodge, veteran of *Middlemarch* (dir. Anthony Page, 1994) and *Vanity Fair* (dir. Mira Nair, 2004). Finally, the images and the values for which Shakespeare and Austen have respectively come to stand are obviously different: Shakespeare represents range but Austen limitation, as we see very clearly in the very title of Jim Abrahams's 1998 film *Jane Austen's Mafia*, whose point depends wholly on the incompatibility of the two concepts: Abraham's film parodies *The Godfather, Il Postino* and *Jurassic Park* but makes no other mention of Jane Austen, suggesting that she is evoked solely as an icon of the genteel and ineffective, and thus someone whose repertoire could precisely *not* stretch to include the Mafia, while *Macbeth*, say, can easily lend itself to a gangster culture.

Perhaps partly because of these strongly marked differences, there have been a number of liberties taken with Shakespeare that have not been attempted with Austen. One of the most obvious of these is the practice of cross-gender casting. Although this is virtually called for in the case of Shakespeare by its fidelity to the theatrical customs for which he originally wrote, it would not be as foreign to Austen as it might appear. In *Mansfield Park*, Tom proposes swapping Cottager's speeches with Cottager's Wife's (159), and in *Pride and Prejudice* Lydia records that 'We dressed up Chamberlayne in woman's clothes' (248). This is something which has never found a reflection in any adaptation, unless we can see a vague echo in the Andrew Davies 1995 BBC/A&E version, in which, as Erica Sheen points out, Elizabeth plays and sings a version of an aria by Cherubino, the cross-dressing page in *The Marriage of Figaro*; Sheen does suggest that *The Marriage of Figaro* is an appropriate text to invoke in connection with *Pride and Prejudice*, but she does not mention the Chamberlayne episode (Sheen 2000: 24–5). However, there is fact a close parallel between the cross-dressed Cherubino and the similarly cross-dressed Chamberlayne, not least in that both are soldiers or prospective soldiers. It would not, then, be entirely inconceivable to experiment with cross-dressing in Austen, yet to my knowledge it has never been attempted.

A similar distinction between Austen and Shakespeare obtains with the question of colour-blind casting. Though this has no such apparently exclusively Shakespearean warrant of authenticity as cross-dressing has, this too is something which occurs in Shakespeare films (as in the casting of Adrian Lester in Branagh's 2000 *Love's Labour's Lost* or 2006 *As You Like It* or Denzel Washington in his 1993 *Much Ado About Nothing*, or the BBC *Shakespeare Retold* version of *Much Ado* in which Margaret is black) but never, to my knowledge, in any filmed adaptation of Austen proper; only in *Clueless, Bride and Prejudice, Lost in Austen*, and the 1986 *Northanger Abbey* (dir. Giles Foster), which has a black page, are there non-white actors, and they are all playing non-white characters. Shakespeare has also been sent into the future, perhaps most notably and certainly most successfully in *Forbidden Planet* (dir. Fred Wilcox, 1956), which again has never been attempted with Austen (although Elizabeth Bennet and Mr Darcy do visit the present in *Lost in Austen*). Nor has anyone attempted to combine Austen's own dialogue with modern dress, perhaps because Austen herself, in characteristically ironic style, seems to counsel directly against such updating in *Mansfield Park*: 'Mr Rushworth is quite right, I think, in meaning to give it a modern dress, and I have no doubt that it will be all done extremely well' (88).

The flexibility of Shakespeare has been illustrated in a number of modern adaptations. Andrew Davies's 2001 adaptation of *Othello*, directed by Geoffrey Sax, for instance, takes remarkable liberties with the story. Here John Othello is the first black commissioner of the Metropolitan Police, and the sense of contemporaneity is sharply underlined by the fact that the adaptation's Prime Minister and barrister bear a distinct resemblance to Tony and Cherie Blair. The closing sequences in particular develop very differently from in Shakespeare, and not just because Davies has so thoroughly jettisoned the play's language. Even more far-reachingly, he has also changed the nature of the story, firstly by having Michael Cass drunkenly proposition Dessie just before John Othello returns home, and secondly by having Jago assure Othello that DNA evidence taken from his dressing gown confirms the adultery. This entirely blows apart the delicate balance created in the play and leaves Eamonn Walker's Othello with far too little to do. Nevertheless, although Davies's adaptation, for all its eyecatching contemporaneity, thus packs far less emotional punch than the original, it does use Shakespeare to tell us something about the modern world at least as much as it uses the modern world to tell us something about Shakespeare, and is consequently of interest.

Much the same could be said of Don Boyd's *My Kingdom* (2001), an extensively modernised and rewritten version of *King Lear* (for sharp and perceptive commentary on this film, see Lehmann 2006). This offers something of a riff on Julie Taymor's *Titus* (1999), in that we see again an old man and his grandson; however, the grandson is also the fool, and drowns in the Mersey, which is of course emblematic of Liverpool, to which the Lear story has here been transposed. The Liverpudlian setting is further underlined when one of the daughters, Tracy, is bought what seems to be Everton Football Club – certainly its colours are blue and white – while the fact that the grandson is called Jamie inevitably reminds us of James Bulger, the Liverpool toddler who was abducted and murdered in 1993, just as the foul-mouthed choristers remind us that in this society, there is a sell-by date on childhood. (The appositeness of

Liverpool for an apocalyptic vision was underlined the next year when it was used as the setting for Alex Cox's *Revengers Tragedy* [sic], which satirically cast the then Prime Minister's father-in-law, Tony Booth, as a venal Lord Antonio and showed an England whose southern half had been entirely wiped off the map.) As so often in such adaptations, Shakespeare's dialogue is relegated to a bit part: the customs officer (who clearly represents Gloucester) quotes Shakespeare and the Edmund figure, who used to be in the vice squad, refers to 'pleasant vices'. Equally, though, we are once again left in no doubt about the contemporaneity and urgency of the issues that Shakespeare can be made to address.

Mansfield Park (dir. Iain B. MacDonald, 2007)

Austen, though, has never been made to work in this way. In some ways, modernity in the way I am defining it here may seem an entirely artificial category, because several of the adaptations I have already discussed have, of course, been temporally updated. However, an updated setting does not always mean sacrificing the point of a text, even if it is Austen: *Clueless* is undeniably modern, but it keeps the emphasis on behaviour and on thinking of others that is so central to Austen's writing, as when Cher considerately thinks of getting her father and his friends a take-away, and so too does *Lost in Austen*, where Amanda tries hard to put others' interests before her own. For many adaptations, though, Austen's interest in morality is of little or no concern; for them, she has become primarily a figure of romance, sometimes spiced up with a dash of proto-feminism. This is certainly the case in the Andrew Davies-scripted *Sense and Sensibility* (dir. John Alexander, 2008), which Davies described in advance as '*Sex and the City* set in the country' (Sherwin 2007: 31); here 'updating' is crudely signalled by the fact that it opens with a sex scene (between Willoughby and Eliza), and we then cut to a man (Willoughby) galloping away on a white horse, while Fanny says 'Norland Park. Ours at last. Come to bed.' Period feel is further sacrificed when it ends with a kiss, and there is also a duel between Willoughby and Brandon, which Brandon, inevitably, wins. Such minor details as Austen's carefully plotted scheme of family relationships, meanwhile, are cheerfully dispensed with: Marianne calls Fanny, who is her sister-in-law, 'aunt', and John speaks to Elinor of 'your cousin Edward'.

Perhaps the most striking example of this privileging of the broad-brush effect over fine distinction is the *Mansfield Park* directed by Iain B. MacDonald, which inaugurated a three-week 'Jane Austen Season' for ITV. Although there is some subtlety evidenced in the adaptation's deployment of the line 'This is not a very promising beginning', which in the novel is actually used by Mrs Norris to refer to Fanny's behaviour on her arrival at Mansfield (50), it shows no subtlety at all in too many other respects, preferring instead to plump for the entirely and in some cases ludicrously obvious: the Crawfords enter scheming, and Sir Thomas throws the text of *Lovers' Vows* into the fire. This adaptation also completely ignores a number of salient features of *Mansfield Park*. It deviates from the original novel from the very outset, when we hear that 'When I was ten years old my mother decided she could no longer afford to keep me', and the elision of the Portsmouth backstory effected here is carried through when Sir Thomas says to Lady Bertram 'I propose that we leave Fanny behind when we visit your mother'. There is hence no Portsmouth and, as a result of this, neither money nor class can be an issue.

Other changes are even more far-reaching in their effects. Billie Piper's Fanny is very physical and active – although Maria is spoken of as possibly being in danger of a headache, Piper's Fanny never gets one. She also darts and bustles about in a way that Fanny Price as Austen originally conceived her would have been completely incapable of doing: Billie Piper was quoted in an interview as saying 'the director wanted us to be contemporary in the way we moved' (Piper 2007a), and to this end, the adaptation was shot on hand-held cameras, the main effect of which is an unrelenting focus on heaving bosoms (the pre-screening publicity focused strongly on the fact that Billie Piper would be wearing a corset). However, although costumes and setting make it, in this respect and others, all nominally in keeping with the letter of the nineteenth century, the spirit is wholly lacking: indeed Austen herself might well have repeated her dismissive observation that the women in question were 'like any other short girl with a broad nose & wide mouth, fashionable dress, & exposed bosom' (Austen 2004: 58). Sir Thomas, Lady Bertram and Mrs Norris are all improbably young (and Lady Bertram even more improbably engineers Edmund's proposal). The Admiral is the Crawfords' stepfather rather than their uncle, in a nod, presumably, to our modern tendency to broken families. The ball is a picnic, making it surely the first alfresco dance scene in Austen (although not quite the only, since the adaptation of *Persuasion* two weeks later concluded in similar fashion, albeit, as we shall see, with slightly better logic). It is Sir Thomas in person who announces Maria's elopement – there is apparently no newspaper, no world outside Mansfield Park. Propriety is outraged when Sir Thomas leaves Henry and Fanny alone and when

Edmund comes in while she is washing her hair, and thereafter she flirts with him; most ludicrously, Fanny quite likes Henry's proposal at first, then says 'I can't believe a word you say. I've seen you do all this before' – bringing the supposed subtext obtrusively to the surface as so many recent adaptations have apparently felt it their business to do, most notably Betsan Morris Evans's 2000 adaptation of *Lady Audley's Secret*. Even details have pointlessly been changed: Henry reads from *The Merchant of Venice* instead of *Henry VIII* (334–5), and Lady Bertram when she sees Fanny says 'Now I shall be comforted' instead of 'Dear Fanny! Now I shall be comfortable' (434).

Most damagingly of all, though, there is simply no moral depth to Piper's Fanny Price, and indeed not much characterisation of any sort; physique has apparently been substituted for personality. Fanny's heroine status is in fact entirely arbitrary, because she does not behave noticeably better than anyone else; and yet a focus on behaviour is the very cornerstone of *Mansfield Park*. The novel builds up careful contrasts such as that between Edmund, who exchanges one of his own horses for one that will carry Fanny (70), and his sisters: 'the Miss Bertrams regularly wanted their horses every day, and had no idea of carrying their obliging manners to the sacrifice of any real pleasure' (69). It is also careful to discriminate between really good behaviour and the mere outward show of it, as we see in two telling passages about the Bertram sisters. First we hear of Maria that

> her good manners were severely taxed to conceal her vexation and anger, till she reached home. As Mr Rushworth did *not* come, the injury was increased, and she had not even the relief of shewing her power over him; she could only be sullen to her mother, aunt, and cousin, and throw as great a gloom as possible over the dinner and dessert. (100)

Later a similar exposé is performed on Julia:

> The politeness which she had been brought up to practise as a duty, made it impossible for her to escape; while the want of that higher species of self-command, that just consideration of others, that knowledge of her own heart, that principle of right which had not formed any esential part of her education, made her miserable under it. (119)

Most tellingly, perhaps all that we need to know about Mary Crawford is encapsulated in her notorious remark that 'Of *Rears*, and *Vices*, I saw enough. Now, do not be suspecting me of a pun, I entreat' (91). Elizabeth Bennet's flippant comment to Mr Darcy that 'To be sure, you knew no actual good of me – but nobody thinks of *that* when they fall in love' (388) is characteristically ironic, and should be treated with the same scepticism as her declaration that she first fell in love with Darcy when she saw Pemberley; in fact, whether or not he knew any good of her is certainly something Edmund should have considered when he found himself attracted to Mary Crawford, and something which the Fanny of the book most definitely does consider.

Nor does the Fanny Price of the adaptation refuse to act, as she does in the novel when she simply declares 'No, indeed, I cannot act' (168), a statement which many critics have seen as the key to her character. Indeed it would be difficult for Piper's Fanny to be different in this way because the adaptation, apparently thinking it is telling the story of *Jane Eyre* rather than that of *Mansfield Park*, offers us throughout first person narration from Fanny's perspective, so that an observation which in the original novel is given to the narrator – 'Miss Bertram's engagement made him in equity the property of Julia, of which Julia was fully aware, and before he had been at Mansfield a week, she was quite ready to be fallen in love with' (77) – is here given to Fanny. Matters are made still harder by the fact that Julia simply disappears from this adaptation, so there is no contrast possible between her and Fanny; thus when Sir Thomas is confident that Fanny will not disappoint him, it is hard to guess what he can possibly mean, since he can have no conceivable evidence for the assertion. Indeed the whole concept of behaviour here is reduced to a joke by being confined to the mouth of Mrs Norris. Asked to describe Fanny, Billie Piper, who ominously observed elsewhere that 'It was really nice to start reading the books and tap into Austen' (Piper 2007b), said 'She is compassionate and loving, and wants the best for people. You come away wanting to be a better person when you've played Fanny Price' (Piper 2007a). But that is not what Fanny Price is about. She is not in fact notably compassionate, and loves very few people. What Fanny Price stands for is right behaviour, not a warm heart, and indeed Clara Calvo has recently compared her to Cordelia in the extent of her unbending adherence to right rather than affection (Calvo 2005: 87). This, however, is an emphasis wholly foreign to this adaptation.

Becoming Jane (dir. Julian Jarrold, 2007)

To a certain extent MacDonald's adaptation was from the outset a film under pressure, for not only had there already been a recent film adaptation of *Mansfield Park*, Patricia Rozema's 1999 version, but MacDonald's adaptation was first screened while *Becoming Jane* was still in cinemas, and so had to compete for attention in a crowded market. It suffered from this, for the contrast between the two films is instructive. Certainly there are things for purists to quarrel with in *Becoming Jane*. In the first place, it is clear from the way we 'fast-forward' through the sequence towards the beginning of *Becoming Jane* where Jane reads the skit she has written in honour of Cassandra's engagement that we must not be bored by too much actual Austen, while the idea of a narrative bringing together both Jane Austen and wrestling is clearly sheer chutzpah. Secondly, the film cannot resist prettifying: Mrs Austen ludicrously digs her own potatoes wearing very nice tear pearl drop earrings, while Cassandra wears her pearl necklace for a walk on the beach.

More seriously, *Becoming Jane* also takes a probably over-optimistic view of the chances for profitable and successful female authorship. In its closing vignette, Jane, Henry and Eliza listen to a woman singing, who is clearly living by her art, and when Jane Austen herself, with a hairdo eerily reminiscent of Charlotte Brontë's, then proceeds to read aloud from *Pride and Prejudice* to an admiring audience, the implication is clearly that she is in the same category. There are effectively only two brothers, Henry and the disabled George, with the wealthy Edward merely mentioned in passing, so Jane declares that she will live by her pen and apparently does, with no hint of the fact that the real Jane and her mother and sister required financial support from Edward, who had been adopted by distant relations, and indeed from her brothers James and Frank too. This interest in seeing Austen as a commercial rather than merely a literary success is one of the many signs of the film's indebtedness to Jon Spence's biography of Austen, *Becoming Jane Austen* (later relaunched as simply *Becoming Jane*), since Spence insists that Austen wrote for money (Spence 2003: 173). Nevertheless *Becoming Jane*, for all its display of commerce and cleavage and its cricket-playing heroine, does retain the quintessentially Austenian emphasis on behaviour and thinking of others: because Tom Lefroy's younger brothers and sisters are dependent on him, Jane will renounce him, even if to do so breaks her heart. (Interestingly, this view of their relationship is not something derived from Spence's book, where Tom is seen as effectively jilting Jane for reasons that are presumed to be financial but are never really explored.) *Becoming Jane* is also much better researched than MacDonald's *Mansfield Park*, as indeed one would expect from its dependence on Spence's book: Jane 'talks on her fingers' to her brother, echoing the fact that the historical Jane Austen could indeed do this because one of her brothers, George, seems to have been both physically and mentally disabled, and the portrayal of Jane's cousin and eventually sister-in-law Eliza de Feuillide in particular, to whom Spence devotes a great deal of attention, is very carefully accurate in points of detail.

So too are other points. Jane cuts passages out of her own writing with scissors just as Cassandra mutilated her letters, and when Lefroy's uncle asks Jane 'Do I detect you in irony?', a neat tribute is paid to her most famous tool. The film is especially faithful in its use of *Tom Jones*, which Tom Lefroy recommends that she read, and whose preferred method of revelation is echoed by the importance of letters, most notably the one which drops from Lefroy's pocket and reveals his goodness to his family. Jane Austen did indeed note in a letter of Tom Lefroy 'He is a very great admirer of Tom Jones' (Austen 2004: 4), although the suggestion of any very intense attachment to him seems rather belied by the flippant tone of her remark to her sister Cassandra that 'I rather expect to receive an offer from my friend in the course of the evening. I shall refuse him, however, unless he promises to give away his white Coat' (Austen 2004: 5). The film's insistence on the primacy of the Lefroy affair is another instance of its dependence on Spence, who is absolutely convinced that Jane Austen was in love with Tom Lefroy and waited three years in the hope that he would marry her, even if his evidence for this is sometimes rather flimsy: he declares, for instance, that 'The name Bennet comes from Tom Lefroy's favourite novel, *Tom Jones*' (102) although it is, as he concedes, mentioned only once in *Tom Jones*, and suggests that a dream Jane had about Cassandra and their cousin's widower Sir Thomas Williams 'may be a sign of Jane's still yearning for Tom Lefroy to come and take her away, even after all conscious hope was gone' (118). Spence also, in a brief appendix, downplays the 'nameless, dateless romance' on which some others of Jane's biographers have set such store on the grounds that even if it did happen and the gentleman was in love, there is no proof that Jane was (247).

The film's foregrounding of this narrative, then, is testimony to a clear urge to fidelity to its source text, and the urge to fidelity is evident too in other respects. Anne Hathaway (who was 'named in deliberate homage to Shakespeare's wife by her theatre-loving parents') gave proof of her desire to be 'authentic' when she rather endearingly 'moved to a village in England for the month before shooting began. "I lived in a house and had tea every day," she says ... "And I learned how to speak in a British accent. On certain days, I would go off and explore, and pretend to be British, and try to pass." She also ate Marmite' (Benedictus 2007: 8).

This is despite the fact that in her previous films Hathaway has in fact been cast as the polar opposite of Englishness: in *The Princess Diaries* (dir. Garry Marshall, 2001) her character conspicuously fails to live up to the standards and expectations of Julie Andrews, who despite being the Queen of Genovia trails her Mary Poppins persona and dispenses tea at all times; in its even more vapid sequel *The Princess Diaries 2: Royal Engagement* (dir. Garry Marshall, 2004), Prince William and the Duke of Kenilworth appear on her list of potential suitors, and the Duke of Kenilworth (Callum Blue) is happy to oblige because all the marriages in his family have been arranged, thus clearly identifying Englishness with the chilly formality against which Hathaway's character ultimately rebels; and in *The Devil Wears Prada* (dir. David Frankel, 2006), Emily (Emily Blunt), the bitchy assistant against whom Hathaway's character must compete, is British.

This willingness on the part of an American actress to 'become' British is of course reminiscent of Renée Zellweger (and to a lesser extent of Gwyneth Paltrow before her), but actually *Becoming Jane*'s principal debt is less to either *Bridget Jones's Diary* or Paltrow's *Emma* than to *Shakespeare in Love*, with which it shares a shape and an underlying idea. Some of the dialogue closely echoes the earlier film:

> Cassandra: 'How does the story begin?'
> Jane: 'Badly.'
> Cassandra: 'And then?'
> Jane: 'Gets worse.'
> ...
> Cassandra: 'How does it end?'
> Jane: 'They both make triumphant happy endings.'

The debt is most notably visible whenever Anne Hathaway's Jane writes down good nuggets which she has heard. A remark of Lady Gresham's becomes one of Lady Catherine's; Tom Lefroy's slight at the dance becomes Mr Darcy's; Jane herself elopes but comes back, as Georgiana Darcy will effectively do, and the presence of Mrs Radcliffe also serves much the same purpose as that of Marlowe does in *Shakespeare in Love* and is used to shift tone in the same way as Marlowe's death does there, since this reference to the Gothic heralds agitated music, rain dripping off a black angel and the announcement that Cassandra's fiancé is dead. *Becoming Jane*, then, is willing to modernise in some respects, but it also remembers to use a tried-and-tested biopic structure and careful research and to retain a sense of the ethos of Austen.

The borrowing of the *Shakespeare in Love* conceit is not, however, without its attendant oddities. Shakespeare was an author famous for both tragedy and comedy, but more so for tragedy, particularly in the shape of *Hamlet*; yet the authors of *Shakespeare in Love* choose to tell his story in predominantly comic vein, with a dash of the romance mode to which he would turn at the end of his writing career. Conversely, Jane Austen is celebrated as one of the greatest comic novelists in the English language, but her story is cast in a mould of loss, grief and heartbreak on all fronts. Her cheerful, successful sailor brothers are never mentioned; instead we see only Henry, who effectively sells himself in marriage, and George, who is certainly physically handicapped and may well be mentally so, too, and dwell on the grief of Cassandra at the death of her fiancé. Even at the end, there is no hint of the nieces and nephews in whom the real Jane Austen took so much interest, and the film closes with a reminder that she died young. The Jane of this film might perhaps have written *Persuasion*, but could she ever have written *Love and Freindship* or *Sanditon*? This, after all, is a Jane who wants to write 'of the heart', not of the manners and social interplay that many might take to be the arena of the real Jane Austen's achievement.

The *Shakespeare in Love* trick is, moreover, more difficult to pull off with a novelist, for while dramatists inevitably give voice to many different perspectives and positions, novelists tend to construct for themselves a significantly more monolithic authorial identity, and this is not without its pitfalls. Although *Shakespeare in Love* clearly relates what Shakespeare writes to how Shakespeare lives, it cheekily pokes fun at the so-called authorship debate with the mischievous question 'Are you the author of the plays of William Shakespeare?', and it certainly does not subscribe to the theory of exact equivalence between life and works which animates so much of the attempt to put forward alternative candidates, as when Derek Jacobi argued in favour of the earl of Oxford as the real Shakespeare on the grounds that 'I agree that an author writes about his own experiences, his own life and personalities'; the 'Declaration of Doubt', which Jacobi helped to present, 'argues there are few connections between Shakespeare's life and his alleged works' (Doran 2007). *Becoming Jane*, by contrast, is not quite sure where it stands on this issue. Lefroy tells Jane that she lacks 'the history' and must have experience to write, and the source narrative, *Becoming Jane Austen*, is certainly wholly committed to the idea that an author's works are rooted in experience, relating Jane Austen's novels to her own life on every possible occasion and some impossible ones. For Spence, Tom's aunt 'Mrs Lefroy was an ideal that can be discerned behind the faults and imperfections of all Jane Austen's heroines' (Spence 2003: 30–1), and events are regularly narrated in such a way as to invite the reader to see them as foreshadowing specific events in the novels. This is particularly clear in Spence's description of Eliza de Feuillide's first visit to Steventon and the theatricals that took place on that occasion, where we are told that 'if Philadelphia [Walter] would not act she was not welcome at Steventon' (Spence 2003: 44), which obviously invites us to see her as prefiguring Fanny Price, and Spence equally clearly views Egerton Brydges as the prototype for Mr Yates and speculates without any real evidence on James and Henry arguing about which of them should be cast to flirt with Eliza de Feuillide (Spence 2003: 44–5). Even more tenuous is his declaration that

> It was more than twenty years before Austen returned to the theatricals with the acting episode in *Mansfield Park*, but she connected the Steventon and Mansfield theatricals by calling two of the characters in her novel Mr Yates and Mr Norris, the names of real actors who took roles in the London production of *The Wonder!* and *The Chances* – the latter performed at Steventon in July 1788. (Spence 2003: 46)

It is really not easy to believe that Austen should, twenty years after the event, have remembered the names of two actors in productions which she herself had never seen.

Special pleading is equally apparent in Spence's account of the relationship between Austen's brother Henry and her sister and cousin Eliza de Feuillide, to which, like the film, he devotes a great deal of attention:

> During Eliza's visit it came out that Henry was to be a clergyman. He had never revealed this piece of information to her. After writing to Philadelphia about Henry's improvement and their reconciliation, Eliza adds tersely: 'You know that his family design him for the church.' Her wording suggests that his intended profession had never been mentioned to her before but was so generally known that it would come as no surprise to Philadelphia. Eliza's ignorance is odd because she had known Henry quite intimately for six years. (Spence 2003: 70–1)

This is hardly the only or indeed the likeliest interpretation of the phrase 'You know that his family design him for the church'. For one thing, how did Eliza know that Philadelphia knew this? Are we perhaps to posit a conversation along the lines of 'Oh, Henry, you are to be a clergyman! How horrid! To be sure you have already mentioned this to our mutual cousin Philadelphia Walter?'. Surely it is far likelier that Eliza knew that Philadelphia knew this because everybody did, and always had, quite probably since Henry's early childhood, since destining him for the church was due to more to his position in the family than to anything in his own character. Spence, however, wants an Eliza who was ignorant of this and is shocked and bitter to discover it because he wants an Eliza who is like Mary Crawford, since for him, *Mansfield Park* can only have emerged from Jane's observation of her cousin, coupled with a little light reading of a manuscript history of her mother's side of the family:

> The strongest evidence that Jane read Mary Leigh's history comes from the virtuoso opening paragraph of *Mansfield Park* recounting the history of the three Ward sisters. It is derived from the story of the three sisters of Jane's great grandfather Theophilus Leigh. (Spence 2003: 86)

In fact, the story of the three Ward sisters proves to bear a passing but by no means a conclusive resemblance to that of the Leigh sisters, and one is also left wondering what is so 'virtuoso' about the opening of *Mansfield Park* if it is in fact a direct transcription from life. Finally, Spence argues for a connection between Eliza de Feuillide and *Northanger Abbey* on the basis of an episode Eliza described in a letter that Jane Austen is unlikely to have read, and on the assumption that Austen associated with Eliza a name, Susan, which she did not ultimately bestow on the heroine (Spence 2003: 121). The attempt to build a case on such flimsy evidence clearly testifies that the underlying urge can only be ideological rather than empiricist.

The film, however, is noticeably more ambivalent about the idea that a writer's life is directly reflected in her (or perhaps his) works. Mrs Radcliffe says her novels are 'Everything my life is not'; nevertheless, when Jane says she wishes to write 'Of the heart' Mrs Radcliffe asks 'Do you know it? ... In time you will. But if that fails, that's what imagination's for'. The paradox may seem to be partially resolved when, as in *Shakespeare in Love*, the writer must sacrifice love and life in order to write – experience, it seems, can only be in the past, as in Wordsworth's famous definition of poetry as 'emotion recollected in tranquillity'. Nevertheless, Jane's own summing up of Mrs Radcliffe is that her 'inner landscape' is the only thing about her that is remotely picturesque, and indeed no one familiar with *Udolpho* or *The Monk* could possibly suppose their plots to have been founded on their author's own personal experiences. Ultimately, the question is left open, and with it the rather bigger one of what this film is actually *for*, and what it is really interested in exploring.

Perhaps most dangerously, *Becoming Jane* is irresistibly attracted to romance, in a way Jane Austen herself was not (Jeremy Lovering's 2008 *Miss Austen Regrets*, in which there is no hidden love story to uncover and Tom Lefroy was emphatically *not* 'The One', looks like a pointed corrective to this). Christine Geraghty suggests that 'The specter of romance haunts critics of Austen adaptations. Romance is seen as the opposite of Austen's ironic, witty, and complex accounts of the human heart' (Geraghty 2008: 34), and this is, I think, both true and fully justified. *Becoming Jane* uses the romance cliché of initial mutual dislike between hero and heroine, which Austen herself employs only in *Pride and Prejudice*, and it insistently sexualises the relationship between the two in a mode which at times threatens to become positively Mills & Boon. During the game of cricket someone calls 'Be gentle, Lefroy' when he is about to bowl to Jane, and later there is a slushily suggestive patch of dialogue when he is reading Gilbert White aloud to her:

> '... until the female utters ...'
> 'Yes?'
> 'The female utters a loud, piercing cry of ecstasy.'

The whole effect is reminiscent of nothing so much as the recent reissue of all Jane Austen's novels with chick-lit covers and the commissioning of a new 'portrait' of her for Wordsworth Editions' 'deluxe' edition of her works, which Helen Trayler, managing director of Wordsworth Editions, explained as follows:

> The poor old thing didn't have anything going for her in the way of looks. Her original portrait is very, very dowdy. It wouldn't be appealing to readers, so I took it upon myself to commission a new picture of her. We've given her a bit of a makeover, with make-up and some hair extensions and removed her nightcap. Now she looks great – as if she's just walked out of a salon. (Hoyle 2007)

It could well be said that Hathaway's Austen, too, looks as if she has just walked out of a salon, not least since in her first star vehicle, *The Princess Diaries*, Anne Hathaway's own usual appearance is presented as the miraculous result of a makeover by a top Italian hairdresser.

To circumvent the difficulties of reconciling its vision of Jane Austen with her actual achievement and output, the film tries to take two notable detours. Firstly, it subtly but unmistakably writes its heroine into a rôle more normally associated with the hero. This again can be seen as reflecting a marked slant of Spence's biography. First he observes that

> The most striking thing about Henry's situation is that the roles were reversed from what we tend to think of as the usual order of things. Eliza was the 'masculine' figure with the money to buy herself the spouse she wanted; Henry was the 'feminine' figure, poor but with looks and charm for sale. This intriguing inversion would have made a good basis for a story, but Jane Austen could not or would not tell it. (Spence 2003: 79)

Viewed in this light, *Becoming Jane* could indeed be seen as telling the story that Jane Austen 'could not or would not', just as *Shakespeare in Love* self-consciously positions itself within the generic and narrative expectations of a Shakespeare play. Secondly, Spence suggests that Jane herself was in fact more like Darcy than Elizabeth (Spence 2003: 102), and that indeed the reversal of real people's gender is a strategy she often uses in her novels. In the film, the same emphasis is found. Not only does Jane play cricket (perhaps reprising Hathaway's baseball-playing Princess of Genovia), but *she* slights Lefroy at a ball; *he* says 'I'm yours'; *she* kisses *him*.

In the second place, the film invents a very interesting character for whom there is minimal historical warrant or literary analogue. Mr Wisley is to some extent a cross between Mr Collins, the unwelcome suitor of Elizabeth Bennet, and Harris Bigg-Wither, the family friend whose proposal Jane Austen accepted at first but then, after a sleepless night, declined (and who also informs Fanny's initial acceptance of Henry in Rozema's *Mansfield Park*). However, Mr Wisley not only has more about him than either Mr Collins or Bigg-Wither, but he also has structural similarities with Mr Darcy. The Lady Catherine figure is his aunt (his mother's sister, as Lady Catherine was sister to Lady Anne Darcy); Jane has the Lizzie/Lady Catherine conversation with Lady Gresham and only to a lesser extent with Lefroy's uncle; Mr Wisley himself says ''Tis a truth universally acknowledged'. Tom, by contrast, in fact doubles Wickham, not Darcy, when he becomes almost immediately engaged – a parallel which is confirmed when Jane roams the ball looking for Tom and at first finds only Wisley, just as Lizzie at Netherfield looks for Wickham and finds only Darcy. Most notably, Mr Wisley introduces her as 'Jane Austen', as if recognising her by the name by which she has since become famous, and when Jane says of Mrs Radcliffe 'Her inner landscape is quite picturesque, I suspect' Mr Wisley replies 'True of us all', suggesting that he might in fact have the capacity and temperament to understand both Jane and her art. Extradiegetically, too, Laurence Fox, who plays Mr Wisley, is the more Austenian actor, since his cousin Emilia played Georgiana and his aunt Joanna David Mrs Gardiner in the BBC/A&E *Pride and Prejudice*, and he has since married Billie Piper. The film's invention of Mr Wisley thus introduces as many problems as it solves, since it problematises still further the question of how Austen's authorship of *Pride and Prejudice* is related to the events of her own life.

Nevertheless, the idea of *Pride and Prejudice* is central to the film, again reflecting Spence, who declares that *Pride and Prejudice* 'is as closely linked to Tom Lefroy as some of Austen's early work is to Eliza de Feuillide' (Spence 2003: 101). (He thinks she was inspired by the fact that Tom's parents' first five children were all daughters.) Not only is *Pride and Prejudice* the one of her novels that Jane's own life, in this version, most closely foreshadows, and the one she is seen starting to write towards the end, but it is also already associated with Anne Hathaway, since it is one of the books that her character in *The Princess Diaries* is instructed to read as part of her 'princess lessons' (although *The Princess Diaries* themselves take us closer to *Emma*, since the sequences at the high school are very like *Clueless* and Mia also has driving dramas). Moreover, *Becoming Jane* also seems to owe a debt to Joe Wright's *Pride and Prejudice*. The barely-there shabby-genteel life of the Bennets here seems to lie behind that of the Austens in *Becoming Jane*, for we see a pig in the Austens' garden as we do in the Bennets' house, and later, Jane feeds the pigs. Mary in the Wright is seen playing the piano first thing, as Jane is in *Becoming Jane*: in the additional material of the Wright DVD, Louise West from Jane Austen's House declares that 'In the morning Jane would get up early, then she'd go and practise the piano'. (Louise West also declares that 'She fell in love with somebody called Tom Lefroy when she was 20'.) Most suggestive is the interest in both *Becoming Jane* and the Wright *Pride and Prejudice* in the connection between experience and writing. The Wright DVD has a 'Jane Austen's Life and Times' special feature in which the producer says 'She only wrote about direct experience', while Wright himself says 'In an Austen novel you never see a scene that she wouldn't have seen'; similarly in *Becoming Jane* the assumption that art must be based on life clearly underpins the decision that Jane Austen herself must have a pseudo-elopement, since she is notorious for using the device so often in her novels. There is also a clear similarity in the two films' portrayal of the marriages of the two sets of parents, with both seen in bed. The Jane Austen of *Becoming Jane*, then, is very much the Jane Austen who was the author of the Wright *Pride and Prejudice*.

Pride and Prejudice (dir. Joe Wright, 2005)

Unlike *Becoming Jane*, the Wright film itself evinces a repeated refusal to engage with either the practicalities or the protocols that governed life at the time when the novel is set. There are far too many people at the opening ball; it is fortunate indeed that the Darcy of this version does not make his remark about country society being confined, because it would have appeared simply ludicrous. Lizzie and Darcy stop while dancing, locked in conversation, and no one seems to notice; indeed in the next shot all the other couples have melted away, blatantly transporting us into the realms of fantasy, into which Jane Austen herself ventures only as debunker, in *Northanger Abbey*. In other respects, too, the behaviour exhibited would have been simply impossible. Miss Bingley is *too* uncivil:

> 'Good lord, Miss Elizabeth, did you walk here?'
> 'I did.'
> Silence.
> 'I'm so sorry, how is my sister?'

Such rudeness would simply not have been possible in the society of which Jane Austen writes. With equal disregard for forms, the butler announces 'Mrs Bennet, a Miss Bennet, a Miss Bennet and a Miss Bennet'. Mr Bingley is too gauche, as when he has to practise his proposal on Darcy before violating propriety by returning to the Bennets' and saying 'I know this is all very untoward, but I would like to request the privilege of speaking to Miss Bennet immediately – alone', and also too crude, when he clutches at the back of Jane's dress at the Netherfield ball. On the same occasion, Mrs Bennet gets a dirty spoon on a man's coat, something which again shows a lack of trust in Jane Austen's own brand of social comedy, in which the humour is verbal and situational rather than slapstick. Jane seems to go to London sitting on the back of a cart, and Lizzie certainly arrives in Kent alone in an open cart; later she just wanders into the kitchen, having apparently come home on her own. Colonel Fitzwilliam and

Lizzie have their conversation in church during Mr Collins's sermon, while Mr Collins in the pulpit accidentally says 'can only be obtained through intercourse ... forgive me, through *the* intercourse'. Mr Darcy apparently comes to see Lizzie on her own in the evening or indeed at night, and, even more ludicrously, Lady Catherine arrives in the middle of the night, upon which Mr Bennet calmly offers her a cup of tea. But then, as Christine Geraghty notes, the film markets itself from the outset precisely on the grounds of its *in*fidelity to Austen: 'As the trailer ... put it, the film is "from the beloved author, Jane Austen" but is "the story of a modern woman"' (Geraghty 2008: 15–16), an approach which Geraghty sees as also extending to the film's heroine, since Keira Knightley 'is a very modern beauty ... When she does speak, Knightley adopts a light, flat tone with a modern handling of language that contrasts with the drawling of Caroline Bingley and the circumlocutions of Lady Catherine' (Geraghty 2008: 38).

The modernising process noted by Geraghty applies not just to how things are said, but actually to *what* is said. The film repeatedly fails to trust Jane Austen's own dialogue. Charlotte says 'I'm frightened. So don't judge me, Lizzie. Don't you dare judge me'. Darcy refers to 'My honesty in admitting scruples about our relationship', sounding for all the world like a twenty-first century Relate counsellor, while Miss Bingley becomes a nineteenth-century version of John McEnroe when she says 'Charles, you cannot be serious', and when Mr Collins declares 'What excellent boiled potatoes. It's many years since I've had such an exemplary vegetable' it is again clear that the scriptwriter has no faith in Austen's own comedy. At times indeed it sounds as though the dialogue has been mistranscribed by someone who simply failed to grasp the subtlety and nuances of either Austen's syntax or her humour: Elizabeth says of Bingley 'and conveniently rich'; Mr Collins says 'Before I am run away with my feelings', which is simply garbled (he means 'run away with *by* my feelings'), as are Mr Bennet's advice to Lizzie to choose Wickham to jilt her because 'He's a pleasant fellow, and he'd do the job credibly' (he means 'creditably') and Mr Darcy's question 'Do you talk as a rule while dancing?'. All of these instances are objectionable not on the naïve grounds of infidelity but because they evince an insensitivity to the rules of English syntax, the keyboard on which Austen demonstrates her virtuoso technique. Austen's own language is again distrusted when Elizabeth says of Mr Collins and Lady Catherine that 'She could not have bestowed her kindness on a more grateful subject', and when the Gardiners call their destination by its modern title of 'the Peak District' rather than Austen's one of 'Derbyshire'.

The film is also wary of following Austen's plotting too closely. Lizzie tells Darcy about Lydia in front of the Gardiners, obviating the necessity for them subsequently to have to be informed about the state of her relations with him, but also removing much of the delicacy of his behaviour. Peripheral characters are ruthlessly dispensed with, eliminating much of the richness of the social scene: the Gardiners here have no children, and Bingley has only one sister; there are also no Phillipses, no Denny and no Sir William Lucas or Maria. There are some other odd little changes: we are not actually told what Elizabeth's age is when Lady Catherine asks her – the conversation is cut short – and it is *Charlotte*, not Elizabeth, who is told she can play the piano in the housekeeper's room. Most damaging, though, are the changes to Elizabeth herself, who is quite simply too silly: at the opening ball, she breaks the silence by giggling audibly, in one of several instances of the apparent influence of *Bridget Jones's Diary*. Particularly interesting is the fact that there is much less sense here of the Bennets' marriage as dysfunctional: as soon as Mrs Bennet says Jane must go on horseback we hear thunder and then the sound of pouring rain, upon which Mr Bennet says admiringly, 'Good grief, woman. Your skills in the art of matrimony are positively occult', and the likeness to *Bridget Jones's Diary* is strengthened by the fact that Mrs Bennet accepts that she might have been wrong, making her more like Bridget Jones's mother than the Mrs Bennet of the novel in her level of insight. Also like Bridget Jones, Elizabeth is more overtly sexualised than Austen's heroine: in the meeting at Pemberley it is her desire and perspective which are foregrounded rather than Darcy's, and she is much more embarrassed and inclined to gabble, as Colin Firth does in the BBC/A&E version, and again in a way reminiscent of Bridget Jones.

Indeed Elizabeth is not the character who this adaptation appears to find most interesting: oddly, that distinction seems to be shared between two characters in whom the original novel is not very interested, Mr Bennet and Mr Collins. The Mr Bennet of the adaptation is not allowed to do or say various things that the Mr Bennet of the novel does: it is Elizabeth who asks 'Do these pleasing attentions arise from the impulse of the moment, or are they the result of previous study?', and also she who says 'Wickham's a fool if he accepts her with less than £10,000'. Equally Mr Bennet knows in advance that Mr Collins is going to propose and leaves him to it, and later seems to find it very hard and draining to say 'I will never see you again if you do'; even more incredibly, all, including Mr Bennet, listen at the door while Bingley proposes. Conversely, Mr Bennet apologises to Mary, and the UK version of the film ends quite inexplicably with a shot of his face as he contemplates the forthcoming marriage of Elizabeth and Darcy. When it comes to Mr Collins, Tom Hollander's Mr Collins is quite pitiable, being short, nervously anxious to please, and much less pleased with himself than David Bamber in the 1995 version. Most seriously, the exchange between Elizabeth and Jane about Mr Collins towards the end of the film uses him to crack a joke entirely foreign to the spirit of the original book and indeed to most subsequent adaptations: Jane says 'If there was but such another man for you' and Elizabeth, rather than, as in the original novel, reflecting at this point on the superiority of Jane's disposition to her own, replies 'Perhaps Mr Collins has a cousin'. Again, the moral impulse is totally absent.

Instead of morality, we have, as in *Becoming Jane*, romance. The female characters here are sexualised and prettified, much as Jane Austen herself has been in her 'makeover' and in the growing cultural push to accept the prettier but dubious Rice portrait as authentic and thus displace the glum little sketch of her by Cassandra. Thus we see Jane doing Lizzie's hair in a shot apparently designed expressly to provide a close-up of Rosamund Pike's cleavage, and the director soon abandoned his initial fear that Keira Knightley was 'too pretty' to play Elizabeth Bennet. The language works in the same direction, most notably in Miss Darcy's positively salacious remark about duets, 'Brother, you must force her'. One also wonders whether the 'portrait' of Darcy is a marble bust rather than a painting not just because marble statues were what was already to be found in the gallery at Chatsworth but also because so many of the other figures are nude. Certainly the relationship between Elizabeth and Darcy is heavily physicalised: even as she says 'You were the last man in the world whom I could ever be prevailed on to marry' she seems ready for a kiss, and indeed the DVD has an 'Alternate US ending' featuring a kiss outside Chatsworth and Mr Darcy repeating 'Mrs Darcy – Mrs Darcy'. If the lovelorn heroine of *Becoming Jane* is clearly the author of the Wright *Pride and Prejudice*, then *Pride and Prejudice*'s prettified, sexualised heroine with the ultimately salvageable family is equally clearly an influence on Anne Hathaway's Jane.

Northanger Abbey (dir. Jon Jones, 2007)

To some extent the same set of influences is visible in *Northanger Abbey*, scripted by Andrew Davies and directed by Jon Jones as the second offering of ITV's three-week Jane Austen season. *Northanger Abbey*, like the Wright *Pride and Prejudice*, shows signs of having been influenced by

Bridget Jones's Diary. Catherine is strongly reminiscent of Bridget Jones in the way her private world takes over the screen, in the discussion of whether or not she keeps a journal and in the way she and Henry visibly take on conversational rôles while dancing, just as Bridget and Mark do in the kitchen. She even has something of Bridget's pronunciation and characteristically modern rising intonation, and this Catherine, like Bridget, is more pouty and puzzled and less wide-eyed than Katharine Schlesinger in 1986. This version of *Northanger Abbey* was also in some ways eerily similar to *Becoming Jane*: both were shot largely in Ireland; Catherine prefers 'cricket and baseball'; and her mother's remark 'I wonder if it can be good for her, my dear, to read quite so many novels' comes very close to Lady Gresham's comic question of 'Can anything be done about it?' when she sees Jane writing.

There were also pronounced similarities with the 1986 version of *Northanger Abbey* directed by Giles Foster. To some extent, these are masked by some of the rather striking innovations of Foster's version, which was unusually radical for its day, with an extraordinary scene showing women immersed to the neck in the baths while wearing elaborate confections of hats, which went so far as to insinuate that Jane Austen's England was actually faintly ridiculous. Foster's adaptation was heavy on subtext – Catherine's dreams are of General Tilney, not of Henry as in the 2007 version – and he also made some other significant changes: the general has as a confidante a terrifying black-clad marquise (played by Elaine Ives-Cameron), whose husband was guillotined, as the husband of Jane's cousin Eliza de Feuillide was; in a daringly secularising touch, Henry has an estate to go to rather than a parsonage; and its Frederick (Greg Hicks) says he has taught Henry all his tricks, upon which we see them both taking snuff with identical gestures. (In the 2007 version, Eleanor explicitly vouches for Henry's difference from Frederick.) Unusually for a Jane Austen adaptation, too, politics are introduced in the Foster version when Mr Allen is outraged that 'That little shoemaker's been charged with high treason' for planning reform. Nevertheless, the two John Thorpes (Jonathan Coy in 1986 and William Beck in 2007) could have been twins; two blonde Isabellas with cleavages are contrasted with two dark Catherines; the parsonages look very similar and both films make much play with dream sequences – indeed one almost looks directly to have inspired the other when the Catherine of the Foster version dreams of Henry coming riding in on a white horse, and the Henry of the Jones adaptation, twenty-one years later, actually does so. Both are 90 minutes long, and both pick out essentially the same elements to dramatise: the openings in particular are strikingly similar, with a young Catherine, alone, seen fantasising out of doors until interrupted by a younger sibling or siblings announcing the arrival of the Allens, who have come to discuss Mr Allen's gout and invite Catherine to Bath, upon which, in both cases, we cut to the coach journey. In both, too, the heroines burn their copies of *The Mysteries of Udolpho*, and in both the dialogue is largely unchanged and full weight is given to the dreadful horror of the General being kept waiting for his dinner while Catherine is distracted, and subsequently to his table manners and talk.

If *Northanger Abbey* recalls both *Becoming Jane* and its own earlier avatar, however, it could not be more different from *Mansfield Park*. The self-conscious narrator works far better here, as we segue imperceptibly from reality to fantasy and Henry observes 'Northanger Abbey would make a very good title, don't you think?'. Appropriately enough for an adaptation of the most insistently intertextual of all Austen's novels, this is indeed a film that is both self-conscious in its own right, and also knows it is coming after other films – when Catherine is alone in her room at the abbey for the first time, we hear what is either a glockenspiel or a celeste but is certainly reminiscent of the Hogwarts motif in the *Harry Potter* films – and knows too how to deploy a filmic cliché: as Catherine's younger sister excitedly exclaims, 'It's a man on a white horse!'. There are signs of modernising influences – John Thorpe calls *The Monk* 'hot stuff', and there is an invented scene making it clear that Frederick Tilney has seduced Isabella Thorpe – but although Davies injects his trademark sexualisation of Austen, this is done to much subtler effect than *Mansfield Park*'s indiscriminately heaving bosoms: instead Isabella Thorpe, leaning over Catherine when they are alone, saucily demands, 'What would the men think if they could see us now?', a question to which the answer is abundantly obvious.

This adaptation also understands irony, as we see early on in the deliciously comic remark 'Not a soul, John. There's no one here at all' as the characters attempt to squeeze into a heaving Pump Room. Above all, it understands behaviour and codes – indeed Catherine here is far more concerned with right thinking than Billie Piper's Fanny – as well as having a sense of what Regency England might actually have looked like: the bookshop windows, for instance, are suitably cracked and grimy, giving a similar effect of dilapidation as in Roger Michell's 1995 *Persuasion*. Even when it is different from the novel it is interestingly so: its early introduction of Eleanor's future husband sows the seed for her later marriage, and Henry's description of General Tilney as a bloodless vampire does a very good job of supplying the backstory, which the adaptation does not have time to cover. Here too, then, such modern-isation as occurred was sympathetic and intelligent rather than jarring, and, above all, did not attempt to jettison the moral impulse which lies at the heart of Austen's work.

The final adaptation in the Jane Austen Season was *Persuasion* (dir. Adrian Shergold, 2007), and this, too, made surprising changes. Here Anne has the exchange about the relative constancy of men and women the first time she meets Captain *Benwick*, and not towards the end of the novel with Captain Harville, and this immediately warns us that the traditional ending of the novel is no longer available for use. Indeed the end uneasily blurs elements of the cancelled chapter, the received text and a run through the streets which is found in neither, and the film closes with Anne and Wentworth dancing on the grass outside Kellynch, which is his wedding present to her, something that both acknowledges and revises a feature of the original novel in that, as Nora Foster Stovel points out, 'In Austen's last novel, *Persuasion*, com-posed when she herself was long past the dancing stage, her heroine, Anne Elliot, does not dance at all' (Stovel 2006: 187). Stovel notes that 'In the 1995 BBC adaptation ... screenwriter Nick Dear augments the pathos by adding a scene in which Wentworth gives up his seat at the piano to Anne in order to dance with the Musgroves, leaving Anne to play solo accompaniment' (Stovel 2006: 188), but Shergold's takes this one step further, and doing so is not wholly without warrant since, as Stovel observes, 'Austen allows them a metaphorical minuet, as their "spirits danc[e] in private rapture" (240) after Anne reads Wentworth's letter' (Stovel 2006: 188). One might, though, speculate that reasons of economy also lay behind this, since the behind-the-scenes programme which accompanied *Lost in Austen* noted that the filming of its full-blown dance scene stretched across three days. Shergold's Anne also does what Austen's never could have done when she says aloud to her father that Mrs Smith (whose first name is here given as Harriet, as if she had wandered out of *Emma*), is 'not the only widow in Bath with little to live on and no surname of dignity'; later she has an internal monologue, while Frederick carefully explains his feelings to Captain Harville. This makes us aware much earlier of *his* feelings, something which is accentuated as the focus of the camera shifts increasingly from *her* gaze to *his*. *Persuasion*, then, was better and more sensitive than *Mansfield Park*, but it had neither the subtlety nor the creative innov-ation of *Northanger Abbey*, and in general, the series as a whole was def-initely patchy, and clearly illustrated the difficulties and pitfalls of its avowed policy of trying to make Austen accessible to a younger, more 'modern' audience, when modernity is conceived of primarily as an interest in sexuality and a lack of interest in morality.

Shakespeare Retold

Austen's emphasis on codes and manners makes it unsurprising that her texts should find modern *mores* in some respects uncongenial. It may perhaps seem less likely that Shakespeare, 'not of an age but for all time', to borrow Ben Jonson's celebrated description, should sometimes do so too. One area in which his mental landscape no longer obtains, though, is in fact sexual morality, as will be clear to anyone who has ever tried to teach *Measure for Measure* to a group of students who cannot remember a time before the contraceptive pill and for whom tertiary syphilis is something which only happens to characters in Ibsen. It was perhaps inevitable, therefore, that the BBC's otherwise strong *Shakespeare Retold* series, which had something of the same project as the ITV Austen, should be at its weakest in its treatment of *Much Ado About Nothing*, which is so strongly focused on a code of chastity, though it also struggled with aspects of *A Midsummer Night's Dream*. Initially conceived as a freestanding TV series of four 90-minute, extremely free adaptations along the lines of the channel's previous success with *Chaucer Retold*, consisting of *Much Ado About Nothing* (dir. Brian Percival), *Macbeth* (dir. Mark Brozel), *The Taming of the Shrew* (dir. David Richards), and *A Midsummer Night's Dream* (dir. Ed Fraiman), this series was first screened in the UK in this order in autumn 2005 and released on DVD just after Christmas 2006, and as with ITV's Austen season, it is instructive to note which aspects of the original translated easily to the format and which had to be more radically adapted or in some cases jettisoned.

The series as a whole reworked its four chosen Shakespeare plays in much the same spirit as *Forbidden Planet* reworks *The Tempest* or *Clueless* reworks *Emma*. Shakespeare's language is abandoned almost entirely, and when it does surface it is not necessarily from the right play: Oberon quotes from *Romeo and Juliet* – 'My bounty is as boundless as the sea' – and says to Puck, 'You give me some more love-juice, or I will give you a midsummer night's dream where the moon doesn't shine', while the waiter says 'Welcome to the Globe diner, sir' to James as he gives him a Globe-shaped menu. Similarly in *Macbeth* Ella Macbeth says to her husband Joe (James McAvoy of future *Becoming Jane* fame) 'You're too full of the milk of human kindness, Joe' – although she was not allowed her most famous line, asking instead 'Murdered? Here?' – and the health inspector declares that he is more likely to forgive the sins of one who confesses 'than the sins of a bloke what has made me work for my pound of flesh, excuse my Shakespeare'. Cleverest of all is the exchange, also found in *Macbeth*, in which a naïve young chef says 'Very Gordon Ramsay' and is told reprovingly 'We don't use that name in this kitchen. It's bad luck to say it out loud. Just call him "the Scottish chef"'.

The best of the four films was *Macbeth*, which was inventively transposed to a kitchen run by top Scottish chef, Joe Macbeth. This was a *Macbeth* with some startling differences from the original story, not least in that this it answered the questions left implicit or tantalisingly unresolved in the original play. Ella, the Lady Macbeth figure, did have a baby, as she expressly tells us – 'I know how it feels to love a baby, Joe. I know how it feels to have a baby feed at my breast' – but it died. Joe and Ella had not previously discussed the possible murder of Duncan – 'Don't pretend you don't know what I'm talking about ... Didn't tell him about your binmen, did you? Maybe you didn't tell him because you're thinking what I'm thinking'. Ella's cause of death is clarified – she jumped off the roof – and the identity of all those involved in the Banquo figure's murder is clearly established.

Most notable was the fact that this *Macbeth* was set in England, in line with a strongly developed emphasis of the series as a whole: Ramona Wray notes, for instance, that

> Hand-in-hand with the evocations of history and tradition embodied in Shakespeare goes *Much Ado*'s investment in all things English, including Anglican churches, windy seaside promenades and historic country hotels. Similarly, *Taming* makes extensive use of establishing shots of derelict stately homes, Big Ben and leafy London parks, and pauses over images of bandstands and eccentric Etonians, in order to underscore stereotypical national associations and an English heartland unchanging in the face of the trappings of globalisation. (Wray 2006: 186)

In the case of *Macbeth*, the English setting is indicated by the fact that the backdrop to the murder is people waving the cross of St George and shouting the traditional football supporters' chant of 'In-ger-lund', which combines with the presence of the Scottish Joe, an Irish Duncan and some asylum seekers from former Yugoslavia to suggest that this was a narrative which touched on a whole range of people and nations. The sense of contemporaneity and universal applicability was also underlined by the fact that the weird sisters are three binmen, first seen eating restaurant leftovers from the dump. The transposition to a restaurant setting worked superbly in many respects: the scene where a crazed

Macbeth wrestles the diner out of the restaurant perfectly encapsulates the way in which the original play registers the violation of civility and commensality, and although, unusually for *Macbeth*, no violence against humans was shown on screen, this was only because the processes of cooking and food consumption proved so much more horrific. Macbeth cleaves a lobster and cuts up a pig's head, deftly echoing the pig which appears at the feast in Polanski's *Macbeth*; the unsatisfactoriness of Malcolm as Duncan's successor is succinctly conveyed by the information that he was a vegetarian for a year; Ella tells her husband 'You're a knifeman, Joe. You know how it feels'; and the weird sisters' promise is of 'Three Michelin stars coming your way'. Not just food preparation but food consumption is also rendered consistently strange and horrible: Macbeth drains milk from the fridge while watching Duncan's TV cooking show and later spills milk and cuts himself on glass from the bottle; finally he imagines first milk and then oil turning to blood.

Other elements of the play were also smoothly transposed: the fact that Duncan is Irish allowed for the preservation of the Irish dimension of the original play, and in the same mode of creative preservation and dislocation of motifs in the original, Ella's dead baby was delivered by Caesarian section. The binmen tell Joe that everything – 'all our yesterdays' – ends up with them; the ghost of Billy starts as a video message on Joe's mobile, although Joe does then imagine he sees him; and most inventively, the 'flying pigs' which figure as the binmen's version of Birnam wood coming to Dunsinane do indeed arrive, in the shape of police helicopters. (Our willingness to read the police as 'pigs' has been prepared for by the fact there is an ex-con on the staff with form for violence who is sure he will be fitted up for the murder of Duncan, although in fact the outcome is that Joe persuades him to murder Billy and the family of Peter Macduff.) Most interestingly, the adaptation directly negotiates its own relationship with its past in the exchange between Joe and Ella about the two illegal immigrants who are used as fall guys for the murder of Duncan:

'Who are they?'
'Top class washer-uppers.'
'Where are they from?'
'The eleventh century. Also known as the former Yugoslavia.'

Ella employs the Yugoslavians after Duncan has joked that he might be run over by a bus, to which Joe responds that since Duncan goes everywhere in his Mercedes, that is not going to happen. The replacement of a potential bus accident by people explicitly identified as coming from the eleventh century nicely emblematises the way in which modernity is being used here in the service of Shakespearean drama rather than as a replacement for it.

The Taming of the Shrew was another particularly interesting adaptation in this series, not only because of what it did with Kate, but also because of what it did with its Petruchio figure. This Kate, played by Shirley Henderson (Bridget Jones's friend Jude and Moaning Myrtle in the *Harry Potter* films) is a Tory MP with ambitions to be the leader of the party, except that the Tory party prefers its leaders to be married. Her sister, Bianca (Jaime Murray), is a supermodel, and her mother, played by the sixties model Twiggy, is a shopaholic socialite who does not even begin to understand her difficult daughter. (As the adaptation unfolds, the rôle of the widow is also subsumed into that of Kate's mother.) Rufus Sewell's Petruchio figure is an old friend of Bianca's discarded manager/ boyfriend, who fled to Australia to escape the Inland Revenue but had to return because he didn't have a work permit. As soon as he hears of the existence of Bianca's politician sister, who is in need of a husband, he scents money and charges in, just as Petruchio in the original play explicitly targets Katherine because of her dowry.

Petruchio's plan soon runs away from him, though. Firstly, he confesses his motivation to Kate. Secondly, he takes her to see his family home. Dislocated from its moment in the original play, where Petruchio does not take Katherine home until after the wedding, this proved a pivotal moment in their relationship here. Petruchio's home, like Petruchio himself, is in a bad way: he can't afford to maintain it and his father used to keep pigs in the drawing room. But despite the state of the house, this visit operates on Kate's feelings for Petruchio much as Elizabeth Bennet's to Pemberley does on her feelings for Darcy, for it elicits two pieces of information: firstly, that Petruchio's mother ran away when he was small, and secondly, that for all his scruffy appearance, he is in fact the 16th Earl of Charlbury – and that is the sort of thing that is always going to play well with Tory voters. An even more surprising revelation follows at the wedding. At first, Petruchio dresses up in morning suit for this, but then he looks at himself in the mirror and decides he can't go through with it, because there is something he thinks Kate needs to know about him. She finds out soon enough when he turns up at church in tights, high-heeled boots and a skirt: he is a transvestite. As he explains, he is 'not a poof – no fears on that score – common misconception', but he likes to wear women's clothes.

This emphasis on Petruchio's unconventionality and vulnerability rather than just on Kate's does something very radical to the dynamics of the play: it makes the relationship not so much a taming as an accommodation. Both Katherine and Petruchio derive tangible benefits from their marriage, but each has to learn to live with the other and each has to learn to strike a balance between the private face and the face that is presented to the world. In this version, Katherine does deliver the gist of most of her final speech, but only to her mother and sister. She explicitly says she would make the offer of total submission, but only because she knows it will be declined. The real test is that, unlike her sister, whose projected marriage is cancelled as a result, she did not ask for a pre-nuptial agreement. The final sequence shows Katherine and Petruchio as the parents of triplets (one better than Maggie Thatcher's twins as well as one better than the twins so beloved of Shakespearean comedy), for whom Petruchio is the carer while she carries on her career, now as Leader of the Opposition. They have reached an accommodation both in public and in private and although the behaviour of each may be unconventional, it is not only mutually rewarding but has brought life back both to Petruchio's moribund household and to the beleaguered Tories, who have never been properly mothered since the ousting of Mrs Thatcher.

These four versions were all entertaining, and these two best of them offered a genuine critical engagement and in effect a substantially developed reading of their respective plays, since they were able to give such pronounced stress to the elements that they thought important and remove or downplay others. The other two, however, did not work so well, and the ways in which they failed to do so are very revealing of how Shakespeare works or does not work in the modern world.

This was particularly clear in *Much Ado About Nothing*. Some of the transpositions in this were very successful: Dogberry, appropriately enough, is in charge of security, and there is equal appropriateness in all the costuming when Beatrice goes to the party as Elizabeth I, Hero as Marilyn Monroe and Claude and Benedick both as knights after Claude gets two costumes for the price of one – which of course helps the disguise to work. The 'flyting' in particular is cleverly updated, especially when Beatrice tells Benedick that he puts the 'w' into 'anchorman', and the tone throughout is very nicely negotiated. To some extent, indeed, Don's clown disguise acts as a lightning conductor that allows comedy of a more subtle kind to flourish, as later when Benedick says 'Love's just one of those things a man grows into – like jazz and olives'. The overhearing for Benedick's benefit is deftly done through cameras, which works nicely, since we are in a TV studio most of the time, and this also underlines the emphasis on the importance of public image. It is, too, entirely appropriate that Benedick's wooing strategy is to read sonnet 116 to Beatrice, concluding with 'Shakespeare must be right'. However, the adaptation takes a relatively simple view of character: Beatrice is a newsreader on *Wessex Tonight*, while Hero is merely a weather girl, and these obviously contrasting rôles are allowed to carry much of the burden of expressing them both as individuals and in relation to each other. Beatrice's co-presenter Keith is immediately branded as sexist and drunk and a philanderer, and is further condemned by the fact that he smokes. Claude is equally quickly identified as vain, self-obsessed and vacuous, and explains himself that he can never spot jokes. This clearly suggests that the Claudio-Hero relationship is one this modernised adaptation will have difficulty with, and that does indeed prove to be the case. Though Beatrice and Benedick do not sleep together, Hero did sleep with Don; moreover, she will not openly admit it, but merely tells Claude that if he loved her he wouldn't do this to her. Her collapse is caused not by outraged innocence but because she much more mundanely hits her head on the corner of a pillar, and at the end, she wants revenge on Don and won't have Claude back. Ultimately, then, this adaptation has no trouble with creating a suitably feisty Beatrice figure and a suitably commitment-shy Benedick, but it has no more idea what to do with a virginal and forgiving Hero than *Mansfield Park* does with a moral Fanny Price (also played by Billie Piper), and nor does it know how to allow the recuperation of a man who does what Claudio does.

The fourth of the series, *A Midsummer Night's Dream*, was also visibly uncomfortable with some aspects of the play. What are we to make of a version of *A Midsummer Night's Dream* in which the Egeus figure and his wife are the two most interesting characters? On one level, the answer to this is simple: the older generation are more interesting here, as they are in the Wright *Pride and Prejudice*, because despite all the attempts to modernise and sex up Shakespeare and Austen, that is still the generation most likely to be watching adaptations of them, which of course brings us back to the fundamental problem of such adaptations in the first place. Equally, though, it seems that this adaptation finds itself troubled by the lack of psychological depth in the original, and consequently it decided that it had to invent some new characters to give it to. Not only are Theo's – the Egeus figure's – story and feelings far more prominent here than in the play, but his name of Theo presents him as godlike, while his surname of Moon marks him as central to the thematic structure of the play. Certainly the interestingly scripted row between Theo and his wife Polly clearly shows that this is where the dramatic energies of this version are, and Oberon thinks that his main function is not to help the young lovers but to save the relationship of Polly and Theo, whose marriage they blessed 26 years before, when Oberon – who thinks he has a duty 'to spread peace and love and happiness' – talked Theo out of his cold feet, a favour which Theo now reciprocates when he in turn offers Oberon marital advice. (This is certainly much needed, because the disruption of Oberon's and Titania's relationship is having very serious consequences: 'Why do you think the weather's so weird nowadays? You think it's global warming?'.) Notably, the climax comes not when the problems of the lovers are resolved but when Theo writes Polly a truly terrible poem as they renew their vows; this occurs instead of Hermia's engagement party, as in the *Much Ado About Nothing*, where it proves impossible to a modern scriptwriter to resolve the problems in a relationship as swiftly and in as pat a way as Shakespeare had done.

Like the 2007 *Northanger Abbey*, this film is smart: the idea that Sander is much more dashing than James Demetrius is conveyed in strictly metafilmic and intertextual terms when he emerges from the lake like Mr Darcy, a reference further underlined when we are told that James and Hermia, like Bridget and Mark Darcy, used to share a bath. There are also some good TV jokes – Theo says to Polly 'At least give me a sign, I feel like I'm talking to a coma victim in *Holby City'*; Helena tells James that he's clever, and he says yes, he often solves the crimes in *A Touch of Frost* before Del Boy does – as well as a theatrical one: like Henry Irving, Bottom has played the Alhambra in Bradford. Indeed the adaptation is sharply scripted in general: Puck says of the forest 'all this nature, it's unnatural, isn't it?', and Quince proposes that 'It's an engagement party, so I'll open proceedings with the theme from *The Deerhunter'*. Quince also guesses that Bottom's attempted impression of Michael Caine is supposed to be Ruud van Nistelrooy, in the face of which the 'mechanicals' disgustedly dismiss Bottom's supposed disguise with the reproof that 'It's supposed to be an engagement party, not the Edinburgh pigging festival'.

This adaptation struggles, though, with the idea of the supernatural, veering uneasily between various possible strategies for accounting more credibly for what the play simply and unashamedly presents as magic. It starts with a row between Titania and Oberon, but we do not see either of them, just the odd ambiguous light effect, until Puck, who looks like a hobo, slants a dropper towards the screen and we do then see Titania and Oberon, costumed more like weirdos than fairies; later, in a similar effect, Titania magics the audience rather than Bottom's act, so that although his jokes remain pitiful, they begin to be much better received. This idea of mind-bending substances is developed elsewhere too: Theo asks 'Is he on drugs? He's talking squiggle'; Puck goes in search of apparently magic mushrooms; and Polly says of the lovers, 'Tripping off their heads, every one of them'. We also see magic tricks, which replace the 'Pyramus and Thisbe' playlet, and Bottom's transformation, which affects only his ears and teeth, is presented very much in terms of what can credibly be achieved with stage make-up. Finally, the idea that there might in the real world be a holiday location called Dreampark is put forward as a partial mediator between the fully real and a rather nebulously-defined 'spirituality' – for want of a better word – that taps into what is for us a much more recognisable discourse of the strange: Helena says to Sander 'You have got some serious commitment issues. Get some help', Theo calls Polly's ideas about love 'New age drivel', and Polly wants to set up a flotation studio. All of these ways of negotiating the gap between reality and the magical are clearly fully in tune with the series' overall project of modernised retelling, but the sheer fact that so many modes are tried does indicate a fundamental unease with the basic idea of the supernatural by which the original play was blissfully untroubled.

What these two sets of overtly or covertly modernised adaptations collectively reveal, then, is that while modern audiences may be thought likely to be uncomfortable with a few very specific aspects of Shakespeare's art, such as his unabashed use of magic and some aspects of the sexual *mores* he depicts, he proves in general extraordinarily amenable to even quite radical transposition and updating. Austen, by contrast, needs to be much more sensitively treated, for Austen, despite the fact that she uses no magic and hence apparently poses much less of a problem to modern adaptors, is consistently immovable on questions of morality, both sexual and otherwise, and cannot be recoded. With Austen thus connoting such absolute and immutable standards and Shakespeare combining cultural capital with such astonishing flexibility, it is no wonder that they have so often proved to function as the twin prongs of separate attacks on the same cultural targets.

Conclusion

The films I have discussed in this book share a number of common features. Their characters typically inhabit a complex, confusing and potentially violent world to which they feel only tenuously connected, but which conditions their experiences and reactions: for instance, Mark Thornton Burnett remarks that 'the image of a stealth bomber from the Bosnian crisis, which we see on Hamlet's monitor, underscores a key narrative point' (Burnett 2006: 39), and the troubles of former Yugoslavia are gestured at too in *Bridget Jones's Diary* (dir. Sharon Maguire, 2001), the *Shakespeare Retold Macbeth* (dir. Mark Brozel, 2005) and *Clueless* (dir. Amy Heckerling, 1995). As well as the possibility of political violence, there is also, in the more recent films, an emerging sense that the world as a whole is under threat from the destabilisation of its weather patterns: we hear of the El Niño effect in *Bridget Jones's Diary*, of the Pismo Beach disaster in *Clueless*, of global warming in the *Shakespeare Retold A Midsummer Night's Dream* (dir. Ed Fraiman, 2005) and of Elizabeth's employers' concern for their 'footprint' in *Lost in Austen* (dir. Dan Zeff, 2008). Finally, all of them to a greater or a lesser extent pit the values and aesthetics of that which is adapted against those of the vehicle of adaptation, and make, in so doing, their own quiet statement on the question of the importance of fidelity.

To list these similarities in this way might seem to suggest that the element of commonality predominates, and that what we are seeing is the registering of concerns that are pretty much the same wherever they are found, in a typical manifestation of globalisation. But as Mark Thornton Burnett and others have shown, the globalised is always subject to specific inflection by the localised, and in the introduction I quoted Markin Orkin as discussing how 'local knowledges may additionally aid the reading of the Shakespeare text' (Orkin 2005: 112).

That, I have suggested, is what is happening in both the Shakespeare and the Austen adaptations I have discussed. In addition, though, I think that what is in evidence is not merely the 'influence' of India or the West Coast or New York in isolation, but a specific tension between that localised flavour and the significantly different associations of the kind of 'classic' text that I take Shakespeare and Austen to be, a kind of classic whose brand markers are an association with a reified, romanticised 'Englishness' and, as always already in the case of classics, a loosely defined idea of not being tied to any specific time.

The flavour metaphor is not wholly meretricious, for these films do typically present themselves as not only pleasurable but also in some sense beneficial, in the way wholesome cooking might be. In the first place, they typically offer a celebratory and recuperative view of the rituals with which our society punctuates experience (and for which they to some extent stand as surrogates). This is most obvious in *In the Bleak Midwinter* (dir. Kenneth Branagh, 1995), but it is observable too in *Metropolitan* (dir. Whit Stillman, 1990), where, as Joseph Alulis observes,

> On Christmas Eve we are given two images of possible responses to ultimate questions. At the Townsend household we see Tom alone with the television on in the background, with a burning yule log on the screen and a tinny, elevator music version of 'Jingle Bells' playing. In immediate juxtaposition to this, we see Audrey at midnight mass at St. Thomas Episcopal Church. The church's architecture is Gothic and on a scale sufficient to make it an appropriate seat for a bishop; the pews are full of people, a magnificent procession makes its way around the building, and the assembled community is singing 'O Come All Ye Faithful.' The stage direction in the shooting script reads 'Majestic ceremony. Beautiful Christmas music.' (Alulis 2001: 78)

It is even the case in *Bridget Jones's Diary*, where the initially purgatorial rituals of Christmas and ruby wedding parties do ultimately lead to the formation of new bonds rather than merely silently marking old ones. *William Shakespeare's Romeo + Juliet* (dir. Baz Luhrmann, 1996), too, finds solace in liturgy and ritual even if not in theology, and even *Hamlet* is by no means indifferent to the charm of celebratory images of family life, which are indeed central to its vision of the lost past, as its glance, however brief, at the comforting silhouette of ecclesiastical architecture shows. It is, perhaps, in this elevation to the quasi-sacramental, to which both prove equally amenable, that we see the full power of Shakespeare and Austen as cultural icons (as with the screening of *Emma* on the day of Princess Diana's funeral) and what that may have to offer to the films which I have explored in this book.

The idea of iconicity is important, because the films I have been discussing achieve their effect despite – indeed in some instances arguably because of – blatant infidelity to the books. Some of them, most notably *Bridget Jones's Diary, Becoming Jane* (dir. Julian Jarrold, 2007), *In the Bleak Midwinter, Shakespeare Wallah* (dir. James Ivory, 1965), and *Jane Austen in Manhattan* (dir. James Ivory 1980), do not even purport to be 'telling the story' of a Shakespeare or an Austen text, and yet no one could doubt that the figure of Shakespeare or Austen, and the cultural capital he or she commands, is central to them. (*Lost in Austen* is an even more striking example of this, since infidelity lies at the heart of its project, as is nicely emblematised by Amanda's shift of her affections from Michael to Darcy.) In these cases, the dominant effect is one of what John Wiltshire, in a passage I have already quoted in the introduction, defines as ' "transcoding" ... a kind of borrowing that plays fast and loose with the original but is, it might be argued, redeemed by its lightness of touch' (Wiltshire 2001: 2). Even those that do present themselves as a version of a Shakespeare play or an Austen novel are not afraid to take wide-ranging and far-reaching liberties with their source text. Almereyda's *Hamlet, William Shakespeare's Romeo + Juliet* and *Shakespeare Retold* are all transplanted to a future that Shakespeare himself could never have recognised; *Bride and Prejudice* (dir. Gurinder Chadha, 2004) takes Austen to India; Joe Wright, Amy Heckerling and the directors of the ITV Austen season all set out unashamedly to modernise her. These films are, in short, hybrids, and the true value to which they pay allegiance is not fidelity but contemporaneity, to which end they are perfectly at ease drawing on cultures, genres and resonances entirely foreign to their originals. Some of these new elements, like the alienating modern city of the Almereyda *Hamlet* and *William Shakespeare's Romeo + Juliet* and the sassy self-consciousness of *Bridget Jones's Diary* and *Lost in Austen*, are themselves beginning to emerge as crucial syntactic elements in a developing grammar of adaptation as that becomes increasingly established as a mode in its own right.

This is perhaps best illustrated by *Lost in Austen* (dir. Dan Zeff, 2008), which begins with a statement both of intent and of self-definition, 'It is a truth generally acknowledged that we are all longing to escape', uttered by the heroine, Amanda Price, who sums up the appeal of Austen as 'the names and language ... the courtesy ... I have standards', and the stark difference between her tastes and her boyfriend's aligns Austen with Mozart versus football and wine versus beer. Here contemporaneity is the keynote throughout. Bingley, Mr Collins, Darcy and even Caroline all fall instantly for a modern girl who has £27,000 a year and paracetamol, and Elizabeth is having too good a time in modern Hampstead to come back. Most eerily, the series seemed to have done a bit of time-travelling on its own account, since it chimed uncannily with two press stories surrounding the Republican vice-presidential candidate Sarah Palin: in the first episode, first broadcast the week after John McCain chose Sarah Palin as his running mate, Elizabeth says 'I've never heard of Alaska', and in the second, first broadcast during the week when Barack Obama got into trouble for his 'lipstick on a pig' remark, Jane declared that 'Lady Ambrosia looks, sounds and smells like a pig. When the time comes, I dare say she shall taste like a pig. I call her a pig'. In these moments, Austen merged seamlessly into the very heart of 2008.

In one sense, of course, these films were always hybridified, since as Emma French remarks,

> The marketing campaign for *Shakespeare in Love* provides ... evidence that the degree of success achieved when marketing Shakespeare on film resides in the simultaneous promotion of both high culture and popular elements in order to make filmed Shakespeare adaptations profitable commodities. If this hybrid, winning blend of high and low is not found, then the film will be a relative commercial failure. (French 2006: 133)

Throughout this book, I have tried to suggest that it is not only commercial success to which such hybridity contributes, but that it also enables the release of new energies, allowing these narratives to engage with topics of which their authors could not originally have conceived.

The films that I have discussed, though, are hybridified in another way too, for by bringing together old stories and new places, they allow us, at their best, to savour elements of different cultures that have been brought together creatively but in a way that still lets their source elements speak, sometimes all the more clearly for the contrast between them. In so doing, they have enabled Shakespeare and Austen texts to speak to a wide variety of issues. In *William Shakespeare's Romeo + Juliet* and *Clueless*, the use of *Romeo and Juliet* and *Emma* allows for a discussion of the relationship between nature and culture, while Jane Austen's adaptation of Sir Charles Grandison and *Hamlet* prove, in the hands of the Merchant Ivory team and Almereyda respectively, ideally adapted for a metatheatrical exploration of modes of representation. Two modern riffs on Austen and Shakespeare texts respectively, *Bridget Jones's Diary* and *In the Bleak Midwinter*, allow for a musing on the relationship between England and America, while *Shakespeare Wallah* and *Bride and Prejudice* use Shakespeare and Austen texts to figure relations between England and India. Even adaptations which are much freer, such as some of those I have explored in my final chapter and *Lost in Austen*, serve ultimately to reveal the closeness of the fit elsewhere, and the reasons why Shakespeare and Austen have not only proved already to be such powerful tools for addressing such a wide range of issues, but seem primed to carry on being so, since they have shown themselves to be so effortlessly capable of renewing themselves and reaching new audiences.

Works Cited

Abbate, Alessandro. '"To Be or Inter-Be": Almereyda's End-of-Millennium *Hamlet'*. *Literature/Film Quarterly*, 32.2 (2004): 82–9.

Albanese, Denise. 'The Shakespeare Film and the Americanization of Culture'. In *Marxist Shakespeares*. Ed. Jean E. Howard and Scott Cutler Shershow. London: Routledge, 2001. 207–26.

Alulis, Joseph. 'In Defense of Virtue: Whit Stillman's *Metropolitan'*. In *Doomed Bourgeois in Love: Essays on the Films of Whit Stillman*. Ed. Mark C. Henrie. Wilmington, DE: ISI Books, 2001. 63–83.

Anderegg, Michael. *Cinematic Shakespeare*. Lanham, MD: Rowman & Littlefield, 2004.

Austen, Jane. *Emma*. Ed. Ronald Blythe. Harmondsworth: Penguin, 1966.

——. *Mansfield Park*. Ed. Tony Tanner. Harmondsworth: Penguin, 1966.

——. *Pride and Prejudice*. Ed. Tony Tanner. Harmondsworth: Penguin, 1972.

——. *Jane Austen's Sir Charles Grandison*. Ed. Brian Southam. Oxford: The Clarendon Press, 1980.

——. *Selected Letters*. Ed. Vivien Jones. Oxford: Oxford University Press, 2004.

Aylmer, Janet. *Darcy's Story from Pride and Prejudice*. Bath: Copperfield Books, 1996.

Belsey, Catherine. 'The Name of the Rose in *Romeo and Juliet'*. In *Romeo and Juliet: Contemporary Critical Essays*. Ed. R.S. White. Basingstoke: Palgrave, 2001. 47–67.

Benedictus, Leo. 'Calamity Jane?' *The Guardian*. 2 March 2007. 8.

Berton, Danièle. '*In the Bleak Midwinter* de Kenneth Branagh. Le Miracle de Noël: le cinéma, le théâtre et la religion en interaction'. In *Écrits et expression populaires*. Ed. Mireille Piarotas. Saint-Étienne: Publications de l'Université de Saint-Étienne, 1998. 223–31.

Bowman, James. 'Whit Stillman: Poet of the Broken Branches'. In *Doomed Bourgeois in Love: Essays on the Films of Whit Stillman*. Ed. Mark C. Henrie. Wilmington, DE: ISI Books, 2001. 39–46.

Branagh, Kenneth. *A Midwinter's Tale: The Shooting Script*. New York: Newmarket Press, 1995.

Buchanan, Judith. *Shakespeare on Film*. New York: Pearson Longman, 2005.

Buhler, Stephen M. 'Double Takes: Branagh Gets to *Hamlet'*. *PostScript*, 17.1 (1997): 43–52.

Burnett, Mark Thornton. *Filming Shakespeare in the Global Marketplace*. Basingstoke: Palgrave, 2007.

——. ' "I See My Father" in "My Mind's Eye": Surveillance and the Filmic *Hamlet'*. In *Screening Shakespeare in the Twenty-First Century*. Ed. Mark Thornton Burnett and Ramona Wray. Edinburgh: Edinburgh University Press, 2006. 31–52.

Burnett, Mark Thornton and Wray, Ramona. 'Introduction'. In *Shakespeare, Film, Fin de Siècle*. Ed. Mark Thornton Burnett and Ramona Wray. Basingstoke: Palgrave Macmillan, 2000. 1–9.

Burt, Richard. 'Backstage Pass(ing): *Stage Beauty, Othello* and the Make-up of Race'. In *Screening Shakespeare in the Twenty-First Century*. Ed. Mark Thornton

Burnett and Ramona Wray. Edinburgh: Edinburgh University Press, 2006. 53–71.

Calvo, Clara. 'Rewriting Lear's Untender Daughter: Fanny Price as a Regency Cordelia in Jane Austen's *Mansfield Park'. Shakespeare Survey,* 58 (2005): 83–94.

Carroll, Laura. 'A Consideration of Times and Seasons: Two Jane Austen Adaptations'. *Literature/Film Quarterly,* 31.3 (2003): 169–76.

Cartmell, Deborah. *Interpreting Shakespeare on Screen.* Basingstoke: Palgrave Macmillan, 2000.

——. 'Film as the New Shakespeare and Film on Shakespeare: Reversing the Shakespeare/Film Trajectory'. *Literature Compass,* 3.5 (2006): 1150–9.

——. 'Theater on Film and Film on Theater in *Hamlet'.* In *Shakespeare's World: World Shakespeares: Proceedings of the VIII World Shakespeare Congress 2006.* Ed. R.S. White, Christa Jansohn and Richard Fotheringham. Newark, NJ: University of Delaware Press, 2008. 171–81.

Chadha, Gurinder. 'Interview for "Celluloid Ceiling: Ask the Experts"'. *The Observer Review.* 4 March 2007. 10–11.

Chakravarti, Paromita. 'Modernity, Postcoloniality and *Othello*: The Case of *Saptapadi'.* In *Remaking Shakespeare: Performance across Media, Genres and Cultures.* Ed. Pascale Aebischer, Edward J. Esche and Nigel Wheale. Basingstoke: Palgrave, 2003. 39–55.

Chaudhry, Lubna and Khattak, Saba. 'Images of White Women and Indian Nationalism: Ambivalent Representations in *Shakespeare Wallah* and *Junoon'.* In *Gender and Culture in Literature and Film East and West: Issues of Perception and Interpretation.* Ed. Nitaya Masavisut, George Simson and Larry E. Smith. Honolulu, HI: College of Language, Linguistics and Literature, University of Hawaii, 1994. 19–25.

Chekhov, Anton. 'The Seagull'. In *Chekhov: Plays.* Trans. Elisaveta Fen. Harmondsworth: Penguin, 1951. 117–83.

Crang, Mike. 'Placing Jane Austen, Displacing England: Touring between Book, History, and Nation'. In *Jane Austen and Co.: Remaking the Past in Contemporary Culture.* Ed. Suzanne R. Pucci and James Thompson. Albany, NY: State University of New York Press, 2003. 111–30.

Daileader, Celia R. *Eroticism on the Renaissance Stage: Transcendence, Desire, and the Limits of the Visible.* Cambridge: Cambridge University Press, 1998.

Davies, Anthony. 'Shakespeare on Film and Television: A Retrospect'. In *Shakespeare and the Moving Image: The Plays on Film and Television.* Ed. Anthony Davies and Stanley Wells. Cambridge: Cambridge University Press, 1994. 1–17.

Dobie, Madeleine. 'Gender and the Heritage Genre: Popular Feminism Turns to History'. In *Jane Austen and Co.: Remaking the Past in Contemporary Culture.* Ed. Suzanne R. Pucci and James Thompson. Albany, NY: State University of New York Press, 2003. 247–59.

Dole, Carol M. 'Austen, Class, and the American Market'. In *Jane Austen in Hollywood.* Ed. Linda Troost and Sayre Greenfield. Lexington, KY: The University Press of Kentucky, 1998. 58–77.

Vanessa Thorpe 'Coalition Aims to Expose Shakespeare'. *The Observer.* 9 September 2007.

Ellington, H. Elisabeth. ' "A Correct Taste in Landscape": Pemberley as Fetish and Commodity'. In *Jane Austen in Hollywood.* Ed. Linda Troost and Sayre Greenfield. Lexington, KY: The University Press of Kentucky, 1998. 90–110.

Elliot, Kamilla. *Rethinking the Novel/Film Debate*. Cambridge: Cambridge University Press, 2003.

Everett, Barbara. '*Romeo and Juliet*: The Nurse's Story'. In *Romeo and Juliet: Contemporary Critical Essays*. Ed. R.S. White. Basingstoke: Palgrave, 2001. 153–65.

Fielding, Helen. *Bridget Jones's Diary* [1996]. London: Picador, 1997.

——. *Bridget Jones: The Edge of Reason*. London: Picador, 1999.

Ford, John R. 'Pursuing the Story: Piecing out Conventions in Loncraine's *Richard III*, Luhrmann's *Romeo and Juliet*, and Pacino's *Looking for Richard*'. *Shakespeare and the Classroom*, 6.1 (1998): 62–9.

Forde, John Maurice. 'Janespotting'. *Topic*, 48 (1997): 11–21.

Foster, Verna Ann. ''*Tis Pity She's a Whore* as City Tragedy'. In *John Ford: Critical Re-Visions*. Ed. Michael Neill. Cambridge: Cambridge University Press, 1988. 181–200.

Fowler, Karen Joy. *The Jane Austen Book Club*. London: Viking, 2004.

French, Emma. *Selling Shakespeare to Hollywood*. Hatfield: University of Hertfordshire Press, 2006.

Fuchs, Cynthia. 'Interview with Michael Almereyda'. Online: www.popmatters.com/film/interviews/almereyda-michael.shtml

Fullbrook, Denise. 'A Generational Gig with Jane Austen, Sigmund Freud, and Amy Heckerling: Fantasies of Sexuality, Gender, Fashion, and Disco in and Beyond *Clueless*'. In *Jane Austen and Co.: Remaking the Past in Contemporary Culture*. Ed. Suzanne R. Pucci and James Thompson. Albany, NY: State University of New York Press, 2003. 179–209.

Geraghty, Christine. *Now a Major Motion Picture: Film Adaptations of Literature and Drama*. Lanham, MD: Rowman & Littlefield, 2008.

Giddings, Robert, Selby, Keith and Wensley, Chris. *Screening the Novel: The Theory and Practice of Literary Dramatization*. Basingstoke: Macmillan, 1990.

Goldberg, Jonathan. '*Romeo and Juliet's* Open R's'. In *Romeo and Juliet: Contemporary Critical Essays*. Ed. R.S. White. Basingstoke: Palgrave, 2001. 194–212.

Greenfield, John R. 'Is Emma Clueless? Fantasies of Class and Gender from England to California'. *Topic*, 48 (1997): 31–8.

Greenhalgh, Susanne and Shaughnessy, Robert. 'Our Shakespeares: British Television and the Strains of Multiculturalism'. In *Screening Shakespeare in the Twenty-First Century*. Ed. Mark Thornton Burnett and Ramona Wray. Edinburgh: Edinburgh University Press, 2006. 90–112.

Hamilton, Lucy. 'Baz vs. the Bardolaters, or Why *William Shakespeare's Romeo+Juliet* Deserves Another Look'. *Literature/Film Quarterly*, 28.2 (2000): 118–24.

Harding, D.W. 'Regulated Hatred: An Aspect of the Work of Jane Austen'. *Scrutiny*, 8 (March 1940): 346–62.

Harris, Jocelyn. '"Such a Transformation!": Translation, Imitation, and Intertextuality in Jane Austen on Screen'. In *Jane Austen on Screen*. Ed. Gina MacDonald and Andrew F. MacDonald. Cambridge: Cambridge University Press, 2003. 44–68.

Hatchuel, Sarah. *Shakespeare, from Stage to Screen*. Cambridge: Cambridge University Press, 2004.

Heckerling, Amy. 'Interview with Amy Heckerling at the American Film Institute'. 14 September 1995. Online: www.jasa.net.au/study/ahinterview.htm

Higson, Andrew. *English Heritage, English Cinema: Costume Drama since 1980*. Oxford: Oxford University Press, 2003.

Hill, Reginald. *A Cure for All Diseases*. London: HarperCollins 2008.

Hilton, Julian. 'Reading Letters in Plays: Short Courses in Practical Epistemology?'. In *Reading Plays: Interpretation and Reception*. Ed. Hanna Scolnicov and Peter Holland. Cambridge: Cambridge University Press, 1991. 140–60.

Hindle, Maurice. *Studying Shakespeare on Film*. Basingstoke: Palgrave, 2007.

Hodgdon, Barbara. 'Baz Luhrmann's *William Shakespeare's Romeo + Juliet*'. In *Romeo and Juliet: Contemporary Critical Essays*. Ed. R.S. White. Basingstoke: Palgrave, 2001. 129–46.

——. 'Re-Incarnations'. In *Remaking Shakespeare: Performance across Media, Genres and Cultures*. Ed. Pascale Aebischer, Edward J. Esche and Nigel Wheale. Basingstoke: Palgrave, 2003. 190–209.

Hopkins, Lisa. 'The Transference of *Clarissa*: Psychoanalysis and the Realm of the Feminine'. *Critical Survey*, 6:2 (1994): 218–25.

——. 'How Very Like the Home Life of our Own Dear Queen: McKellen's *Richard III*'. In *Spectacular Shakespeare: Critical Theory and Popular Cinema*. Ed. Lisa Starks and Courtney Lehmann. Fairleigh Dickinson University Press, 2002. 47–61.

Howlett, Kathy M. 'Playing on the Rim of the Frame: Kenneth Branagh's *A Midwinter's Tale*'. *The Upstart Crow*, 19 (1999): 110–28.

Hoyle, Ben. 'How to Shift Those Books if the Author is Plain Jane', *The Times*, 23 March 2007.

Hudelet, Ariane. 'Incarnating Jane Austen: The Role of Sound in the Recent Film Adaptations'. *Persuasions*, 27 (2005): 175–84.

Hutcheon, Linda. *A Theory of Adaptation*. London: Routledge, 2006.

Jess, Carolyn. 'The Promethean Apparatus: Michael Almereyda's Hamlet as Cinematic Allegory'. *Literature/Film Quarterly*, 32.2 (2004): 90–6.

Kaye, Heidi and Whelehan, Imelda. 'Introduction: Classics Across the Film/Literature Divide'. In *Classics in Film and Fiction*. Ed. Deborah Cartmell, I.Q. Hunter, Heidi Kaye and Imelda Whelehan. London: Pluto Press, 2000. 1–13.

Kendal, Geoffrey, with Colvin, Clare. *The Shakespeare Wallah* [1986]. Harmondsworth: Penguin, 1987.

Ko, Yu Jin. ' "The Mousetrap" and Remembrance in Michael Almereyda's *Hamlet*', *Shakespeare Bulletin*, 23.4 (winter 2005): 19–32.

Lane, Maggie. *Jane Austen's Family: Through Five Generations*. London: Robert Hale, 1984.

Lanier, Douglas (2002a). ' "Art Thou Base, Common and Popular?": The Cultural Politics of Kenneth Branagh's *Hamlet*'. In *Spectacular Shakespeare: Critical Theory and Popular Cinema*. Ed. Courtney Lehmann and Lisa S. Starks. London: Associated University Presses, 2002. 149–71.

——. (2002b). 'Shakescorp *Noir*'. *Shakespeare Quarterly*, 53.2 (summer 2002): 157–80.

Lehmann, Courtney. 'Shakespeare the Savior or Phantom Menace?: Kenneth Branagh's *A Midwinter's Tale* and the Critique of Cynical Reason'. *Colby Quarterly*, 37.1 (2001): 57–77.

——. *Shakespeare Remains*. Ithaca: Cornell University Press, 2002.

——. 'The Postnostalgic Renaissance: The "Place" of Liverpool in Don Boyd's *My Kingdom*'. In *Screening Shakespeare in the Twenty-First Century*. Ed. Mark

172 *Works Cited*

Thornton Burnett and Ramona Wray. Edinburgh: Edinburgh University Press 2006. 72–89.

Lehmann, Courtney and Starks, Lisa S. 'Making Mother Matter: Repression, Revision, and the Stakes of "Reading Psychoanalysis Into" Kenneth Branagh's *Hamlet*'. *Early Modern Literary Studies*, 6.1 (May 2000). Online: www.shu.ac.uk/emls/06–1/lehmhaml.htm

———. 'Introduction: Are We in Love with Shakespeare?'. In *Spectacular Shakespeare: Critical Theory and Popular Cinema*. Ed. Courtney Lehmann and Lisa S. Starks. London: Associated University Presses, 2002. 9–20.

Loehlin, James N. ' "These Violent Delights Have Violent Ends": Baz Luhrmann's Millennial Shakespeare'. In *Shakespeare, Film, Fin-de-Siècle*. Ed. Mark Thornton Burnett and Ramona Wray. Basingstoke: Macmillan, 2000. 121–36.

Loomba, Ania. *Gender, Race, Renaissance Drama*. Delhi: Oxford University Press, 1992.

Lynch, Deidre. '*Clueless*: About History'. In *Jane Austen and Co.: Remaking the Past in Contemporary Culture*. Ed. Suzanne R. Pucci and James Thompson. Albany, NY: State University of New York Press, 2003. 71–92.

Maley, Willy. ' "A Thing Most Brutish": Depicting Shakespeare's Multi-Nation State', *Shakespeare*, 3.1 (April 2007): 79–101.

McAleer, John. 'What a Biographer Can Learn about Jane Austen from *Emma*', *Persuasions*, 13 (1991). Online: www.jasna.org/persuasions/printed/number13/mcaleer.htm

McFarlane, Brian. *Novel to Film: An Introduction to the Theory of Adaptation*. Oxford: The Clarendon Press, 1996.

McLuhan, Marshall. *Understanding Media: The Extensions of Man*. New York: Routledge & Kegan Paul, 1964.

Middleton, Thomas and Rowley, William, *The Changeling*. Ed. Joost Daalder, 2nd edition. London: A & C Black, 1990.

Modenessi, Alfredo Michel. '(Un)Doing the Book "Without Verona Walls": A View from the Receiving End of Baz Luhrmann's *William Shakespeare's Romeo+Juliet*'. In *Spectacular Shakespeare: Critical Theory and Popular Cinema*. Ed. Courtney Lehmann and Lisa S. Starks. London: Associated University Presses, 2002. 62–85.

Mompalao de Piro, Joseph C. *The MADC Story 1910–1985*. Qormi: Imprint, 1985.

Monaghan, David. '*Emma* and the Art of Adaptation'. In *Jane Austen on Screen*. Ed. Gina MacDonald and Andrew F. MacDonald. Cambridge: Cambridge University Press, 2003. 197–227.

Mulvey, Laura. *Visual and Other Pleasures*. Bloomington, IN: Indiana University Press, 1989.

Nachumi, Nora. ' "As if!": Translating Austen's Ironic Narrator to Film'. In *Jane Austen in Hollywood*. Ed. Linda Troost and Sayre Greenfield. Lexington, KY: The University Press of Kentucky, 1998. 130–9.

Nixon, Cheryl L. 'Balancing the Courtship Hero: Masculine Emotional Display in Film Adaptations of Austen's Novels'. In *Jane Austen in Hollywood*. Ed. Linda Troost and Sayre Greenfield. Lexington, KY: The University Press of Kentucky, 1998. 22–43.

Orkin, Martin. *Local Shakespeares: Proximations and Power*. Abingdon: Routledge, 2005.

Parrill, Sue. *Jane Austen on Film and Television: A Critical Study of the Adaptations*. Jefferson, NC: McFarland & Co., 2002.

Pilkington, Ace. 'Zeffirelli's Shakespeare'. In *Shakespeare and the Moving Image*. Ed. Anthony Davies and Stanley Wells. Cambridge: Cambridge University Press, 1994. 163–79.

Piper, Billie (2007a). 'Interview'. *TV and Satellite Guide*, 17–23 March 2007.

———. (2007b). *The Sheffield Star*. 17 March 2007.

Prawer Jhabvala, Ruth. *Heat and Dust*. London: John Murray, 1975.

Pym, John. *The Wandering Company: Twenty-one Years of Merchant Ivory Films*. London: British Film Institute, 1983.

Richardson, Samuel. *Sir Charles Grandison*. Ed. Jocelyn Harris. Oxford: Oxford University Press, 1986.

Rothwell, Kenneth S. 'How the Twentieth Century Saw the Shakespeare Film: "Is it Shakespeare?"'. *Literature/Film Quarterly*, 29.2 (2001): 82–95.

Rowe, Katherine. '"Remember Me": Technologies of Memory in Michael Almereyda's *Hamlet*'. Online: www.brynmawr.edu/filmstudies/SampleScholarlyEssay.htm

Roy, Parama. 'Reading Communities and Culinary Communities: The Gastropoetics of the South Asian Diaspora'. *Positions: East Asia Cultural Critique*, 10.2 (2002): 471–502.

Ryan, Kiernan. 'The Murdering Word'. In *Romeo and Juliet: Contemporary Critical Essays*. Ed. R.S. White. Basingstoke: Palgrave, 2001. 116–28.

Shakespeare, William. *Romeo and Juliet*. Ed. T.J.B. Spencer. Harmondsworth: Penguin, 1967.

———. 'Twelfth Night'. In *The Arden Shakespeare Complete Works*. Ed. Richard Proudfoot, Ann Thompson and David Scott Kastan. London: Thomson Learning, 2001. 1191–1217.

Sheen, Erica. 'Introduction'. In *The Classic Novel from Page to Screen*. Ed. Robert Giddings and Erica Sheen. Manchester: Manchester University Press, 2000. 1–13.

Sherwin, Adam. 'BBC's Austen Will Be a Rural Sex and the City'. *The Times*. Friday 13 April 2007. 31.

Sinyard, Neil. '"Lids Tend to Come off": David Lean's Film of E.M. Forster's *A Passage to India*'. In *The Classic Novel from Page to Screen*. Ed. Robert Giddings and Erica Sheen. Manchester: Manchester University Press, 2000. 147–62.

Smith, Emma. '"Either for Tragedy, Comedy": Attitudes to *Hamlet* in Kenneth Branagh's *In the Bleak Midwinter* and *Hamlet*'. In *Shakespeare, Film, Fin-de-Siècle*. Ed. Mark Thornton Burnett and Ramona Wray. Basingstoke: Macmillan, 2000. 137–46.

Snow, Edward. 'Language and Sexual Difference in *Romeo and Juliet*'. In *Shakespeare's Rough Magic: Renaissance Essays in Honor of C.L. Barber*. Ed. Peter Erickson and Coppélia Kahn. Newark, NJ: University of Delaware Press, 1985. 168–92.

Solender, Elsa. 'Recreating Jane Austen's World on Film'. *Persuasions*, 24 (2002): 102–20.

Spence, Jon. *Becoming Jane Austen*. London: Hambledon, 2003.

Stern, Lesley. '*Emma* in Los Angeles: Remaking the Book and the City'. In *Film Adaptation*. Ed. James Naremore. London: The Athlone Press, 2000. 221–38.

Stovel, Nora Foster. 'From Page to Screen: Dancing to the Altar in Recent Film Adaptations of Jane Austen's Novels'. *Persuasions*, 28 (2006): 185–98.

Thompson, James. 'How to Do Things with Austen'. In *Jane Austen and Co.: Remaking the Past in Contemporary Culture*. Ed. Suzanne R. Pucci and James Thompson. Albany, NY: State University of New York Press, 2003. 13–32.

Tibbetts, John C. 'Backstage with the Bard: Or, Building a Better Mousetrap'. *Literature/Film Quarterly*, 29.2 (2001): 147–64.

Trivedi, Poonam. 'Reading "Other Shakespeares"'. In *Remaking Shakespeare: Performance across Media, Genres and Cultures*. Ed. Pascale Aebischer, Edward J. Esche and Nigel Wheale. Basingstoke: Palgrave, 2003. 56–73.

———. '"It is the Bloody Business Which Informs Thus": Local Politics and Performative Praxis, *Macbeth* in India'. In *World-wide Shakespeares: Local Appropriations in Film and Performance*. Ed. Sonia Massai. Abingdon: Routledge, 2005. 47–54.

———. '"Filmi" Shakespeare'. *Literature/Film Quarterly*, 35.2 (2007): 148–58.

Troost, Linda and Greenfield, Sayre. 'Introduction: Watching Ourselves Watching'. In *Jane Austen in Hollywood*. Ed. Linda Troost and Sayre Greenfield. Lexington, KY: The University Press of Kentucky, 1998. 4–12.

Turim, Maureen. 'Popular Culture and the Comedy of Manners: *Clueless* and Fashion Clues'. In *Jane Austen and Co.: Remaking the Past in Contemporary Culture*. Ed. Suzanne R. Pucci and James Thompson. Albany, NY: State University of New York Press, 2003. 33–51.

Walker, Elsie. 'Pop Goes the Shakespeare: Baz Luhrmann's *William Shakespeare's Romeo + Juliet*'. *Literature/Film Quarterly*, 28.2 (2000): 132–9.

———. 'Shakespeare on Film: Early Modern Texts, Postmodern Statements'. *Literature Compass*, 1 (2003): 1–5.

Wayne, Valerie. '*Shakespeare Wallah* and Colonial Specularity'. In *Shakespeare, the Movie: Popularizing the Plays on Film, TV, and Video*. Ed. Lynda E. Boose and Richard Burt. London: Routledge, 1997. 95–102.

Wilson, Cheryl A. '*Bride and Prejudice*: A Bollywood Comedy of Manners'. *Literature/Film Quarterly*, 34.4 (2006): 323–31.

Wiltshire, John. *Recreating Jane Austen*. Cambridge: Cambridge University Press, 2001.

Worthen, W.B. 'Fond Records: Remembering Theatre in the Digital Age'. In *Shakespeare, Memory and Performance*. Ed. Peter Holland. Cambridge: Cambridge University Press, 2006. 281–304.

Wray, Ramona. 'Nostalgia for Navarre: The Melancholic Metacinema of Kenneth Branagh's *Love's Labour's Lost*'. *Literature/Film Quarterly*, 30.3 (2002): 171–8.

———. 'Shakespeare and the Singletons, or, Beatrice Meets Bridget Jones: Post-feminism, Popular Culture and "Shakespea(Re)-Told"'. In *Screening Shakespeare in the Twenty-First Century*. Ed. Mark Thornton Burnett and Ramona Wray. Edinburgh: Edinburgh University Press, 2006. 185–205.

Young, R.V. 'From Mansfield to Manhattan: The Abandoned Generation of *Metropolitan*'. In *Doomed Bourgeois in Love: Essays on the Films of Whit Stillman*. Ed. Mark C. Henrie. Wilmington, DE: ISI Books, 2001. 49–62.

Filmography

10 Things I Hate About You (dir. Gil Junger, 1999)
About a Boy (dir. Paul Weitz, 2002)

Amadeus (dir. Milos Forman, 1984)
American Psycho (dir. Mary Harron, 2000)
As You Like It (dir. Kenneth Branagh, 2006)
The Bad Sleep Well (dir. Akira Kurosawa, 1960)
Batman (dir. Tim Burton, 1989)
Becoming Jane (dir. Julian Jarrold, 2007)
Beginner's Luck (dir. James Callis and Nick Cohen, 2001)
Bend it Like Beckham (dir. Gurinder Chadha, 2002)
Bhaji on the Beach (dir. Gurinder Chadha, 1993)
The Birdcage (dir. Mike Nichols, 1996)
Blade Runner (dir. Ridley Scott, 1982)
Bride and Prejudice (dir. Gurinder Chadha, 2004)
Brideshead Revisited (dir. Michael Lindsay-Hogg and Charles Sturridge, 1981)
Bridget Jones's Diary (dir. Sharon Maguire, 2001)
Bridget Jones: The Edge of Reason (dir. Beeban Kidron, 2004)
Brief Encounter (dir. David Lean, 1945)
Casablanca (dir. Michael Curtiz, 1942)
Clueless (dir. Amy Heckerling, 1995)
The Devil Wears Prada (dir. David Frankel, 2006)
Dil Farosh (dir. D.N. Madhok, 1937)
Elizabeth (dir. Shekhar Kapur, 1998)
Elizabeth: The Golden Age (dir. Shekhar Kapur, 2007)
Emma (dir. Diarmuid Lawrence, 1996)
Emma (dir. Douglas McGrath, 1996)
Escape from New York (dir. John Carpenter, 1981)
The Far Pavilions (dir. Peter Duffell, 1984)
Fast Times at Ridgemont High (dir. Amy Heckerling, 1982)
Forbidden Planet (dir. Fred Wilcox, 1956)
Fortunes of War (dir. James Cellan Jones, 1987)
Four Weddings and a Funeral (dir. Mike Newell, 1994)
From Here to Eternity (dir. Fred Zinnemann, 1953)
Hamlet (dir. Kenneth Branagh, 1996)
Hamlet (dir. Michael Almereyda, 2000)
Heat and Dust (dir. James Ivory, 1983)
Henry V (dir. Laurence Olivier, 1944)
The Householder (dir. James Ivory, 1963)
In the Bleak Midwinter (dir. Kenneth Branagh, 1995)
The Incredibles (dir. Brad Bird, 2004)
Indiana Jones and the Last Crusade (dir. Steven Spielberg, 1989)
Indiana Jones and the Temple of Doom (dir. Steven Spielberg, 1984)
The Jane Austen Book Club (dir. Robin Swicord, 2007)
Jane Austen in Manhattan (dir. James Ivory, 1980)
Jane Austen's Mafia (dir. Jim Abrahams, 1998)
Jane Eyre (dir. Franco Zeffirelli, 1996)
Jane Eyre (dir. Robert Young, 1997)
Jesus of Nazareth (dir. Franco Zeffirelli, 1977)
The Jewel in the Crown (dir. Christopher Morahan and Jim O'Brien, 1984)
Kaliyattam (dir. Jayaraaj, screenplay Balram, 1998)
Kandukondain Kandukondain (dir. Rajiv Menon, 2000)

Kannaki (dir. Jayaraaj, screenplay Sajeev Kilikulam, 2002)
King John (dir. William Pfeffer Dando and William K.L. Dickson, 1899)
La Cage aux Folles (dir. Edouard Molinaro, 1978)
Lady Audley's Secret (dir. Betsan Morris Evans, 2000)
Look Who's Talking (dir. Amy Heckerling, 1989)
Look Who's Talking Now (dir. Tom Ropelewski, 1993)
Look Who's Talking Too (dir. Amy Heckerling, 1990)
Lost in Austen (dir. Dan Zeff, 2008)
Love Actually (dir. Richard Curtis, 2003)
Love's Labour's Lost (dir. Kenneth Branagh, 2000)
Macbeth (dir. Roman Polanski, 1971)
Macbeth (dir. Mark Brozel, 2005)
Macbeth in Manhattan (dir. Greg Lombardo, 1999)
Mansfield Park (dir. Patricia Rozema, 1999)
Mansfield Park (dir. Iain B. MacDonald, 2007)
Metropolitan (dir. Whit Stillman, 1990)
Middlemarch (dir. Anthony Page, 1994)
A Midsummer Night's Dream (dir. Ed Fraiman, 2005)
Miss Austen Regrets (dir. Jeremy Lovering, 2008)
Much Ado About Nothing (dir. Kenneth Branagh, 1993)
Much Ado About Nothing (dir. Brian Percival, 2005)
My Kingdom (dir. Don Boyd, 2001)
Northanger Abbey (dir. Giles Foster, 1986)
Northanger Abbey (dir. Jon Jones, 2007)
Nostromo (dir. Alastair Reid, 1997)
Notting Hill (dir. Roger Michell, 1999)
O (dir. Tim Blake Nelson, 2001)
Omkara (dir. Vishal Bharadwaj, 2006)
Othello (dir. Geoffrey Sax, 2001)
A Passage to India (dir. David Lean, 1984)
Persuasion (dir. Roger Michell, 1995)
Persuasion (dir. Adrian Shergold, 2007)
Peter's Friends (dir. Kenneth Branagh, 1992)
The Phantom Menace (dir. George Lucas, 1999)
Pride and Prejudice (dir. Robert Z. Leonard, 1940)
Pride and Prejudice (dir. Simon Langton, 1995)
Pride and Prejudice (dir. Andrew Black, 2003)
Pride and Prejudice (dir. Joe Wright, 2005)
The Princess Diaries (dir. Garry Marshall, 2001)
The Princess Diaries 2: Royal Engagement (dir. Garry Marshall, 2004)
The Producers (dir. Mel Brooks, 1968)
Prospero's Books (dir. Peter Greenaway, 1991)
Purab Aur Pachim (dir. and screenplay Manoj Kumar, 1970)
Raiders of the Lost Ark (dir. Steven Spielberg, 1981)
Revengers Tragedy (dir. Alex Cox, 2002)
Richard III (dir. Laurence Olivier, 1955)
Richard III (dir. Richard Loncraine, 1995)
Romeo and Juliet (dir. Franco Zeffirelli, 1968)
Sense and Sensibility (dir. Ang Lee, 1995)

Sense and Sensibility (dir. John Alexander, 2008)
Shakespeare in Love (dir. John Madden, 1998)
Shakespeare Wallah (dir. James Ivory, 1965)
She's the Man (dir. Andy Fickman, 2006)
Some Like It Hot (dir. Billy Wilder, 1959)
Stage Beauty (dir. Richard Eyre, 2004)
The Taming of the Shrew (dir. Sam Taylor, 1929)
The Taming of the Shrew (dir. David Richards, 2005)
Taxi Driver (dir. Martin Scorsese, 1976)
The Tempest (dir. Percy Stow, 1908)
The Tempest (dir. Derek Jarman, 1979)
Tempest (dir. Paul Mazursky, 1982)
The Tempest (dir. Jack Bender, 1998)
Throne of Blood (dir. Akira Kurosawa, 1957)
Titanic (dir. James Cameron, 1997)
Titus (dir. Julie Taymor, 1999)
To Be or Not To Be (dir. Ernst Lubitsch, 1942)
Tom Jones (dir. Metin Hüseyin, 1997)
Twelfth Night (dir. Tim Supple, 2003)
The Two Towers (dir. Peter Jackson, 2002)
Vanity Fair (dir. Mira Nair, 2004)
West Side Story (dir. Jerome Robbins and Robert Wise, 1961)
William Shakespeare's Romeo + Juliet (dir. Baz Luhrmann, 1996)
You've Got Mail (dir. Nora Ephron, 1998)

Index